Three Dreams on Mount Meru

François Devenne

Three Dreams on Mount Meru

TRANSLATED BY

Lauren Yoder

The Toby Press

The Toby Press LLC

First English language edition 2007
Three Dreams on Mount Meru

POB 8531, New Milford, CT 06776-8531, USA
& POB 2455, London W1A 5WY, England
www.tobypress.com

Originally published in French as *Trois rêves au Mont Mérou*

ISBN-10 1 59264 173 3, ISBN-13 978 1 59264 173 4, *paperback*

A CIP catalogue record for this title is available from the British Library.

Printed and bound in the United States by Thomson-Shore Inc., Michigan.

One of man's most touching and beautiful attributes is that he aspires both after what he desires and what he has lost.

Alexander von Humboldt

Chapter one

Today, in the year 1170 of the Hegira, as I finish the narration of my journey to Mount Meru, I can't help thinking about Omui. He was the best storyteller in all Mombasa. The fabulous stories he would tell every Friday in the square in front of the grand mosque always enchanted me. I keep the memory of that man alive within me. I like to think that I'm made of the same stuff and that like him, I too belong to the race of enchanters. Of course, I'm guilty of pride to think that, especially since I write my words out with a pen, whereas his were spoken. But my inspiration, just like his, comes from the turbulent waters of language. We skim off the foam and decorate the somber parchment of existence with our sentences.

Omui's stories were always captivating. After prayers each Friday, people would gather on the square in front of the El-Rani mosque, near the tree that sheltered the old man from the sun. I never missed one of these sessions, nor the gatherings at Omui's house, and I didn't care if my friends made fun of me. As they saw it, the real motive for my being there was Omui's niece, who lived with her uncle. They were jealous that a boy could love the girl his family had chosen to be his wife. It's true that I've always associated Omui's name with Hasmahani's. I had known her since we were kids. Our friendship began to develop during my fifteenth year. Deep affection brought us together, and curiously, our love was born from a broken vase.

I had come to see her brother. He wasn't there and I was invited to wait for him in the living room. I sat there alone. I could hear the sound of the sea merging with the shouts of children playing in the street outside. Specks of dust were dancing in the sun's rays as they streamed through the windows. I loved that atmosphere, and letting myself drift into a dream world, I ended up dozing off. A quiet greeting drew me from my somnolence. There stood Hasmahani at the far end of the room, her back to the window and a large vase in her hands. She had come silently into the room, and it was as if her silhouette against the window, wrapped as it was in a light veil, had just stepped out of a dream. She set the vase down on a table and slipped away before I could utter a word. I hadn't expected her to disappear so quickly. I gathered my wits, stood up, and walked over to the vase as if I needed to find out if it had all been a dream. There was indeed a vase on the table; an Indian or Chinese vase. These oriental vases that Arab merchants carry in the holds of their ships are unusual in Mombasa. This one was made of white porcelain and very beautiful, but a crack marred its surface. It had been broken and glued back together. It seemed strange to display a defective vase like that here in the living room. The rareness of the piece couldn't hide its current imperfection.

Hasmahani once again lifted up the cloth that hung in the doorway and stood there right in front of me with a bouquet of hyacinths in her hand. At first she stepped back in surprise, but then walked over and put the flowers in the vase.

"Why do you keep a vase that's cracked like this?"

"Well, because it's cracked it's able to love the flowers it holds. And that makes them even more lovely," she answered melodiously.

"How does that make them prettier?"

"The vase lived through a catastrophe, and it realizes that it's fragile. So it pays attention to sensitive creatures. That's why I give it flowers. It will unveil their beauty."

As she finished the sentence she smiled with a little movement of her head and then lowered her eyes. The idea captivated me. A smile grew in my heart without ever making it to my face. Happiness filled me, and finally I smiled and then even burst into laughter. I knew that I was a little cracked like the vase, even though I wasn't quite sure what flower I might be carrying around within me. But the fleeting emotion was enough to open a little door.

A month went by. I loved Hasmahani but had never told her so. One morning, I decided to take her some flowers. I was in luck and found her home. Omui was absent. One of his wives invited me in. She was surprised to see me carrying flowers and left me alone with the girl.

"Hasmahani, I've brought you some flowers."

"Flowers? Why flowers?"

"For the vase."

"The vase doesn't need any flowers."

"Well, they're more for the woman I love than for the vase."

The girl waited a moment before speaking. "Only a man knows how to love, Bayu, and you're just a boy."

"No, I'm a man."

"You? A man?" Her laughter rang out light as a bell. I was vexed and showed her my hands.

"Just look at my fingers, Hasmahani. They can write the Koran and they'll soon be sculpting the doors of your house."

"You're dreaming, Bayu. You're dreaming, but you still haven't dreamed enough since you haven't made the journey to Mount Meru."

"Who gave you the right to talk about that?"

"The woman I'll be. Without completing that journey you can never be a man."

"That's my clan's business! You don't know anything about our rituals!"

"One thing I do know is that young men of your clan can't get married until they come back from Mount Meru. Before they give someone flowers, they've dug in the ground and found its roots. You haven't."

Her impudence hurt me. She was only a kid, two years younger than I, and she said things like that. I put the flowers down and left furiously.

I found myself walking through the tiny streets of the city, so angry that I didn't even greet the people I knew. As I came around a corner, the wall of the Kilindini mosque appeared before me. I could see the branches of the fig tree in front of the mosque. It was a real surprise to find myself near that tree. It was as if Hasmahani's words had led me there. For the fig tree's unusual history is related to the story of my own clan. And to the journey to Mount Meru that every male in the El-Mudi family must undertake.

The fig tree in front of the Kilindini mosque is centuries old. It stands there backed up against the façade of an ancient mosque in the middle of an esplanade paved with black and white stones. The white ones are cut from limestone that comes from the interior of the continent, whereas coral brings the sea's black desires to the darker stones. They form a chessboard on which the fig tree is the only piece, in the game of sunlight and shadow played by the sun and the leaves. A garden and its stone wall surround the esplanade. The first thing you notice when you enter the esplanade is the fig tree. It protects the place. Its multiple trunks twist and form voluptuous poses that compose the tree's branches. Its thick foliage, its air roots hanging down like vines, and the insects swarming around the figs give the tree a wild expression, the kind of savagery that we normally associate with animals or men but never with plants. And so it's a real surprise for a Muslim who walks through the mosque gate for the first time and stands face to face with this tree that's come straight from some obscure forest. The visitor is even more surprised when he sees the pool for libations and the *mihrab* and the *minbar* right there shaded by the tree. For he has just realized that the tree's foliage is like the vault of a prayer room!

If he asks how all this has come about, he'll hear a very strange story. Eight generations have come and gone, but the El-Mudi clan still clings to the memory of that strange story. It's like the glowing embers of a fire that will never die out among us.

When the Sultan Abdallah planned his pilgrimage to Mecca, he decided to glorify his return by inaugurating a new mosque. He entrusted the job to Badrani Nyuni El-Mudi, for the El-Mudi family always supplied the city's best artisans and architects. Rather than building a brand new mosque, they decided to enlarge the old mosque, tearing down some buildings around it in order to do so. They agreed to lay out a garden so that they could hear birdsong as they walked to prayers. The sultan gave Badrani complete authority, and he opened his coffers and authorized soldiers to do some of the heavy work. His only requirement: everything had to be finished by the time he returned. Three months seemed like a short time, but they weren't much of a constraint for Badrani given his freedom to work. He would be able to act at will, without interference from the imam, who was going along with the sultan, or from the regent, who had been chosen because he was too weak to plot against the sultan. It was said that the regent was intelligent enough to counter any intrigues planned by other family members, but stupid enough not to conspire against the sultan himself. Even if the regent had expressed some reservations about Badrani's architectural plans, Badrani would have stood up to him. The El-Mudi clan's reputation is as old as the clan itself. We are noble. And the lion doesn't need to ask the bird to sing. He simply listens to it.

So Badrani was free to plan the new mosque's structure without any constraint except that of creating a garden. A crazy idea was beginning to germinate in his mind, an extraordinary idea. Only a man like my ancestor could ever have come up with it. It came from a dream that he had had when he was a child. In the dream, he was out walking in a sun-drenched savannah, past skinny trees whose thorny branches had no leaves. The ground was scorching, and the air was hot and dry. Fatigued to the bone, he was looking for a place to rest, and coming around a hill he saw a gigantic tree. Its branches were raised toward the heavens and then slowly bent down like a praying man, and it looked like an immense parasol covering the earth. Some blue flowers were growing in the tree's peaceful shade. A fountain was bubbling under the tree, with some sunlight reflecting off its little white stone wall even though it was partially shaded, and it seemed to be there to quench travelers' thirst as well as to invite them to offer libations before they prayed.

He started running toward this cool haven, but then suddenly stopped in his tracks. In his haste he hadn't noticed the animal on the white stone wall, a leopard whose spotted coat blended with the scattered patches of light projected on the ground through the foliage. His first instinct was to run, but the water, protected there by its stones, seemed to beckon to him. Though he couldn't see the water, he could certainly sense it. The water would quench his thirst, flow into his body and relieve his senses that were bruised by the dry air. He moved forward. Motionless, the leopard let him approach. Its yellow eyes, split like black almonds, stared at him.

"Good morning, leopard," he said.

"Good morning, little man."

"I'm very thirsty, leopard, and I think I see a fountain there."

"Yes, you do, little man. There is a pool full of water. Since I stand guard over it day and night, I can no longer hunt and I am very hungry. What will you give me if I let you drink?"

"I have nothing to give you, leopard. I'm only the son of an artisan. But I can caress you. Have you ever been caressed by a man?"

"Once, I believe. A man placed his hand on my head. But he let go when I ripped open his throat with my fangs."

"That must not have been a caress, leopard. I'm talking about the feeling on your body when a hand glides lovingly over your fur like the evening breeze after the day's heat."

"The caresses my sisters give me are enough. Your hand is made to be eaten."

"But leopard, I'm offering you the unique opportunity to feel the extraordinary softness of a man's hand on your coat. My caress will make every spot on your fur open up. It will be just like the first raindrops penetrating the ground at the end of the dry season."

"The human hands I've encountered up to now haven't been so well intentioned. They've always been holding lances or bows and arrows. One of those hands had a good aim and I felt a strange burning."

"The desert rose germinates in the burning sun, O leopard. So far, you've known only its thorns. Let me give you the flower."

The leopard turned its head slightly and said: "Fine. Come ahead."

He moved toward the leopard. The leopard couldn't see the knife behind the boy's back, sheathed in his belt. He had planned that once he had the leopard's attention, as he stretched his hand out to caress it, he would be able to grab his knife with his other hand with one swift movement and slit the leopard's throat. He made ready to act. But when he moved his hand toward the leopard's head he realized—and it was like a revelation—that the animal had had the same idea. It was getting ready to rip him to shreds with its claws. But there was no turning back. His hand was already touching the animal's head. Both the boy and the leopard started slightly when the boy's palm made contact with the creature's fur. A feeling of wellbeing spread through both bodies, a feeling of peace radiating from the point of contact between man and beast. A great quietude filled them and wiped out their desire to kill. Both the boy and the animal smiled.

With the smile still on his lips Badrani Nyuni El-Mudi woke up, leaving the sea of dreams.

Although he was only a child, Badrani was marked by that fantastic dream that remained firmly anchored in his memory. Its meaning remained obscure until the day the sultan proposed the mosque project. As soon as the sultan explained what he wanted, Badrani's excitement rose, because he finally understood what his dream had meant. But he was careful not to talk about it and pretended to listen attentively to the sultan. He left the palace still excited by the idea that had stunned him at the beginning of the conversation. The mosque would be like the tree in his dreams, the mosque would *be* that very tree. As he walked through the palace gates he looked instinctively out at the sea and broke into a smile. For there off the Mombasa coast lies an island covered with exuberant vegetation. No boat had ever put ashore, because its name—*kisiwa cha chui,* Leopard Island—had been enough to keep sailors away. It was directly on the route to Socotra, and many travelers had seen a leopard resting in the trees as they passed by. Nobody knew how the wild animal survived, nor how it got onto the island in the first place, because several leagues separated the island from the mainland. The animal had been seen on many occasions climbing into a fig tree, and even the tree was an enigma because it was a variety that grew only in the hinterlands and was unknown along our coasts. The fig tree's presence added mystery to the island. All sorts of rumors floated around, and they changed with every boat that passed near the island before docking in Mombasa. The general opinion was that a sorcerer lived on the island and could turn himself into a leopard to frighten away sailors.

After the sultan left for Mecca, Badrani gathered the artisans in the family together and told them about his plans.

"The mosque will be made from the fig tree on Leopard Island. We will go dig up the tree, bring it back by boat, and then we'll plant it in the soil of our island that is blessed by Allah. It will be the vault of the prayer room. Beyond the shade it casts at midday, we'll create the garden. Our prayers will begin as soon as we enter the park. There's no reason to build walls. Allah's work itself is enough."

Consternation filled everyone's face. What had smitten Badrani? What man in his right mind could imagine turning a tree into a mosque? And what a crazy idea to go dig up a tree on an island inhabited by evil spirits!

His brother was the first to speak. "How can you ever dig up the tree if it's guarded by a leopard? Nobody is going to be willing to go along with you."

"Tomorrow I'll go to the island. I'll stay a week. When I come back, the leopard will no longer be dangerous."

"May the leopard devour you so that I won't have to see my brother swinging from a rope," Badrani's brother replied.

He stood up and walked out. The other men hurried out as well. Badrani was left by himself, but he wasn't too worried by his friends' and relatives' reaction. When he got back alive, their surprise would be so great that they would let Badrani carry out his plans. For a man who conquers a leopard must surely be allied with supernatural forces! (I must say right now that the El-Mudi family has never practiced witchcraft. In human memory, nobody has ever heard about any man of the family dabbling in sorcery. It's true that Ahmed Mauli was found dead in strange circumstances after he had insulted a clan member in public. But all honest men agree that poisoning is not an act of witchcraft.)

Badrani's prediction came true. He came back in one piece from the island, and that impressed them all so they let him pursue his work. The big subject of discussion in the city was what the sultan's reaction would be. Would he massacre the entire family or would he be content to just torture Badrani? Some members of the clan left Mombasa to go to Malindi or Kilwa, seeking protection from the disaster that Badrani was bringing down upon them. As people walked by the mosque under construction, all they could say was that Badrani was building his own scaffold.

During one meeting, in which Badrani ordered the workers to build a crane and get a dhow ready to go get the fig tree, there was but one question on everyone's lips, but nobody dared ask it. Finally a young man got up the courage.

"What has become of the leopard?"

"The leopard is no longer dangerous."

"Did you see it?"

"Yes."

Silence.

"How did you tame it?"

"I became a leopard myself."

Silence.

"You became a leopard?"

"Yes, I became a leopard."

Badrani didn't say anything more about it. His victory over the leopard conferred on him a great deal of prestige. The courage he had displayed was all the more admirable because old visceral fears and the memory of battles between men and leopards still disturbed the souls of the people living in Mombasa.

Badrani worked vigorously to build the mosque. The *mihrab*, the niche pointing in the direction of Mecca, was made with bricks covered with ceramic and marble. The *minbar*, the pulpit from which the guide delivers his sermon on Fridays, was made from teak and cashew wood, and came from one of our family's workshops. Slaves cut the paving stones for the prayer room. The sultan's gardeners were requisitioned to create the park. Finally, no fewer than one hundred men set out for the island. They set up camp near the fig tree where so many sailors had seen the leopard. No animal calls could be heard in the woods around them. The men were no longer terrified, but there was still mistrust in the air. It began to dissipate, however, as the excavation moved along. A difficult task faced the men.

First they attached the fig tree to the crane and then began to dig around roots that were so deep they seemed to form a new tree buried in the ground. The workers' amazement was great. First lassitude set in, and then fear took over. Mightn't the mass of wood, ripped out of its earthen sheath, dripping mud, smash them to pieces if it fell, even though strong ropes held it to the crane? Badrani had to go back to Mombasa and buy some slaves from an Arab merchant who had been about to send them to Arabia. Along with some soldiers, he took them to the island. The soldiers used their whips and the slaves finished the labor. Four goats were sacrificed so the earth might forgive them for taking away something precious.

Transporting the tree to Mombasa was easy because Arab dhows have wide holds that are able to carry heavy cargoes. Hadn't they even carried some giraffes to China?

Back in Mombasa, Badrani's success excited everyone. They all watched eagerly as the boat arrived in the port and the fig tree was hauled to the mosque. The project's master gained enormous popularity. Crowds pressed around the work area when the tree was replanted. The fig tree stood gracefully above the paving stones, casting a large shadow in the middle of the sun-drenched park. On the wall of the former mosque they could see the new *mihrab* and the new *minbar*, and it seemed perfectly normal to begin praying there.

Badrani realized that he had succeeded when the tree began to bloom. The blooms were just the little timid flowers that fig trees produce, but they still proved that the tree would survive. Badrani was a happy man, even if a shadow did sometimes drift over his joy—what would the sultan think?

Days passed. One morning a sail appeared on the horizon, a brown triangle filled out by the trade winds and by one man's pride. Crowned with the title of Hadji, the sultan was coming back to take possession of his kingdom, his island, the pearl on the edge of the continent. His joy in returning was tempered somewhat by the fear that a plot against him was being prepared on the island. He was reassured to see the huge crowd there to welcome him and all the important people waiting on the quay. His last suspicions faded away when he entered his palace. Order reigned. None of the people close to him had been poisoned. The regent had been able to counter his brothers' and cousins' vague desires for power, and the rival factions had neutralized each other. The Lion was home again. The mass of people surrounding him so obsequiously held no importance for him as long as they remained docile. He sat down in front of a row of men waiting eagerly to drink in his words like a child drinking at his mother's breast. He told them about his trip, transforming it into a major exploit so they would all realize that the success of his journey was due to the work of Allah. Then he enquired about several items, but first about how his homecoming celebration had been organized. He didn't ask about the mosque. He took leave of his guests by saying that the next day he would go to the mosque for prayers. Nobody dared speak.

The following day, the men gathered at the mosque's entrance, sheltered from the sun by the garden wall. To everyone's surprise, Badrani had shown up. At least his honor was safe. The sultan appeared, responded to their greetings and stepped through the gate. He stopped in his tracks. Nothing had really changed and yet nothing was as before. There was indeed a pleasant garden in the square and a path lined with young flame trees. The flowers' bright colors directed his eyes to the expanse of grass interlaced with paths. But all these paths led toward the former mosque where he saw a tree growing. It couldn't have been uglier, covered as it was with vines and encumbered by birds and insects. It was a fig tree, one of those trees under whose shade blacks from the interior liked to sit and talk. No sign of a new mosque. Instead of a majestic building with its proud minaret standing tall, there was nothing at all except the old mosque and that hideous tree.

"Where is the mosque?" the sultan asked.

Finally Badrani broke the embarrassing silence.

"The mosque is the tree you see here before you, sultan."

"That tree? A mosque?"

"The tree forms the vault of the prayer room. Already it provides protection from the sun, and in a few decades its foliage will be so thick that even the rain won't be able to get through."

"How about that!" exclaimed the sultan.

And he grew silent. Amid the confusion that filled him, there was something he didn't understand, some question still unanswered. His mind had formulated the question but then it slipped away. Submerged under a wave of emotions, the sultan was unable to recall what it was. Finally, he remembered:

"Where does this tree come from?"

"From Leopard Island," answered Badrani.

So Badrani had not only committed the sacrilege of turning a tree into a place of prayer, he had gone to an island inhabited by sorcerers to get it! The sultan's anger would have exploded if he hadn't been so worried. For although he was a good Muslim and held the title of Hadji, the man was deathly afraid of sorcery. Even if you pray five times a day, fast regularly and give alms, profess the oneness of Allah and the prophet's mission, and undertake the pilgrimage to Mecca, it's still wise to protect yourself against sorcerers. The sultan paused to reflect. His advisors, that band of imbeciles, those sons of infidel women, hadn't said one word since he arrived and there they sat motionless, frozen by fear. Badrani was known for the liberties he took with religion—hadn't he even carved a bird on the lintel of a door destined for the mufti's house?—but his family was above reproach. No possible links with sorcery.

"Did you and your men manage to dig up that tree and bring it all the way here?"

"Yes, sultan."

The sultan swallowed. His saliva tasted bitter in his throat, tightened as it was by anguish and irritated by his anger. He had come back from Arabia inspired by his prayers in Mecca. He had circled the Kaaba tower seven times and then kissed the black stone in the ultimate act of submission. In communion with the thousands of faithful, his consciousness had been absorbed into something far greater and truly ineffable. Faith illuminated his thoughts. His dream was to anchor Mombasa to the Orient, turning it into an outpost of civilization, and now these people in Mombasa had just reminded him that the island really belonged to Africa.

"And what has become of the leopard?"

"The leopard has remained what it was."

The sultan began to think. Badrani was the city's best artisan because he combined obvious artistic qualities with a solid architectural background. He had decorated the houses of several notable citizens with magnificent carved doors and had mastered the techniques of building high minarets. He was perfectly competent to build the new mosque. And yet here, instead of carving birds, Badrani was planting trees to attract them.

"Come, Badrani. Let's look more closely at the tree."

The two men walked toward the tree and sat down on one of the mats spread out over the stones. Badrani could sense the sultan's wrath and didn't open his mouth. Yet in spite of his anger, the sultan looked around at the unusual prayer room, contemplated the *mihrab* and the *minbar*. He too was silent. And then suddenly he asked a question.

"Badrani, why did you plant this tree?"

"To make my dream come true, sultan."

"What dream?"

"A dream that I had when I was a child and this tree appeared to me like a mosque. Since then I have never stopped trying to understand my dream. And now I know."

"What do you know?"

"That life is a tree."

"A tree?"

"And we are all dreams."

"Badrani, I'm still not sure I'll spare your life. But tell me, why did you go to that island to get the tree?"

"In my dream there was a leopard."

"Oh, that's why…and…didn't the leopard do anything?"

"It didn't dare attack the men. It stayed hidden back on the island."

Relief spread over the sultan's face. There wasn't a trace of sorcery in this business. The family *mganga* would organize a ceremony to chase away any spirits that might still be hanging around the tree and there would no longer be any danger.

"You're a strange man, Badrani. The next time, maybe you'll go look for a tree on Mount Meru!"

In those days, Mount Meru was the furthest point in the hinterlands that the caravans had reached.

"Come on," he said, as if to keep his anger from getting the upper hand now that his anxiousness was fading away.

The two men reached the garden gate. A huge crowd was massed near the exit. The sultan wondered why, until he realized that all these men had come for prayers. He turned toward Badrani and looked him in the eyes for the first time.

"Badrani, I'll spare your life. But you must leave. You are banished from Mombasa for…for three years. Go wherever you like…."

Badrani left Mombasa without revealing a word about his destination, much to his family's great displeasure, for they were furious that he would sever all ties so abruptly. And it didn't help that he didn't send back any news for three years. Eventually he reappeared in a caravan loaded with ivory, wax, and iron. He brought back some big wooden beams cut from trees unknown in Mombasa. They were lovely pieces of wood with a dense compact texture, ideal for making doors and bas-relief sculptures. They had been cut from conifers that grew only in the African uplands.

The wood came from Mount Meru. That's where Badrani had spent his time in exile, away on that far-off mountain that was almost inaccessible in those days and still not very well known today. Beyond Mount Meru stretches an immense savannah inhabited by wild animals and evil spirits.

While Badrani had been absent, his prestige had grown. He was seen as a man of integrity who had stood up to the sultan to achieve his destiny. His forced exile didn't seem justified any more, except perhaps to shore up the reign of a potentate who couldn't stand for anything or anyone to cast a shadow on his own power. The mosque and the fig tree became a place of prayer and conviviality. Badrani's return was celebrated as a victory for the El-Mudi family. The clan's notoriety increased and along with it more orders for carvings. Badrani set up trade with the Swahili caravans going to Mount Kilimanjaro and Mount Meru, and they brought back precious wood. His standing increased within the clan. In just a few years he became the most listened to and the most influential man among the elders. And that's when he imposed the ritual that all the male children of the El-Mudi clan must follow. He announced that to become an adult, every boy would have to make a journey to Mount Meru so he could dream three dreams. Our young men needed to be tested and to gain strength on the difficult path. There were fears that some might disappear en route. But even in Mombasa the clan wasn't safe from harm. Smallpox decimated the clan from time to time, the plague almost wiped us out, the Portuguese killed several of our men, the city was besieged by African warriors, and finally even the bloody rivalries that sometimes shook the sultanate also affected the El-Mudis.

So people accepted the idea of an initiation journey. They did raise the objection that it seemed strange for Muslims to turn toward the interior of the continent where black pagans lived. Badrani answered:

"The sun rises in the east but sets in the heart of Africa." And he added: "Muslims or pagans, we're all black."

So most of the men accepted Badrani's proposal. They all agreed, however, that they would keep the boys home until they had fully mastered the secrets of wood. That way they wouldn't lose their refined senses during the journey. A generation after that decision, most of the adults had made the journey, and nobody questioned the rite of passage which distinguishes the El-Mudis from the other Mombasa clans. The practice has continued up to our day. But we have to admit that its purpose is mysterious. For what does it mean to dream? The elders don't have much to say about dreaming when they give advice to the novices about their upcoming voyage. They stick to very concrete advice about which itinerary to follow and how to act. It's up to the future initiate to understand the meaning of the ritual he will undertake. He will plumb the depths of his dreams. And he's free to take from them whatever he wants. But he does need to learn to listen.

And thus the boy sets off, leaving his native island and taking a path toward another life.

Hasmahani's attitude had annoyed me so much that I refused to see her for several weeks. But I had an important piece of news I wanted to share with her.

We saw each other at a wedding, but within the commotion of all the guests it wasn't easy to speak. During the evening banquet I was the one who started a discussion. The discussion was about the baobab standing in the market square. Its trunk looked like a swollen hand that had been stung by a wasp. It was said to have hidden a family during the sack of the city by the terrible Zimbas. The water in its trunk quenched the fugitives' thirst and they were able to live on the tree's fruit. Little good it did them in the end, because the

Zimbas noticed the fruit was disappearing and climbed up into the tree. The unfortunate people were found and killed. I've often wondered how we ever learned that story, because the Zimbas devastated the city without leaving any survivors. Then they went on to Malindi, but there they were wiped out by the warriors of that region. Since there were no survivors, I would like to know who started the story about the baobab. Really, the only living survivor after the Zimbas left was the baobab. I brought this point up during the wedding, and then everybody tried to come up a solution; with some witness who had escaped the massacre, inventing some hiding place, like in a house that hadn't even been built yet or proposing some name that we heard then for the first time.

At the end of that conversation, Hasmahani came up to me and whispered in my ear:

"The baobab passed on the story to the market women, to the pregnant market women."

When she saw my incredulous look, she smiled and raised her eyebrows. And then, adjusting her veil that had slipped down from her hair, she walked away.

I caught up with Hasmahani as she was walking home with her brother. He let me accompany her home. It was already dark. The rising moon cast its light on the streets.

"Hasmahani, the clan elders have decided that with the next full moon I'll leave Mombasa for Mount Meru."

"That's good."

"The elders have also confirmed that our two families would like to see us get married when I return."

She didn't answer, but pulled her veil over her chin. It seemed to me that she was smiling.

"What would you like me to bring you from Mount Meru?"

She stopped and looked at me. In the darkness I couldn't see her face very clearly, framed as it was by her veil that hung down over her djellabah. Her silhouette resembled the tree trunks that were sculpted in my father's workshop. My desire had made her breasts stand up deliciously under the cloth, but I hadn't done enough woodcarving to bring out her face. I didn't like the portrait the night was painting before my eyes, in spite of Hasmahani's charm. There was something still missing. The easy thing would have been to blame the darkness, but I had the vague feeling that the girl's true beauty was at stake. Her grace escaped me, because my true sight hadn't yet been born.

Hasmahani answered:

"A flower. The flower that you will give birth to."

"I thought that only women could give birth."

"Aren't you an artist?"

"I'm an artisan. I can carve only those designs that my father has taught me. That's not the same thing as creation."

"How about your ancestor Badrani Nyuni El-Mudi? He was surely a creator, since he was inspired by the island leopard."

"The leopard? Nobody knows how he got rid of it. Probably by force."

"By force! The leopard called to him in a dream and he went off to hunt it! You don't get it, Bayu. Were it not for that leopard, you wouldn't be one of the best wood carvers in Mombasa."

"I don't understand."

"The leopard is what nudged your ancestor to turn toward creating."

"The leopard! It's such a dangerous animal!"

"All creation carries with it some risk."

"Hasmahani, you are really strange. You're only a girl and yet you claim to know about the origin of the El-Mudi clan. You shouldn't be acting like this. Your family would be embarrassed if they knew how you were speaking to your future husband."

"My future husband is an El-Mudi, just like my sons will be. They will need to understand that the leopard is the creative breath of their clan."

What strange words. I didn't know how to respond, but it seemed to me that there was some truth in what she was saying.

"All right, Hasmahani. Maybe you're right that I can't be a man until I complete the journey to Mount Meru. I hope that I'll live to know you as my wife, for it's a perilous journey. There's no guarantee that I'll make it back."

Hasmahani didn't say anything.

Her house, located near the water's edge, wasn't very far away. We could hear the sea. The sea smells wafted over us like the perfume of incense from a far-off country that gives the ocean its name. The sound of the waves, the wind's caress, and the smell of algae were inebriating.

When we started down the last tiny street toward her house, I had the strange sensation that something was out of whack. The path grew hazy, and the road we were walking on scarcely seemed real. It was as if I was out of step, out of synch with the real world.

I heard a voice.

"I do hope you come back, Bayu."

I nodded absentmindedly, because I had already set out on the path toward Mount Meru.

Chapter two

I looked back one last time toward Mombasa Island, a coral tortoise with a city on its back, separated from the continent by a narrow sound. The evening breeze still hadn't dissipated the veil of heat draping the island. Squeezed in between the dark walls, the houses looked like little sun-bleached bones in an open-air grave. And it's true I was burying my childhood.

I took the path along the gorge that cut through the cliff, stepping around the fallen rocks. The mineral world of these heat-oppressed slopes stood in stark contrast to the green strip of trees along the water. Birdsong echoed between the canyon's walls, and the river murmured along its banks. Gusts of wind carried along damp earth smells. The walls on both sides of the gorge were beginning to get steeper and vegetation was now sparser. Candelabra trees raised their bouquets of armored branches skyward, and cacti greeted me with their atrophied, leprous arms. They brought to mind fallen genies that some curse had planted there.

The trail climbed toward the Zimba pass, a narrow passage on the plateau that governs access to the gorge. Behind the escarpment, the plateau opens onto a wide plain dotted with acacia trees, announcing the monotonous expanses of the great continent.

The sound of my steps on the bare rock reverberated from wall to wall. The sound would disappear momentarily whenever sand or small pebbles covered the bare rock. The clan elders had told me about the unusual echoes in the gorge. The strangest phenomenon occurred near the Zimba pass at the end of the ravine.

"When you get to the Zimba pass, shout out your name," one of my uncles had told me, "and after a very long time your name will come back as an echo. Your voice won't be the same when you hear the echo, neither your voice nor you yourself. In any case, Bayu, what you need to know is that your trip will finally begin when you walk through the Zimba pass."

My sack was quite heavy. It held a blanket, some clothes, a flint and a piece of iron for making fires, my sculptor's chisel and hammer and a Koran, as well as some dried fish and a goatskin of water. I was also carrying a machete and a hunting knife, more as a deterrent than for actual use. When you grow up in a family of craftsmen you don't usually learn much about handling weapons.

It was near the end of the afternoon when I got to the Zimba pass. The gorge's walls spread open, revealing a bit of sky. It was as if a blue door stood before me, inviting me into another world, a world without end. I understood why the elders said that's where the voyage would truly begin. For the Zimba pass is surely the first border an initiate has to cross. The countryside opened up, a verdant plain covered with twisted trees and thick bushes. I decided to shout out my name in the gorge as the elders had advised. The echo would come back to me a long time later.

"Bayu," I shouted.

"Here I am," another voice answered immediately.

To my great astonishment, a silhouette materialized out of the cliff wall. There stood a young man I hadn't seen previously.

"Who are you?"

"Bayu," my voice echoed back.

"Yes, I'm Bayu, the son of old Ojalu," the boy continued.

"Peace be with you. I'm the son of Safwani Ibrahim el-Mudi, the son of Ibrahim Issa el-Mudi, who was the son of Issa Waduud el-Mudi. My given name is Bayu, just as yours is."

"May God bless your family. Are you from Mombasa?"

Truly, it wasn't enough for the boy to appear as if by magic. He also asked strange questions.

"Why do you wonder if I'm from Mombasa? Don't you know the El-Mudi clan?"

"No," he answered simply.

I was dumbfounded. He claimed not to know one of Mombasa's most illustrious families.

"We're the best craftsmen on the whole island. How can you not know who the El-Mudis are?"

"It's just that I never go to Mombasa."

And he sat down. I was annoyed by the boy's air of self-importance. Though younger than I, he wasn't showing the proper respect.

"How about you? What are you doing here?"

"I'm watching these goats and cows."

There was indeed a herd doggedly nibbling at the spindly bushes on the plateau slopes. Further down, on the rich grass of the plain, some cows were grazing along a river that stretched out like a lazy ribbon.

"Where do you come from?"

"From Kinya."

"Kinya? Where's that?"

"It's a village on the plain, a day's walk up river. Don't you know Kinya?"

"No," I had to admit.

"So you don't know either my village or my family," he noted.

I looked away, out over the plain. After a moment of silence, I said: "What are you doing so far away from your village?"

"Looking for grass," he said with a smile. "There are no dangerous animals around here, so I can relax. And how about you? You're from Mombasa, but where are you going?"

"I'm going to Kobekobe. There I'll be joining a caravan heading toward Mount Meru."

"You're trying to go to Mount Meru?"

"Yes," I answered proudly.

"But that's so far! I don't understand. The caravan starts out from Mombasa. Why didn't you travel with it?"

"That's part of the ritual."

"The ritual?"

"Yes. The clan elders are sending me. First I must reach Kobekobe alone."

"What a strange ritual! Of course, Kobekobe is only a two day's walk away and it's not very dangerous. If you make a good fire at night even the genies won't bother you. Where will you sleep tonight?"

"Right here."

"Fine. Then we'll be together. I plan to sleep closer to the river. I was just waiting for the sun to go down a little before I went back to my camp. You're welcome to join me."

And so I spent my first night away from Mombasa in the company of a young shepherd. He knew lots of poems, and listening to him was a pleasure in spite of his poor Swahili.

The last stars were still twinkling in the sky as dawn invaded. The dark mass of the plateau escarpment, broken where the gorge cut into it, was still drowned in shadows. Bayu would have been glad to accompany me if he hadn't had to keep an eye on his herd. I said my goodbyes to the young shepherd near the ford in the river.

"So this is where the Zimbas came through to attack Mombasa," I said.

"Yes, they made an alliance with the crocodiles."

"With the crocodiles? Which crocodiles?"

"You see, one of the Zimba ancestors was himself a crocodile and they've kept up friendly relations with the animals. That's how they crossed the lake."

"There used to be a lake?"

"Back in ancient times a lake infested with crocodiles lay at the edge of the plateau. This whole plain used to be a swamp. The crocodiles wouldn't let anyone go beyond the gorge, and so the people of Mombasa thought they could safely stop guarding the pass. That was a fatal mistake, because the Zimbas had no problem crossing the lake. They considered the crocodiles their brothers and could talk to them. They held a ceremony to gain their good graces and then started out across the lake. People say that they didn't even need to use their pirogues because they crossed the lake on the crocodiles' backs. And when they reached Mombasa they caught the sultan's army by surprise."

The shepherd smiled, showing a row of white filed teeth that reminded me of crocodile jaws.

"There aren't any crocodiles in the river now, are there?" I asked with some concern.

"No, not around here. It's too dry. There aren't any crocodiles or any Zimbas. Just their souls that sometimes wander through."

"Their souls wander—"

"Yes, but don't worry. They're harmless. You can hear them moving. They breathe a little and then continue on. In fact, I'm not sure if they're Zimba souls or if they're genies. The bush"—and with a gesture he indicated the vast wooded space extending beyond the river—"is full of genies."

With these last words, I became filled with apprehension. Bayu must have noticed, for he added:

"They won't bother you. Personally, I've never had any problems."

I stared out at the grassy expanse dotted with trees waiting there for me.

"It's time for you to leave. Goodbye, Bayu."

"Goodbye," I answered half-heartedly. And I crossed the river.

It was simple enough to follow the track left by passing travelers and animal herds. There was no danger of getting lost. A light breeze came up, bringing with it the smells of the ocean still not so far away. It was pleasant to feel the breeze caressing my skin, reminding me of the humidity in Mombasa. Perhaps it was an illusion, but it seemed to me that I could hear words. They tasted like sea salt.

"Remember me," the sea was saying. "Don't forget, Bayu. I'm carrying the island of Mombasa and all his inhabitants on my back, and the city walls are the cloth I wrap myself in to protect you. Since your birth I've never failed to cradle you."

The words faded away. The sea breeze caressed my skin, and its breath was as wet as were my mother's eyes when I set out.

The countryside, at first covered with large trees, mimosas and acacias, became more barren. I reached a dry rocky plateau where cacti and euphorbia grew. At its base, large stones stood upright here and there. They looked like the vestiges of a city destroyed by a hurricane. The euphorbia raised their hydra heads above the stony labyrinth, conquerors on a devastated field of battle.

As I walked along, I began to feel a little afraid. My journey would be hard, even painful. The elders hadn't spared any details. I could already sense the contrast between my city's vitality and the plateau's desolation. I knew that some of the clan's young men had perished on the journey. The two brothers Athinani and Mahfuudh set out a year apart but neither returned. Isaam, an uncle just a little older than I was, and my cousins Jaafar, Hadith and Nasser, the last of whom was seen on Mount Meru before disappearing, were all dead, having succumbed to some accident, been devoured by wild animals or killed by equally wild men.

I was distracted by little songbirds hopping from stone to stone. One bird, hidden behind a rock, began a song of marvelous beauty. Hoping to see it, I walked around a big block of stone that came up to my chest. Imagine my surprise to discover that the song was pouring forth from the rock itself! I was a little worried and stepped back in astonishment as the song seemed to be calling me. I hesitated, uncertain what to do. Was it a real song or a genie's manifestation? If a bird was imprisoned in the rock, I needed to free it. With my hammer and chisel, I began to pound on the rock along a crack that ran around it. I heard the song again and grew more confident. The rock was hard, and chips flew. I worked doggedly, hammering relentlessly. Finally the rock gave way, splitting in two and laying bare a bird fossil. The preserved shape was graceful: Short beak, thin wings and a long tail. The song ceased immediately. I didn't know what to think of what I had done. Had I condemned the song by trying to listen to it? Was it sacrilege to expose that image buried in stone by Creation? Having no answer, I set off again.

It was astonishing to me that rock could preserve traces of life. To my mind, only wood, the material best suited for sculpting, was endowed with memory. Isn't it the craftsman's task to bring out the tree's loveliest memory?

After the stones I came to a carpet of grass and some small acacia trees not much taller than a man. If they hadn't been so numerous, I would have assumed they were young. With their sparse foliage the thorny trees formed a shadeless forest. They barely had trunks, just stalks decorated with a double row of thorns, like the teeth of vertical jaws. On their branches there were some black swellings, like tumors, about the size of figs, poisoning the woody stems. The sparseness of the acacia's foliage made them seem even less attractive, like a pitiful army of soldiers with arms emaciated from their miserable life. If I could have chosen, I would have preferred the harshness of the rocks, closed up around the secret of their genesis, to these fleshless plants without souls.

I was a little nervous, especially because I kept hearing a strange sound. It was a faint intermittent whistle, not very loud but quite shrill. You let it out of your mind a moment, and then it reappeared. The sound was definitely there, or rather there was somebody or something making the sound. Even though I would often whirl around to look back at the skinny acacia trees, I never caught sight of one single animal or human. But the whistling continued. My mind filled with stories of enchantments and genies inflicting misfortune on friends or relatives. The strange whistling probably came from some angry genie, upset because I had invaded its territory. I should have made an offering before crossing this land, but nobody had suggested that. I grew more fearful with each step I took. I picked up my pace, hoping to get away from the insidious sound. Once, I thought it was gone, but then, perfidiously, there it was again. Not a living soul around to help me.

I took off running and then stopped after a moment to look behind me. I felt someone grab the back of my shirt! It must be the genie! I turned around with a scream and found myself face to face with a thorny acacia tree. Its sharp-clawed branch had snagged my shirt. I stood there panting, looking dumbly at the tree with its trunks, thin as a girl's wrist, covered with those strange protrusions and their tiny holes. An ant came out of one of the holes. The wind picked up and the protrusions started whistling. I was overwhelmed to think that nature could produce such a sound using those tiny holes in a gall. So that's what was causing the whistling that had put me in such a state! I felt like an idiot. What would the rest of my journey be like if the first sound I heard in nature disturbed me so?

Since evening was coming, I began looking for a place to sleep. I gathered a supply of branches and built a fire large enough for me to feel safe. I swallowed a piece of dried fish and rolled up in my blanket. For the first time in my life I would be sleeping all by myself, with no other person near me. Nobody else I could talk to! Fortunately I began to get sleepy. The lively fire brightened the night, and I could feel its warmth. Crazed by the flames, insects were letting themselves be devoured by a fire chameleon.

In the middle of the night I woke up. The majestic sky was traversed by the starry river that flows through night's infinity. The Indians in Mombasa call the heavenly river the Milky Way. Perhaps they were weaned too soon. Maybe that's why they invented this expression in which the night is brightened by a feminine magic that gives shape to our dreams.

I drifted back to sleep and a few hours later woke up once more. The fire had burned itself out, and the river filled with milk was no longer flowing. It must have poured itself out in far off India, where it was surely nourishing the dreams of the brothers of Mombasa bankers and shipowners.

At dawn, when I opened my eyes, I felt sullen, almost angry at being alone and not having anyone to talk to. My most pressing goal was to get to Kobekobe and meet some people. Clearly people had marked the trail I was following, but it wasn't enough for me to follow the tracks they had left on the plateau. I wanted to speak to some real flesh-and-blood person. Around noon I came to a field, lying fallow. Vegetation had reclaimed some parts of the field, whereas in other parts the stalks left after harvest still covered the ground. I noticed some beehives hanging in the branches of a tree and then the full heads of some sorghum in a field nearby. Then, finally, I saw Kobekobe village, protected by a wall, on a hilltop. It was a great relief to see other human beings. There were men talking in the shade of a mango tree and women washing clothes in the river at the base of the hill. One branch of the river meandered off to form a wide shallow pond filled with reeds. The two tortoises that had given their names to the village—*kobe* means tortoise—must have come from that pond. I greeted the men, conversed with them a little and then asked them to take me to the village chief.

"There's no chief here," they answered. "There is a master of the land, a master of ancestor worship and elders for each clan's affairs. Tell us what your problem is and we'll take you to one of the elders."

"I want to join the caravan leaving for Mount Meru."

"The caravan left this morning."

"It's already gone?"

"Yes. They arrived yesterday evening and set out again this morning."

"But they were supposed to spend a day in Kobekobe," I said, and my voice betrayed my concern.

"Perhaps they were, but the caravan leader, Abdul…maybe you know him since he's a Swahili, not very tall. Anyway, Abdul the chief decided not to wait since the animals didn't seem to be tired."

"Well, that's no problem" said another man. "You can catch up with them tomorrow. They're not moving so fast that a man walking alone can't catch up with them."

"How can I find their tracks?"

"The trail is easy to see, and you just follow the donkey droppings."

"What if I get lost?"

"That'd be hard to do. Doesn't your name come from the word

bayuwayu, meaning swallow? Have you ever seen swallows get lost even though they come from distant lands?"

The man talking to me called a boy over and asked him to give me hospitality for the night. The boy invited me to follow him. We took a path through the fields leading around the hill. The ripe sorghum, red in the sun, swayed as we passed. Here and there full ears of corn stood high on their stalks among the sorghum. Some of the manioc plants were already as big as bushes.

"Your manioc is really big!"

"That's not manioc. It's *mpira*. We feed its leaves to our goats. There's some manioc over there. We don't grow much manioc, and when the father of our clan first arrived there wasn't any here at all."

"Who was the father of your clan?"

"His name was Tiediji and he came from the east. One day, when he was tired from walking, he leaned up against a tree. Two tortoises came out from the roots. That's a sign of fertility, so he founded the village right here."

"Did you know that swallows came from far away?" I asked.

"I've never thought about it. It's true that in Kobekobe we never see swallows except at the end of the rainy season."

"Yes, like in Mombasa. Why do they come here?"

"This is where their life is."

We entered the village. It seemed to me that I was coming back home and that everything had changed. The rectangular houses made of wood, clay and thatch looked like some of the houses in Mombasa. There was the same activity as in my native city's tiny streets, and yet nothing was as before.

They woke me up in the middle of the night. It was still dark when the boy and I left the village. Without his help I would never have been able to find the trail, for it was still drowned in darkness. The contours of the trees surged forth like wrecked ships. The horizon began to glow red. Irresistible light invaded the sky. An explosion of birdsong celebrated the moment when night turns to day.

Cultivated fields gave way to tall grasses, and the caravan trail cut through them. It was the only road from the coast to the continent's interior. Little birds busied themselves around the droppings left by the convoy that had passed by the day before. They would fly off as we approached and then regroup after we passed. On Mount Meru, my uncle Daudi had met an old man who had seen the first caravans arrive when he was young. The man said that along with the caravans some songbirds appeared that had been completely unknown when he was a child. They fed on donkey and camel manure.

We walked along briskly, for I was in a hurry to catch up with the convoy. As we talked, we reached the top of a hill. Through the morning mist, we could see clear to the horizon. Ahead was a grassy plain without many trees, just a few acacias, and their shadows cast by the rising sun stretched out toward the west, showing me which way to go.

"Bayu, here's where I'll leave you. All you need to do is follow this trail and you'll catch up with the caravan by this evening. Have a good trip, and don't forget to stop and see me on your way back."

Chapter three

From the hilltop I looked out over the immense expanse I would need to cross to join the caravan. The grass was very tall, the height of a man. The wind was drawing ever-changing designs on the grass's surface, ephemeral signs on the prairie's huge canvas. I was about to enter an unknown country, and I was nervous and even a little frightened at the prospect of the trip ahead of me. I walked down the hill and started off through the bush.

I kept up a rapid pace, quickly breaking out into a sweat. The further I went, the more my apprehension grew, because I could see so few animal droppings, so few indications that the caravan had gone that way. My life's big journey, the journey that was supposed to make a man of me, was starting out as a quest for dung.

The heat was becoming more and more unbearable, but I didn't want to waste any time resting. I was in a hurry to catch up with the caravan. Then I came to a fork in the trail. I hadn't expected that! Which path had the caravan taken? Why hadn't my hosts in Kobekobe told me about the fork? A little annoyed, I looked around for dung, hoping to see which way the caravan had gone. Some birds led me to a little heap of dung on one of the paths. I saw some more a little further along. So that's the direction I chose. I walked the entire afternoon, eager to find the caravan. The grass was growing thicker, and often I would lose the trail. As evening fell, there still was no trace of the caravan, and the path had almost disappeared. It was clear it was the wrong trail. I was lost, and it was too late to turn back. A lump rose in my throat, and though I did my best to keep from crying, my eyes brimmed with tears. I was filled with resentment. The people in Kobekobe had led me astray in this undertaking, just like the clan elders. Why had the elders not let me leave Mombasa with the caravan? It's as if they wanted to be sure that I would have to undertake my journey alone. Now I was beginning to see things in a new light. I remembered the time they spent explaining the properties of certain plants that didn't even grow on Mombasa Island. We had gone far out into the countryside, and my father and uncles had taught me how to identify edible plants and those plants that showed where you could find water or those that could heal wounds and bites. A true initiation for wilderness survival! Then there was all the advice about finding one's way and information about the regions I would be crossing: the Teïta Mountains, Usumbare and Pare, Taveta country, the area around Kilimanjaro, as well as the Pangani and Umba Rivers. Surely that's how they had done things because their goal was indeed to teach me how to travel alone.

I was condemned to follow the trail without a companion. Just thinking about how alone I was gave me chills. My sense of honor prevented me from going back to Kobekobe to wait for another caravan. I had no choice but move forward and complete my journey all by myself.

I sat down on the ground, bitterly replaying all those thoughts in my head. A shiny insect, a golden beetle, caught my attention. I picked up the insect, and immediately it drew its legs up to its body as if it were dead. The poor beetle jumped up and down a few times on the palm of my hand before I set it back down on the ground.

Then it went on its way, continuing its quest that was so foreign to the human mind. Another beetle came to mind; earrings my father had given my mother when I was just a small child. One day, my mother appeared in the doorway all in a dither. I was playing with the other children in the yard. She called out to us.

"Children, I've lost one of my beetle-shaped earrings. I can't find it anywhere. Perhaps it's out here in the yard somewhere. Help me look for it."

Right away we began to search for the piece of jewelry, looking all over the yard, especially in those places my mother liked to sit and rest. But we had no luck. My brothers, sisters and cousins all gave up and went in. Before going back in the house, I decided to look in a part of the yard we hadn't scoured. And that's how I found the earring, lying on the leaf of a succulent plant. What jubilation! I immediately ran toward the house, holding the precious piece of jewelry in my hand.

When she saw me coming, my mother squatted down and held her arms out to me.

"So, here's my little prince."

I rushed up to her, but stopped short when I saw her face up close. I took a step backward.

"What's the matter, dear?" my mother asked in surprise.

She was wearing both of her beetle-shaped earrings! I was unable to move and looked solemnly at her.

"What do you have in your hand? Show me."

I put my hand behind my back.

"Come on, show me!"

I held out my hand and opened it.

"Oh! What are you doing with that insect? Is it a beetle? Why have you squashed it? It's so beautiful. Come now, throw it out."

With that memory in my mind, I set up camp, for the sun was setting over the horizon.

It had been a strange idea for my father to give my mother earrings shaped like a beetle. Didn't he know about the religious ban on representing living creatures? Unless he was trying to copy our clan's ancestor, Badrani Nyuni el-Mudi, who dared carve a bird on the mufti's door! In the Koran, only Jesus, the son of Mary, has such authority:

> "From clay, you create a bird form,
> with my permission.
> You breathe into it, and it becomes a real bird,
> with my permission."

Badrani had committed a serious mistake, and he probably paid dearly for it on Judgment Day. It's strange that the elders never dwell on such details when they tell about the clan's origins. And asking about our origins was a waste of time.

"You'll understand after you've had three dreams on Mount Meru," was all I ever heard in answer.

I slept all alone for the second time in my life.

At dawn I set out once more.

All morning long I walked through a smooth grassy sea. Total calm reigned. The plains were so silent that that seemed deserted by all life forms. I couldn't hear any animal calls, any birdsong, and of course never the voice of any genie. Not even a breath of wind to make the tall grass rustle. Sometimes the path would disappear in the mass of vegetation and then reappear as a thin furrow on the ground, though I never knew whether it really was the trail or just an animal path. Finally the trail ended against a wall of grass as tall as a man. I was clearly lost. Not terribly worried, but a little nervous all the same, I began to cut my way through the grass. The elders had taught me how to use the sun for direction. What I needed to follow wasn't some path other men had made, but rather my own way.

It wasn't really that I was walking through the high grass but more as if the grasses were drawing me in and then closing back up behind me. They bent as I stepped on them, but there was no snapping or any other sound. I kept walking as the sun rose in the sky. Its intensity multiplied as it reached its zenith, spreading a suffocating blanket over the plains. Weighted down by the heat, the wide expanse lay quiet.

I sat down, trying to take advantage of what coolness there still was at ground level. That's when I heard a scream behind me. I leaped to my feet and fled. The long drawn-out cry was coming from somewhere in the thick grass. The sound continued as I ran. But nothing was pursuing me. Finally, out of breath, I stopped running. The veins in my temples were throbbing so hard that I couldn't hear anything at all. For my first reflex was to listen. The plains were silent, and the ground was breathing quietly beneath the heat. The troubling cry I heard hadn't upset the earth at all. I had never heard such a scream. It seemed to gather together the misery of the entire world. What frightened me most was its human intonation, when surely only an animal could produce a scream like that. I made no further effort to find out what it was, and in spite of the heat I started walking again. Even if I had tried to rest, my nerves were too taut and I wouldn't have been able to relax. I walked for hours under the leaden sun. Hunger didn't bother me much, and I managed to keep thirst at bay. Finally, dead tired, I collapsed on a grassy carpet in the shade of an acacia tree. My legs were weak and my ears were ringing. Gradually the ringing began to subside, and as my senses were dulled, all I could hear was background rustling.

I dreamed I was walking through a swamp. My feet were sinking in the mud and the dampness tickled my skin. At first, the unpleasant tickle didn't impede my progress, but soon it became hard to ignore and was almost unbearable. I woke up and found that a porcupine was digging in the ground beside me and rubbing against my legs. It ran off into the grass, its path marked by the waving grasses as it scurried away. That was my first dream since I left Mombasa. It seemed insignificant, but it caught my attention. For wasn't my goal to reach Mount Meru so I could dream?

Very near me, I heard a bird call. A small bird rose in full song toward the sky, beating its wings in fluttering flight. Then it folded its wings and dove back down into the grass. I noticed that my surroundings were beginning to change. The plains had shaken off their torpor and now were alive with cries, birdsong and indistinct sounds made by other animals. The plains gave shelter to a variety of animals, and that made me a little nervous. I could hear some barking off in the distance, probably a pack of those wild dogs that eat their victims while they're still alive. The barking worried me a little, because I knew I would be easy prey for such carnivorous animals. Then I heard loud laughing, thank Allah, some distance away, following by equally macabre screaming that made my blood curdle. I recognized the sound of hyenas. My cousin Jawaad hated the creatures and had described them for me. He claimed that his brother Nasser, who had disappeared on his way to Mount Meru, had been eaten by hyenas. He based his belief on a dream he had had a few weeks after Nasser had left home. A man out on the savannah, being attacked by a pack of wild animals, was calling out to him. That night the dream hadn't bothered him much, but the dream became a nightmare two years later when the family finally realized that Nasser wasn't coming home. Even though Nasser, whom I had never known because he was fifteen years older than I was, had been spotted on Mount Meru by the leader of a caravan starting back toward Mombasa, Jawaad was convinced his brother had perished out on the savannah and never made it to the mountain.

So, as soon as the hyenas started screaming out on those plains, I was frozen with fear. I built a fire as I prayed and recited the *shahada*, our profession of faith. I realized I had neglected my afternoon prayers because I had been so intent on covering ground. The effect of the prayers was to dissipate my fear, as if faith in Allah had restored my confidence. Let the hyenas come! I'd keep them at bay with a burning branch.

I set off walking again. But I must admit that having to travel alone was unbearable. I began to complain aloud about my fate, calling on myself as a witness as if I could show compassion to myself. I would have loved to see some adult appear and reach out his hand to me, but all I could hear were hyenas laughing. I would need to get hold of myself, and the first thing I needed to do was to listen to my famished body.

The next day, the savannah still extended as far as the eye

could see. The acacia trees with their flattened tops looked as if some giant had leveled them off with his hand. And of course there was lots of grass, unending grass. The best part about the grasses was the wind creating waves through them that reminded me of the sea near Mombasa. But these particular waves were in fact pushing me away from my hometown toward an uncertain future. As for the trees, their thin twisted trunks were worthless as wood for sculpting. As I walked, I noticed a huge baobab tree, its branches looking like claws ready to seize prey. The thought came to me that I might be able to find some water in the tree and that perhaps I could refill my goatskin. I drew closer.

It was an old whitened baobab, on the threshold of death. There was no longer any foliage on its branches, and the branches themselves were faded by the sun and rain. The huge trunk was swollen like a yam root. Deep down under layers of sap lay the tree's heart, and no axe would be strong enough to reach it. It was an ancestral tree, a king made of wood who had carved his own throne. My steps crossed the shadow the highest branch cast on the ground. On my side of the tree, the branches were too high to reach, so I would have to go around to the other side. Surrounding the tree was a halo of silence that made it even more impressive. When I brushed up against its bark, the silence was so penetrating that it seemed as if I was entering a cavern. And yet the wind in the branches was producing a slight whisper, as if someone was breathing. A huge branch hung down low and offered the means for climbing up into the tree. When I got near the branch I glanced at the side of the baobab that had been hidden from sight as I approached.

And that's when I saw it.

Right out of hell, with its body reddened by the sun and its fiery mane, the lion was stretched out on a large horizontal branch. Its paws with their sharp claws were hanging down on either side, and its head rested on the branch. Its tail waved intermittently to chase away clouds of flies. With its mouth open, the lion breathed with a rasping noise I had mistaken for the wind. It yawned, exposing a worrisome set of teeth.

Its eyes turned toward me, and I would be able to remember them if a dark fog hadn't suddenly risen to hide them. The sight of the lion seared my eyes and struck me blind. But I continued walking, and soon I could see the tall grass opening up before me again. As my sight was restored, bits and pieces of my thoughts came back as well: I was running from the lion, but soon its heavy pads would be pounding the ground behind me like a funeral drum. Like Nasser, I was going to die, torn apart by some wild beast's claws. My painful cry would reach the dreams of my cousin Jawaad as the lion ripped my body apart.

I heard a growl behind me and then the sound of rustling grass nearby. My eyes could make out a shape. There the lion was beside me! It was just walking calmly along. I felt my legs weaken. The lion passed me. Its back was swaying slightly behind its big furry head. I was sickened by the odor, for its gaping mouth exhaled horrible smells of raw meat. I began to follow the lion and my fear dissipated. It had overtaken me so that I could follow its trail. Perhaps the lion was trying to be my guide. It turned away from the direction I had been going, heading more to the south. The grassy wall bent down as the lion passed, and I followed in its wake. When facing the wind, it would sometimes look back. Fate had placed me on the lion's path so it could show me the way over the immense plain. I was clearly under its protection.

Later that afternoon the lion stopped and lay down in the shade of a bush. I found some cactus fruits whose spiny skins were stretched over pulp filled with water and was able to quench my thirst. The lion's stench kept me from trying to rest too close to it. I dozed under a bush some distance away. A growl aroused me from my torpor. The animal was already moving off through the grass. I fell in behind it as if we were childhood friends. It seemed like I had been its companion ever since leaving Mombasa.

We were still walking when a glow spread over the plain. A sheen appeared on every blade of grass, on every leaf, branch and trunk. Every color turned to gold. Dusk was falling. It would not be a dusk during which Bayu would be devoured by a wild animal, but rather one marked with a grand, life-creating movement of stars. The lion looked back at me and growled, then climbed up into a tree. The day's journey was over. I lay down at the foot of the tree, and the lion above me lay staring at the oval sun as it sank out of sight.

I slept soundly, although a strange dream dominated the night. Tall aquatic birds were silently flying by before my eyes. They had long necks, made longer still by their bills, and their legs extended back on the same axis as their bodies. Their broad wings were beating slowly. There were multitudes of them, flying very close together. Through the space between their bodies I could catch glimpses of the star-filled sky. Probably the Milky Way I had seen on earlier nights. The birds were following that great starry river that flowed toward an unconscious sea, rimmed with fertile deltas.

The next morning, there was no trace of the lion. It was simply gone. I climbed the tree to inspect my surroundings but I could see no traces of where it had walked through the grass. It was a great disappointment. I would have liked the lion to keep guiding me over the plains.

In Mombasa, there are many lion stories, including the one about Iffat, a woman who became a model of courage.

On the Somali coast, there's a cove that used to shelter a port, built so long ago that nobody knew exactly when, but long before the revelations to the Prophet. Nothing is left of the town except a tower. A stairway spirals up around the outside, and the tower is wider at its base than at its top. There's not an architect on the Swahili coast who would be able to construct such a building now. According to legend, the people living in the town kept a fire on the top, and the flame burned night and day, although nobody has ever figured out why there was a tower and a fire. Eventually all memory of the town was nearly lost, and the tower alone was left to resist the ravages of time.

Nonetheless, a man from Malindi moved with his family to the forgotten town. He was a *mganga*, a magician doctor, and it was said that he enjoyed the company of wild animals and could communicate with them. Rumor had it that he had concluded a pact with lions by giving them his firstborn son, and it was said he could become a lion himself. On several occasions people had indeed seen a lion prowling near his home at dawn. The terror those sightings caused in the community made him decide to leave Malindi. And yet nobody accused him directly of sorcery. Although there was a rumor of infanticide, everyone recognized the *mganga's* great healing powers. His reputation extended all the way to such distant cities as Mogadishu and Kilwa, and people would come from that far away to be healed. In Mogadishu, one of the sultan's wives was barren, and it was a great boost to the *mganga's* reputation when he helped her conceive. He would send his sons to Malindi to sell his medicines, but those who were really sick needed to consult him in person.

After four years of being married without getting pregnant, Iffat went to see him. The *mganga* asked her lots of questions, examined her and then announced that he would need to consult his ancestors. The ceremony took place two weeks later on a night when the moon was full. The *mganga* went into a trance and disappeared into his hut while Iffat went to stay with one of his wives. Her sleep was troubled by the *mganga's* spirit-inspired cries. She even thought she could hear a lion roaring just before dawn. The *mganga* stayed hidden away all morning long. Finally in the afternoon he summoned her. He was calmly smoking his pipe under a shade tree.

"I believe I can heal you." He exhaled a puff of smoke while she sat there, waiting expectantly for what he would say. "In fact, I'm certain I can heal you. But there is one problem, and it's a serious problem."

He looked at her. She listened with her eyes lowered.

"Look at me," he said. "If you accept my medicine, you'll get pregnant within two or three moons. You'll become pregnant and you'll give birth to twins, a boy and a girl."

The woman smiled. "Thank you," she said.

"Don't thank me, because what I must now tell you will be more painful than if you had gone away with no hope at all of having a child. When your daughter is two years old, you'll bring her to me."

The woman stared intently into his eyes.

"You must bring me your child, and I'll feed her to a lion."

The woman said nothing, but she couldn't keep her hands from trembling.

"I'll give you three days to think about it."

Those three days were horrible for Iffat, but when the deadline came she went back to see the *mganga*.

"*Mganga*," she said, "I accept your proposal."

"You are a brave woman. May your son live until the end of your days. I have one little piece of advice to give you. Don't keep your daughter with you after she's born. Give her to some relative to take care of. That will make her disappearance less painful."

Iffat went back to Mombasa with the medicines she was to take and never said a word about the agreement she had made with the *mganga*. She did become pregnant and gave birth to twins, a boy and a girl. Her husband chose the son's name, but Iffat wouldn't allow him any say in what the girl's name would be. She gave her the surprising name Mkono, which means "hand" in Swahili. In spite of what the *mganga* had recommended, she raised her daughter herself.

When Mkono turned two, her mother did nothing at all. She kept living in Mombasa and learned to deal with her worry. Evidently the *mganga* hadn't forgotten anything, and six months later he sent his son to Mombasa to speak not to Iffat, but to her husband. It was only a brief meeting.

"Tell your wife that my father still expects what she promised him."

And the *mganga's* son went away without another word.

Iffat's husband, when he got back home, bombarded her with questions. But she wouldn't tell him anything. Two months went by, and the woman still had made no move to go back to see the *mganga*. And then Iffat had a strange dream in which the doctor appeared to her, saying: "The stream that refuses to flow to the sea ends up dying in exhaustion on land."

A few days later, several people, panicking, talked about having seen a lion prowling around in the city. The lion appeared twice more, near Iffat's house. The whole city was in turmoil. The sultan immediately summoned Iffat, whom rumor held responsible for the evil spell that had smitten the city. He scolded her roundly, asking her to explain what was happening, but she refused. He even threatened to have her stoned if she wouldn't obey. Finally she said:

"Very well, sultan. Since your city walls and your army are unable to keep a big cat from terrorizing the people, I, Iffat, who gave birth twice in one night, I myself will go face the lion."

The next day she left on a dhow, armed with a sharp sword, but leaving her daughter behind.

A fine drizzle was falling over the abandoned town. Like a large screw, the spiral tower rose out of the ground, dominating the vegetation that had swallowed up all the other buildings. The atmosphere was heavy. The clouds parted a little, showing a patch of blue sky and letting just one ray of sunlight reach the ground. The *mganga*, waiting beneath a tree, saw the sun's reflection on the sword Iffat was carrying even before he could identify the young woman's silhouette.

"Here I am," she said.

"You've come without your daughter."

"I've come alone to face the lion."

The *mganga* burst out laughing.

"Crazy woman! Do you think you can kill a lion with that miserable sword?"

"I'll not be fighting with a man's strength but rather with a woman's will."

"Well, well. What a noble declaration, if you don't mind being devoured in place of your daughter. I don't know whether I should admire you for your courage and willingness to combat the lion or scorn you for your cowardliness at not giving up your daughter."

He thought for a while.

"Since that's the way it is, since you claim to be able to change fate, you'll combat the lion. That will happen during the full moon, in a few days. Until then, you shall be my guest. You may move in with one of my wives."

The young woman started to walk away.

"Iffat!" the doctor called.

She turned around.

"You must realize that I am not responsible for the terms of the contract I needed to make with the lion in order to heal you."

The days went by. And the night of the full moon arrived.

The *mganga* sent word to Iffat to get herself ready that night. And then when it was dark, he summoned her.

"Iffat," he said, "you must climb to the top of the tower, and there you'll await the lion. There's a fire burning up there. You can keep it going."

She followed the staircase winding around the tower and reached the platform. At the back of the platform, facing the sea, a fire was burning. Branches were piled up nearby. Iffat waited in the night's darkness a long time. As she was leaning out over the parapet she thought she saw a shadow slowly inching forward beneath the trees. An animal was moving through the darkness, in the underbrush where only a little moonlight could reach. The animal started across the large clearing around the tower and Iffat recognized the big cat's silhouette. It was an enormous lion with a heavy mane. It stopped in the middle of the clearing and looked up toward the top of the tower. Iffat pulled back from the parapet, but not before she had seen the animal's gleaming eyes. She didn't dare take another look. She thought she could hear the sound of its pads on the ground, and then on the stairs. Her heart was pounding. She backed up near the fire, and with her back to the flames, she stood facing toward where the stairs opened up onto the platform. The big cat appeared. Iffat's long shadow touched it. The fire illuminated its face.

Iffat conquered her fear and spoke to the lion.

"I salute you, O Lion. You have come, and I am here. Please don't think that I've forgotten the oath I made to your friend the *mganga*. I'm not the kind of woman who tells lies. I swore to bring him my daughter."

And with those words, she took two steps forward.

"So, I tell you that my daughter's name is Mkono. Here. I give this to you."

And then she lifted her sword. She extended her left arm, then brought the blade down on her wrist. Her hand was cut off cleanly.

My first activity that morning was to try to find some food, and I was rewarded by happening upon a breadfruit tree standing by itself among the acacias. The flesh of the breadfruit cooked over hot coals is delicious, and fills your stomach like a platter of yams. The savannah always provided sufficient food even if its resources seemed sparse. Had I been able to catch some small game, my ration wouldn't have been so meager. The francolin and guinea fowl hurrying off whenever I got near made me dream of a tasty stew, even though that kind of game is never used in Mombasan cooking. What would I have not done for a dish of spicy rice, a nice *biryani* prepared by a woman's hands, together with a sea bream, its scales coppery-red from the hot oil. Its white flesh, filled with bones, that appears when you pull back the skin. The smell that fills your nostrils when waves of heat rise from roasted flesh. My thoughts spread out tasty platters on the altar of my famished stomach, but reality condemned me to meager fare. I had to settle for the fruits and wild plants the elders had taught me to identify.

I continued my journey across the savannah. My only companions were those thorny trees, and they seemed as alone as I was out on that grassy prairie. I was sorry the lion wasn't around.

I thought again about Iffat's story. She survived her wound and managed to get back home to her children. A few weeks later, a traveler gave her a small package from the *mganga*. She opened it and discovered the ring she had worn on her left hand.

Memories of my family came to mind ceaselessly, in the form of an image, a voice, a word. My body had stocked thousands of long-forgotten impressions and anecdotes, engraved into a memory whose existence I was unaware of. The past, sometimes distant, sometimes recent, came back to mind, providing an unexpected tableau of my life in Mombasa. I felt very homesick. I missed Mombasa.

Off in the distance I caught sight of the Teïta Mountains, mountains located to the west of Mombasa, crossing the plains.

Their heavy silhouettes, worn down by time, seemed to be moving over the horizon. The gray domes reminded me a little of mosques without their minarets. I let them continue on their voyage. I had other concerns, and the first among them was the swamp I was getting bogged down in. Dazed by the sun, I had kept my eyes on the ground carefully enough, but it was beginning to give way under my feet. The tufts of rushes should have given me a clue. The water-soaked ground was scattered with puddles that reflected the fleecy clouds above. The breeze rippled the water without managing to disturb the insects meshed on its surface. Above the reeds, swarms of gnats flew in clouds, and swifts were darting through them, punctuating their flight with strident cries. I wasn't keen on continuing out on that strip of stinking earth. A termite hill provided an observatory from which I could seek out the shortest path across the swamp.

The first thing I noticed was the Teïta Mountains. They had gotten closer. Now they were resting not far from me in the grass, and the idea came to me that perhaps they weren't really even mountains. I thought I could make out a minaret. It rose into the air and then suddenly dropped back down along with a great trumpeting.

I had never seen elephants before, and my discovery made me curious. All I could see above the tall grassy curtain was the pachyderms' backs. I had to wait until the elephants reached a gap in the tall grass before I could see them clearly. Their bodies seemed carved roughly out of stone blocks. Their legs, like pillars at a mosque, held up an enormous mass of flesh. Their flanks were covered with mud. Little birds looking for parasites were clinging to their rough hides. The strangest thing was the pair of ears like huge badly-shaped leaves framing their heads. In Mombasa, where caravans unloaded their ivory, lifeless trophies without soul, I never imagined that elephants could be so noble and majestic. These animals radiate great strength along with a truly feminine gentleness. They take us back to an ancient world. Their beauty moves us because it links us with our own prehistory. There's no doubt that ivory's white gold has been secreted from somewhere deep within their being.

The sight of those peaceful mammals was comforting. I stood

watching them a while, and then I crossed the swamp and continued on my journey.

I slept near a river. At dawn I woke to see spider webs glistening in the sun like jewels scattered over the dewy grass. I moved down to the water's edge, taking great care for fear of meeting some dangerous animal. Reeds, shaded by a curtain of trees, protected the deserted shore. We were in the middle of the dry season, and the sluggish water course wound through a mosaic of puddles and sandbanks. A plump tilapia was trapped in one of the puddles. I hurriedly gathered together some firewood and cooked the fish. I thoroughly enjoyed my catch, feeling only a faint regret that it wasn't served with rice and the proper spices.

As I was getting ready to start off, some trampled grass caught my attention. Some mammal had been lying there while I was sleeping. Among the broken stalks of grass I could pick out a lion's paw print! The tracks were deep and led straight toward where I had bedded down. A big cat had watched over me as I slept and must be prowling somewhere nearby. Might it be the lion from the baobab?

I didn't see the lion that day, nor the days that followed. However, several times its roar echoed out over the plain. I was amazed by its fury, by its strength and virulence. I would listen, with bated breath. The roar would reach its climax and then slowly die out in a long rasping moan.

Lions were not the only animals out on the plains. The fauna hidden by the tall grasses never ceased to disturb me. Animals I knew nothing about lived there on the savannah. I was hearing their calls, wails, and growls for the first time. I could always feel how close they were, and I couldn't let down my guard for a minute.

I was quite alone, and my solitude, something new for me, was hard for me to deal with. I had to learn how to live like that, waking up without one single smile to share, going to sleep without saying one single word.

One evening, as I was digging in my bag, I came across my mother's mirror. I had completely forgotten about it. She had given it to me the day I left. With tears in her eyes, she had given it to me, wishing me a safe trip. "*Na rudi salama*. And come back in peace." Those had been her last words. And then she had turned away with her typical modesty, pulling her veil down over her tear-streaked face as if to indicate that she was turning the page on the childhood I had spent under her protection.

I must point out that my mother was caught by surprise when the council of elders approved my father's decision. She was hoping that the men of the clan would refuse to let me embark on the trip since I was so young. She vainly tried to persuade my father to delay my departure.

"But he's only fifteen years old!" my mother protested.

"That's old enough! He needs to leave this year if I expect to take him with me to Mecca in two years."

"He's only a child."

"A child! He's already as strong as a father with children."

"Will he ever come back?"

"Of course he'll come back! He's an El-Mudi!"

My father, clearly angry, had begun to shout. And he added:

"He cannot wait. In two seasons, I'll receive payment for the palace doors and I'll be rich enough to take the trip to Arabia. We'll marry Bayu to little Hasmahani as soon as he comes back, and then we'll leave for Mecca. With the title of hadji, Bayu will be respected by all the great Mombasa families and his reputation will reflect on our own family and on our clan."

"The Koran doesn't mandate a trip to Mount Meru," my mother dared to say.

"It's our clan's tradition."

With that memory in my mind, I looked into the mirror my mother had given me. What reflected back at me was unrecognizable. My face was tired and emaciated, and my head was a mat of dirty hair. Hunger had hollowed out my cheeks. The once confident smile on my lips had disappeared. Gone were my laughing eyes with which I looked condescendingly over my little Mombasa world. Feverish eyes stared at the unfamiliar person in the mirror.

I had already been walking for several weeks over the grassy savannah. Time was flowing by, and it seemed to me that my path was leading me further from Mombasa yet bringing me no closer to Mount Meru. The *nyika*, that dry region separating the coast from the rich mountainous interior, was never-ending. The days were mournful and without savor, all that occupied me was my fear of the wild animals. I was suffering. My pain seemed unjust to me, but it compelled me to reflect. Now I was evaluating everything I had been given. I had grown up surrounded by my family, living off their generosity. I never had to work hard for anything except for learning how to sculpt. Along with what I knew about the Koran, my mastery of wood appeared to me the only quality I had. Everything else was superficial. And yet the more I felt threatened in this hostile savannah, the more I discovered what new strengths I had. They were helping me endure all sorts of tests while little by little a necessary change was coming about. My childhood was over. I was walking toward my adult life.

One day, tired of walking, I stopped near a fallen tree. The trunk lay uprooted in the tall grass. A thorny bush had taken possession of some branches that had broken when the tree had fallen. Along the tree trunk was a border of white flowers, among which were some grippingly beautiful orchids. At first I didn't notice the bones lying there among the flowers. It was the rib cage, with orchids growing up through it, that first caught my attention. And then when I stood up I could make out the whole skeleton hidden beneath the mass of white petals. Its head turned up toward the sky, the skeleton was contemplating the clouds that covered its body with a shroud of passing shadows. Death was displaying its face in the middle of a bouquet of orchids. Death was completely indifferent to my undertaking, my obstinate crossing of the plains, and it had already prepared a grave for me, a grave with white flowers. Might this man be my cousin Nasser, Jawaad's brother? The crushed leg bones and the missing arms seemed to confirm what Jawaad's dream had revealed.

A lovely blue flower, a perfect symbol to carve in a door frame in Mombasa, had grown up through one of the eye sockets. Its stem had started up through the bony frame and was climbing toward the sunlight. A wasp landed on the flower. At that moment I sensed the presence of something behind me. Some living creature, either animal or human, had been watching me ever since I had stopped near the skeleton. My stomach tightened, and I took some deep breaths to relax. I could smell a musky odor. My legs felt paralyzed, but suddenly I managed to leap across the skeleton. Behind me a lion's roar exploded, propelling me even faster. I took several steps into the tall grass, but didn't keep running. I turned around to face it, raising my machete. An enormous lion loomed up before me, but instead of attacking me, it turned away into the grass with a grunt, as if it were inviting me to follow. I thought it would perhaps show me the way to Mount Meru, for it looked very much like the lion from the baobab. Confidently, I followed it. As it had the first time I encountered it, the big cat chose a different direction than I would have.

I followed the lion all afternoon without stopping, in spite of the heat. The sun was beating down on the plains. I was so tired that I hardly even kept my eyes on the lion, happy to follow at a distance. Suddenly, the lion's head grew bright, and its mane flamed up like a torch. That lasted a few moments and then it regained its former appearance. We continued walking as if nothing had happened.

Night fell. The cat climbed up into a tree, and I lay down under it. When dawn came I was alone. The lion had left during the night, returning me to my solitude.

It's strange that a lion, the animal we most fear, became my guide. "Mother lied to me," I thought. For during my early years, whenever she was exasperated with my foolishness and wanted me to stay close to her, she would call out that a lion was coming. The city of Mombasa also mystified me. Standing arrogantly behind its high walls, it claimed to be the center of the world, scorning the interior of the continent onto which it projected its own fears. And now the bush haunted by spirits had accepted me. I was still alive, protected not by an army of slaves in Mombasa's pay, but by a big cat.

Since the plain was a source both of boredom and concern, I turned to look at the sky. Looking at the sky brought support to me daily and gave me courage to endure my trials. Especially the night sky. It may be surprising to hear that night time in the bush can be enjoyable. I did often hear sinister ululations. Like white specters, owls sometimes flew past me in the night. One evening, one of the specters landed on a branch near where I was lying. In fright, I cried out, and the owl flew off.

But when I could forget the earthly world, its evil forces and dangerous spirits, when I turned my gaze toward the night's heavens, the starry vault filled my soul with its beauty.

As I observed the firmament, I discovered a new star, south of Orion. The night was already far spent. I could see it sparkling joyously as if it were sending me a direct signal. I had never seen that star in Mombasa in spite of the many nights I had spent watching the heavens. So I imagined that it was shining for me, and that I was the single solitary reason for its appearance. That's a weird idea, I know. But the world I was now passing through was so strange to me that the idea, like a star rising out of my own shadows, didn't surprise me at all. I decided to name the star Hasmahani.

I never stopped thinking about Hasmahani as I crossed the plain. The girl had surprised me a few days before I left when she had said I was an artist. The El-Mudis are only craftsmen and have been craftsmen from father to son, following what our elders have taught us. The shapes we carve out of wood represent Arabic geometrical figures or Indian-inspired interlacing. We use such figures to decorate door jambs and panels and arrange them on door frames and mantels along with inscriptions glorifying the Prophet. That's not the same thing as creation.

I enjoyed recalling the beginning of my love for Hasmahani. Even before we were engaged, I was often able to see her because her brother was a friend of mine. We frequently went as a group to walk on the beach at the foot of the little cliff under which the imposing fortress walls rose up. We would sit up at the top of the escarpment, looking out over the sandy white beach with its coconut trees. Their trunks rise up along the steep cliff and their branches spread out above it. Some trees are so close to the rocks that we could leap out, grab their trunks and slide down to the beach. That was the boys' favorite sport when there were girls around to watch their acrobatic moves. I didn't enjoy those demonstrations of juvenile virility very much. In fact, that's how Youssef broke his leg. But my sisters kept pushing me to try. I don't know what joy those two idiots could have gotten from egging me on like that. I never dared refuse with other girls around. When I would ask my sisters later in the evening what some girl thought of what I had done, they would inevitably answer: "Oh, she said you climb like a monkey," with sometimes some subtle variations, like "She said: 'He has the name of a bird but he climbs like a monkey.'"

Sometimes I would be alone, that is, without any other male friends around, and would sit with the girls hoping one of my friends would show up. Like any self-respecting Swahili woman, Hasmahani was (and still is) as talkative as a magpie. So conversation always flew thick and fast between her and the other girls—my sisters, my cousins and their friends. I let them jabber on, watching the reflected coloration the sea takes on as evening draws near, in the wake of the dhows returning to port.

Fresh water gushed out from a spring in the cliff. During the dry season it only oozes a small amount of water, darkening the rock, but during the rainy season the spring makes a small waterfall, and the water digs a narrow little channel in the sand beneath it. I've always liked the sound the spring makes. I loved to listen to the water's pleasurable movement, murmuring words to the stone as it makes its escape. The girls' tinkling laughter beside me wasn't loud enough to cover the music of the water. Sometimes, a different voice stood out to accompany the cascade's melody with a higher pitch. I would listen to the voice without paying much attention to its words. I loved to hear the gay, liquid sounds weaving around the water's song. It was like music played by two instruments, guiding my spirit out to the open seas where ships were gliding under full sail. The voice belonged to Hasmahani.

One day when the tide was high we walked out on the rocks looking for shells and any fish that might be trapped in the little pools. We waded into the water up to mid-thigh, careful not to step on sea urchins. The girls followed us, lifting up their djellabahs, the long robes they wore, and exposing their legs. They pretended to try to be modest, but their shining eyes gave them away. As I dug around on a rock I was able to put my hand on a nice oyster. Not without difficulty, I pulled it off the rock, in great anticipation because sometimes there's a pearl in an oyster shell. My friends were busy catching a lobster that was trapped in a hole, and when I announced my find, nobody came except Hasmahani.

"Wait," I told her. "I want to see if there's a pearl inside." I tried clumsily to pry open the shell with my hands.

"You're going to break it. Here, let me do it." Hasmahani took the shell, plunged it into the water and then brought it up to her mouth. She stuck out her tongue, her lovely pink tongue, and licked the fold of flesh between the hard mandibles. The oyster opened up immediately and she was able to stick her fingers between the shells, delicately prying them apart.

"Oh, there is a pearl!" I shouted.

And indeed, there lay a shiny white pearl on a bed of mother-of-pearl. I reached out to pick it up, but suddenly Hasmahani's hand turned the shell over.

"How sad! You dropped it!"

I quickly picked the oyster back up, but there was no sign of the pearl.

"The pearl is gone! Quick! Help me find it!"

All the sand our feet had stirred up made it hard to see. I bent over and felt around on the bottom with my hands, but Hasmahani didn't lift a finger. The pearl could have fallen anywhere and been carried off by the current. I scratched through the sand, inspecting the rocks and passing my hands over the seaweed growing on the rocks. Suddenly, my fingers came across a strange object made of something I was not familiar with. I realized almost immediately that it was Hasmahani's foot. I straightened up to apologize. But why hadn't she moved away? The girl simply looked at me in embarrassment.

"I'm afraid the pearl is lost," I said.

"What pearl?"

"The pearl that was in the oyster, of course."
"Oh, yes," she said dreamily.
And she gave me a smile.

Chapter four

I had walked all morning long, and was looking for a place to spend the hot afternoon hours, when I heard a guttural sound and raised my head. A flock of black storks was passing overhead. Immediately I recognized they were the same aquatic birds I had seen in my dream after that day of walking with the lion from the baobab. Now the storks were flying with their flight feathers still colored by ink from the dream out of my night and into the light of day. Their nocturnal feathers were still black with night and their diurnal feathers already brightly white. Their legs and beaks were red like the desire that links dawn to dusk. What beauty there was in those birds! The storks formed their flight pattern, lined up one behind the other, and they began to gain altitude. As I watched them soar, I recognized the outlines of a mountain! A gray-blue cone I had taken for sky rose above the plains. Like a reef, the mountain emerged from a sea of vegetation, from the great plains of anxiety. For a moment I doubted that it could be Mount Meru. At such a distance it could only be one of the other tall peaks in that region. It was solitary, not as massive as Kilimanjaro and nothing like the Pare and the Usambara mountain chains. The only thing I knew about these mountains was from descriptions given by the elders in my family. The dark shape suffused with blue light I was now looking at could indeed be the Mount Meru of those legends.

Finally I had reached my goal! Intense joy filled me, a message of delight coursing through my body.

The mountain's shape made me think of a limpet, a type of shell shaped like a hat that the sea deposits in great numbers on the shore. Impossible not to think of the Mombasa beaches. The Indian Ocean deposited its images of foam and sand on the shores of my consciousness. The warm flux of the waves washed over my thoughts, and their salty taste entered my mouth. Vague memories invaded my mind. My tension evaporated. There was a moment of calm, as after a storm. For at times like those the ocean becomes a sea of glass in which the sky can repair its distorted face. The sand seems to be covered with brilliant scales, for many shells are coated with mother-of-pearl. The most beautiful of all the shells is the nautilus. Its chalky, streaky spiral likely hides a treasure down in its inaccessible hollow, down where the walls seem to have been painted with dried blood. Stripes like thin veins transport saline blood toward its secret heart. You can hear the shell breathing when you hold it up to your ear. From the deep cavity arises an ancient word, a love song we recite in multiple tenses at the moment between past and future.

My joy didn't leave me. I savored my victory. I had made it to Mount Meru all by myself! Wild animals, anxiety, hunger and thirst had been unable to stop me. I was proud to have safely completed such a long journey in good health. I was going to fulfill my destiny, to reach Mount Meru and dream three dreams.

I began to head straight toward the mountain.

The land rolled softly, with unfamiliar, sensual shapes. A string of hills—large grassy knolls—broke the monotony of the plain. I spent the night at the top of one of the knolls. It was a pleasant, dreamless night, filled with assurances of victory. The wind moved my grassy bed, creating a slight shimmering of the hill's surface, as if it were breathing. We slept together. Dawn found me joyous, with a feeling of pleasure I hadn't felt since leaving Mombasa. I set out through the dewy grass, walking briskly as if the ground were carrying me. I don't know if I was a waking witness to the earth's slumber or a sleepwalker lost in its night, but I was happy.

For two days I kept up my enthusiasm. Then the difficult progression through the bush and thorns began to dampen my ardor. I had to be contented with just looking at Mount Meru out on the horizon. The bluish mass of the mountain seemed to sway in the whirlwinds of heat rising from the plain.

Mount Meru lay due south of me. The mountain is due west of Mombasa, and all the trails leading to it end not on the north but the south slope. So it was clear that I had walked too far north. Fortunately the lion had twice put me back on the right path. Without the lion's help, I would have gotten totally lost. Unless the mountain itself has moved. Isn't there an Arab legend saying that Kilimanjaro travels over the plains, explaining why the volcano is so hard to see? And Mount Meru is never more than a week's march from Kilimanjaro. Why wouldn't it follow its big brother's example? And in fact I hadn't seen Kilimanjaro on this trip. It had gone off on some secret trail, and its white, round hat, the hat we call a kofia, remained unknown to me.

I use the word kofia in memory of old Mustapha's cutting comment about fat Habib, he who leaped from a dhow into a small boat with such force that he broke through the boat's bottom and drowned. Although Habib never came back up, the sailors just kept on laughing. I don't think that he could have broken the boat's planks with just his own weight, nor that he could really have gone all the way through. We Swahilis like to spice things up so they are more palatable. Yet it's true nonetheless that Habib reposes at the bottom of the sea because he jumped too fast out of a dhow.

Today I can still hear what old Mustapha said. It's as if he were saying it now right in front of me. I was a child, old enough to listen to the men as they discussed things away from the women, but too young to participate. On that particular day the men were speaking about Kilimanjaro. Mustapha loved to talk, and they were listening to him describe the mountain where he had spent two years as a Swahili scholar with the Chagga king. Many times he had seen Kilimanjaro's white peak among the white clouds. When someone asked him what that strange natural phenomenon looked like, he responded jokingly: "like Habib's head." Everyone burst out laughing, except Habib, whose huge bald head was capped with a tiny white kofia.

Kilimanjaro's white peak was the source of frequent questions. Some people claimed that the bright dome standing higher than the clouds is formed by the intense cold that holds sway at that altitude. White must surely be the color the rock turns in the cold's grip. Some people thought just the opposite. They thought the sun scorched the mountain peak, turning it into an ivory jewel set in sunlight. But the most popular opinion in Mombasa is that Kilimanjaro's white mask is made of silver. On the day the men were discussing the subject, fat Habib was the only one who disagreed with all such ideas. He stated that the Arabs hadn't just invented the word "snow" out of thin air (that was the first time I heard the Swahili word *theluji*). "Kilimanjaro is covered with snow," he said. "And that is what happens to water at very low temperatures. It forms when the temperature is lower than we can imagine, like the cold in white peoples' countries." The elders listened patiently to Habib, but I could see on their faces that they were skeptical. Just then the muezzin's call rang out. I saw fat Habib walk away for the last time. A week later he would drown. Now he lies at the bottom of the ocean forever, like the eternal snow on Kilimanjaro.

Every morning Mount Meru's clear outline appeared on the horizon. In the heart of the dry season there were fewer and fewer clouds in the sky. No more cumulus clouds, those clouds that like to show their swollen stomachs to the sun. Cumulus clouds always enchanted me, especially when a falcon's shadow brushed over their radiant faces. Scrubby brush began to give way to swampland. Mount Meru's contours had grown larger, and I could already see the mountain's slopes wrapped, as it were, in a gray-blue *pagne*. The next day a darker crown with a chunk out of the top suggested that there was a forest clinging to the mountainside.

As I neared the volcanic mountain I became more apprehensive, as if something inside me was putting up resistance. I was afraid of that new stranger, that mountain now raising its gigantic face before me. How would I be welcomed by the Merus, those mountain people who live on the south slopes? No one lives on the northern slope I was approaching.

Within just a few days the countryside changed completely, from the first hills announcing the mountain ahead to the volcanic slopes covered with forest. I kept heading south to reach the side of the mountain where people live. I traversed a region of wooded hills interspersed with swampy valleys and natural prairies where herds of buffalo and elephants were grazing. I was careful not to get too close to them, nor did I try to ascertain that the dark masses moving around in the swamps were really hippopotami. I remembered the story of a traveler whose caravan had stopped near a lake. The man tried to reach the water by cutting through some thick brush, not realizing that a hippopotamus was grazing there. When the hippo caught sight of the intruder, it charged in fury. It grabbed the poor man in its mouth and dove into the waters of the lake. The man was crushed by the animal's huge canines and then released, rising to the surface. He floated for a while and then sank.

I was impressed by how tall the mountain was. Its summit seemed to be dozing in a bed of clouds. The mountain's faces rose to attack the sky. They were covered with a mantel whose color kept changing throughout the day.

The volcano would wake up draped in layers of fog moving in wide processions, like ghosts of the dead returning home from their nocturnal visits. Well before noon the sun would burn away the last patches. And then I could clearly see the mountain's massive architecture; a succession of valleys, domes, buttes and escarpments, solid and broken shapes. It was like discovering a gigantic body whose folds were sliding down from the bare summit before disappearing into the fleecy forest. The grand forests seemed to be dancing on the waves of a moving earth that calmed down only when it came into contact with the plains. The sun's course in the sky carved shapes out of the mountainside, shapes that had been completely nonexistent just moments before. From the crests, shadows spread down in large sheets, swallowing up entire sections of the mountainside. New contours appeared in the sunlit woods. White strokes indicating rivers and waterfalls stood out in the valleys and then disappeared beneath the dark forests.

With the afternoon, heat clouds would begin to invade the slopes halfway up the volcano. They dissipated as evening drew near, absorbed by the forest that I imagined must be swollen with water, dripping in the moist heat, the heavy scent of humus hanging in the air. At dusk the summit would re-emerge, like a doomed vessel raising its prow in one last spasm before sinking, swallowed up by the unconscious sea, the long night filled with dreams of Mount Meru.

The volcano's massive form radiated a strong presence. Linked with the mystery of the forest, they made it seem as if the mountain had a true personality, that it was a living being with a soul. Its massive body, clothed with forests and dripping with water, was a sign of fecundity and a source of respect. The mountain's size was impressive, its beauty ravishing, its exuberance daunting.

The initiation rites of the El-Mudi clan are truly hard to understand. How is one to become a man by leaving a magnificent city for a mountain devoted to nature? The trip was taking me back to our clan's creation, and for me, all that was still a mystery. What a crazy idea Badrani Nyuni el-Mudi had to come dream on Mount Meru! In Mombasa, only the wood of the city gates must dream about volcanic forests. Perhaps the genesis of my clan is somehow related to wood, I thought, because for generations we have been craftsmen from father to son. Perhaps our origins lie with the birthplace of wood.

Behind the first foothills I happened upon a hidden waterfall. I couldn't resist my attraction to the moving water or the desire to bath in the clear pool. The falls pounded on the rock below. When I entered the pool, I didn't find the delicious coolness I was expecting. The water was freezing! I had never felt anything so cold. If I had plunged my body under the falls, it would have been an immense shock. I turned to go back down, following the mountain stream.

The stream crossed huge flat rocks that nature had hollowed out in places, leaving natural bathtubs warmed by the sun. With no hesitation, I stripped off my clothes, washed them and spread them out to dry on some bushes. And then I lay down in the deepest of the pools, my head resting on the edge and my body totally submerged. My muscles began to relax. I could see my penis, lying to one side, attached to my groin where some pubic hair was just beginning to grow. Pleased with myself, I must have fallen asleep.

When I regained my senses, my first thought was to put my clothes back on. They should have been hanging on the thorn bush I left them on, but there was nothing there. I looked all around but saw no sign of them. They had disappeared! Distraught, my first reaction was to cover my privates with my hands, as if such modesty could protect me from danger. I remembered my machete and rushed over to pick it up. But I stopped suddenly when I saw two pairs of legs under the leaves. They began to move and two men came out of the underbrush. One was a man in the prime of his life, and the other was just a boy. But the boy compensated for his age with weapons: a lance, a shield and a bow. The older man was carrying a machete, and my clothes as well. I stood frozen, my hands over my penis. The two looked at me with smiles on their faces, especially the older man. His smile widened, and his mouth finally opened up to show a row of yellow teeth and to emit a sound, an interjection, followed by a whole series of sounds. And then the man burst out laughing. He laughed uproariously, holding his stomach.

The man finally stopped laughing and asked me a question in some incomprehensible language. When he saw my stunned silence, he was seized once again by his hilarity. His younger companion kept on smiling. They exchanged a few words in their own language, and then they walked over to me. The boy's face was astonishing. One ear was deformed by a large stretched-out hole in his lobe, and in it metal rings were hanging. There was no jewelry on the other ear, but it too was mutilated. Its lobe had also been stretched, but the boy had folded it back and laid it in the space between the top of his ear and his cranium! His head was shaved, bracelets adorned his arms and anklets his ankles. The older man didn't have the same deformed ears, nor did he have scars like the ones covering the boy's torso. Both wore goatskins around their waists. The man began to speak to me in Swahili.

"I greet you, stranger. My name is Oluti Kamuri, from the Kamuri clan. And you, what family do you belong to?"

"I belong to the El-Mudi clan. I'm the son of Safwani Ibrahim el-Mudi. My name is Bayu."

"What a lovely name!" And he laughed again. "How has this swallow managed to stray so far?"

"I've come from Mombasa."

"You've come from Mombasa!"

Now the man had stopped laughing. He said something to his friend.

"And how did you get here from Mombasa?"

"I crossed the plains."

"Alone?"

"Yes."

Silence followed my answer. The two began to whisper to each other, though there was no reason for them to speak so quietly—I didn't understand a word of their language. Suddenly the boy stepped up to me and touched my chest and then my shoulder. I looked questioningly at the older man.

"He thought you must be a spirit. Don't worry. We don't have the same ideas as Mombasa Arabs do," he told me, alluding no doubt to the slave trade. He handed me my clothes.

"It's not very polite to steal a stranger's clothes," I said.

"Oh, come now. Don't you know it's also not very polite for a stranger to bath in our sacred springs where only sterile women are allowed to come?"

"I didn't know."

The conversation continued in a less distrustful tone. We found out more about each other. The two were not brigands looking for some foul deed to commit, nor were they slave hunters. Rather they were simply two Meru peasants hunting in these game-filled forests. Is there any need to say how happy I was to meet fellow humans? My anxiety turned to joy. Now I was certain I'd be able to reach Meru country, and my two new travel partners, Oluti and his friend, who was armed to the teeth, guaranteed me protection for the end of my journey.

They interrupted their hunt so they could lead me back to their country. We cut across the mountain slopes, walking through dense forested regions that I had previously avoided. They were simply forests with tall, straight trees. Their pale leaves reflected silvery hues in the sunshine. Everything was steeped in silence, but not even the ravines and rivers we crossed could put a stop to my gushing words. It was as if I had to make up for all those days of solitude since leaving Mombasa. My guides were no less talkative than I was, especially Oluti, who understood Swahili. His young companion depended on his translations to communicate with me.

The boy's ears didn't cease to amaze me. I didn't hesitate to ask Oluti about the deformity, and my question might have seemed impolite if the boy had understood Swahili. And then the first thing the man did was to translate my words and burst out laughing along with his friend.

"All Merus, both men and women, wear rings in their ears. They stretch their ears while they're still children."

"But you don't have holes in your ears."

"No, not I. But my children do."

"Why don't you?"

"I'm not a Meru."

"What are you if you're not a Meru?"

"Now I am a Meru, but I was born elsewhere. Fate willed it that I become a slave. I fled from my master and found refuge on Mount Meru. I fled from your city, if you want to know the truth. My master lived in Mombasa. His name was Abdulaziz Mazara."

"Abdulaziz Mazara? The name sounds familiar. But when you fled, why didn't you go back to your own home?"

"Come now. The slavers had ravaged my village, captured all the healthy men and women and killed the old people. They were murderers. I had nothing left."

"So then why did you come to Mount Meru?"

"When I escaped from my master Abdulaziz, the easiest thing to do was to hire on as a bearer in a caravan. In those days the city was full of Kambas looking for work. When we got to the mountain I left the caravan, because I knew it would be impossible to go back to Mombasa since—"

"You've never gone back to Mombasa?"

I know that it's very impolite to interrupt an elder, but because I had been alone so long I could not hold my tongue.

"Last year for the first time. I had some ivory to sell and other things to do."

"And nobody recognized you?"

"What do you think? I was still a child when I escaped. Since then I've had four children of my own, and the oldest is about your age."

"Did you get married on Mount Meru?"

"Of course. I asked the local peasants for hospitality. They aren't savages like your Mombasa traders."

"We aren't savages."

"Well, that man Abdulaziz Mazara, my master, he certainly was. He made me suffer a great deal."

"What did he do?"

"He made me suffer—"

"That name Mazara sounds familiar."

"He was an Arab merchant. He lived in the Al-Qarah neighborhood."

"I've got it! He was murdered last year."

"Yes, that's right. It was while I was back in Mombasa. Have they found his killer?"

"I don't believe so. Several witnesses claimed that a young slave had killed him, almost a child."

"They say that Mazara's penis was cut off."

"Oh, that's the rumor. The family says he was stabbed."

"You know, sometimes rumor is not far from the truth."

Late in the day we arrived at the foot of a hill that Oluti told me marked the boundary of Meru country. From its summit we could look out over a succession of hills covered with forests or grass. I couldn't see any houses in the midst of all that vegetation. There was just bush, then trees, and finally the dense forest of the upper mountain.

"Is that your country?"

"Yes, this is Ussari. And over there, near those hills, that's Mamtara, where we're heading."

"Are there people living here?"

"Of course! Can't you see anything? Look, there are some banana plants." And indeed, in the wooded areas, between the plains and the forest, the light green color of the banana plants stood out among the tree leaves. "And over there, do you see the houses?"

Thanks to the smoke rising from some of the huts, I was able to spot them. So, the Merus lived in the forest! For high above these banana plants and the huts were the tops of big trees. It took me a little more time to pick out small areas here and there where there were no trees; probably some cultivated fields.

"You can also see the protective hedge that separates us from the plains," Oluti explained to me.

"What do you need to protect yourselves from?"

"From the wild beasts that prowl at night, and even from elephants. The hedge is so thick that they can't get through. And then there's always our simmering war with the clans from Masangu."

"You're at war? Why?"

"They found a chief who likes to play at being a king, and he thinks Mount Meru belongs to him. Now and then he launches raids to capture slaves he can sell to the caravans. He also sends his men to hunt elephants. There are many elephants in this area. There are even more here on this side of the mountain than there are near Masangu."

We camped in a clearing for the night, around a fire. I didn't sleep very well and woke up chilled to the bone from the damp, cold air rising out of the ground in the silence of dawn's first glimmers. Fog held the mountain in its grasp. The birds were strangely quiet, as if their songs weren't needed to announce daybreak. The day was slow to break beneath the fog's heavy veil.

We forded a river at the bottom of a cold, damp valley. As we climbed up the other side, a thorn-bush hedge blocked our path. The woody stems were so close together that they formed a true wall. We turned to walk along the hedge, and we could hear children shouting and a cow mooing. We came to a wooden door, and Oluti called out. A voice answered, and the door opened. It was like entering a rat hole, and I had to bend down to get through. We came out into an open space dominated by towering trees and surrounded by banana stalks that looked like an assembly of genies projecting their shadowy designs on me, the stranger. There was manure piled up at the foot of the bananas. From the very beginning my sculptor's eye didn't like the way they stood, their false trunks with no bark separating into long leaves torn into strips near the ends. Not the slightest bit of wood to carve! I felt real aversion for these plants that tried to imitate the tall proud shapes of trees without knowing what they really were. Splotched with green, they stood like priests, but the only offerings they received were animal feces. In fact, real wood was needed to hold up the heavy bunches of bananas that drooped down over the long poles.

The heavy fog dulled the sounds and filtered the light from the rising sun. The guardian at the door wasn't very talkative. My companions set off down a path through the banana grove. I followed close behind, eager to leave the bananas' oppressive vaulted ceiling. But there were bananas everywhere, so thick the earth could hardly breathe. They filled every particle of land, and their clusters of green trunks pierced the ground endlessly. A multitude of trees accentuated the vegetation's domination. My companions slipped through openings in the banana grove, sometimes having to force their way through. Huge trees with massive trunks and luxurious foliage stood enthroned where paths met, immovable in their protective presence. They bore witness to the ancient forest that in places was regaining its foothold.

The path cut through woods untouched by axe or fire, winding through a valley drowned in fog, and the damp air made me shiver. We penetrated deep into a universe of vines, of leaves, of mammoth ferns and of moss-covered trunks. In the banana groves, huge leaves from taro plants spread out like a promise of plenty, and mounds of sweet potatoes plaited the ground like the plaits in the hair of black women. The houses, hardly visible in the mist, stood back, away from the path. We could hear human voices and the sounds of animals. The huts were cone-shaped, and their thatched roofs extended all the way to the ground. They had only one opening, a rectangular door made of wood. In spite of these huts that I could sense more than actually see, everything seemed to be abandoned in the unreal fog. Oluti and his friend were walking fast, eager to reach their home a day's walk away. As for me, so talkative the day before, I didn't feel much like talking. Intimidated by the place, it was all I could do just to follow along.

A few adults appeared. They stood there in the banana groves, often carrying a hoe, and they would watch us pass without greeting us. They all had stretched earlobes, their hair was very short or even shaved off, and their torsos were scarified.

After we crossed a ravine so deep I thought I would never get through, I was astounded to see my dead uncle Daudi come to meet me, reaching out his hand in greeting. Oluti, already starting down the path, spoke to him in Meru without turning around and without waiting for an answer. A little frightened by my uncle's sudden appearance, I wouldn't take his hand, simply raising mine in greeting. It was surely just someone who looked like my uncle. The man stayed beside the path as we went off into the mist. Other men appeared in the fog, their faces always without expression, joyless, almost indifferent, like something supernatural. Long lobes decorated with rings hung down from both ears. I was beginning to doubt that I was really physically in Meru country. Perhaps I was under some evil spell. Bewitched, I was walking through limbo and my cunning guides were leading me to the spirit kingdom. Those men with their deformed ears looked more like souls of the dead than like flesh-and-bone beings.

My cousin Nasser must have known a similar fate. He had

likely been offered up to the spirits of the mountain rather than eaten by hyenas as his brother Jawaad believed. I thought again about my uncle's double I had met on the path. Perhaps he really was my relative! That would be serious. Because meeting one's uncle without the proper greeting, especially if he's already dead, is an offense to the clan. But who could blame me for a mistake like that? Knowing he was dead and believing that I was alive, it was hard for me to understand how my uncle could be coming to meet me.

Everything made it clear that I was under a spell. I remembered that spring of cold water in which I had put my hand. Water that cold couldn't have been real. There must be a spell working.

"You're not very talkative, Bayu. Are you sad?"

Oluti was speaking to me. His voice sounded very human and brought me out of my reverie.

"No, no. I'm just looking. There are so many banana stalks."

Oluti started laughing. "That's what we eat."

"And what's this plant?" I asked, pointing to a luxuriant plant, some kind of dracaena, omnipresent in the bushy hedge along the banana groves.

"That's the *mshale*, a sacred plant. It grows on the mountain."

"Aren't there any fields?"

"What do you mean? We've been walking along fields the whole time!"

"No, what I mean is, aren't there any fields of grain?"

"You'll see. Here we grow mostly bananas, but down lower there's finger millet growing."

A ray of sunlight broke through. The fog's cape opened. The growing heat began to dissipate the filaments of fog that were still attached to the tree tops. What a pleasure it was to feel the sun's caress! The vegetation began to take on brighter colors. The damp leaves and tree-trunks glistened in the sunshine. It was no longer a lugubrious forest inhabited by spirits, but a verdant garden, fertile and prosperous, abounding in produce. Vegetables and grains were growing everywhere beneath the bananas. Bands of flowers extended back into the shade of trees loaded with beehives. Poles propped up plants filled with fruits I had never seen in Mombasa. All it took was the sun shining for a couple of minutes to show how rich the country was and to dissipate my morbid thoughts.

Along with the sun, children appeared. They would run ahead of us and then wait a little off the path to stare at me, the foreigner. They would burst out from between the banana stalks like little naked imps. Three of them ran away suddenly after a few words from Oluti.

"What did you say to them?"

"Ha, ha! I said that you had come from the coast to steal children and suck their blood."

It was clear that Oluti wasn't a spirit! I was beginning to wonder where all the women were hiding when a human shape with a bundle of sticks on its head moved to the side of the path. I couldn't say what most astonished the young woman, the fact of meeting a Swahili or the look of alarm on my face. She was nearly naked, and her breasts were uncovered! Thanks to Allah, a goatskin covered her loins, but her legs were exposed for all to see! I was deeply shocked. But that wasn't the last of my surprises. The path opened up onto a wider one, and there I saw boys leading goats.

"It's market day," Oluti said.

"Will we go past the market?"

"No, we turn off just before. I'll show you the market in Mamtara if you like."

The market place must not have been far away, for I could hear the brouhaha of the market women. A group of women appeared, carrying bunches of bananas on their heads. They were all like the crazy woman I had seen, their breasts and legs exposed! How could a woman put herself on display like that? Others walked past, leaving the market with loads on their heads. Their breasts were all exposed and their legs uncovered.

"Are these women married, Oluti?"

"Of course they're married. If you knew our people, you could tell by the rings on their necks and their bracelets. Look at their breasts. You can see that children have suckled."

So these savages let their women walk around naked! How revolting. How could they look down so on women?

"They aren't dressed?"

"What do you mean? I don't believe they're naked. You must be tired, Bayu. Would you like to stop and rest?"

"No, but, how about their legs?"

"What about their legs?"

"Well...oh, nothing."

"Here, we don't hide legs, if that's what you would like to know. We're not in Mombasa here; we're on Mount Meru."

So, their women went around naked whatever their age. Old women walked past totally unashamed, their breasts hanging down to their stomachs, followed by nubile girls with their breasts just developing. What was worse, some of the girls had their legs uncovered clear to the tops of their thighs! None of the descriptions of the mountain and its inhabitants I had heard from my clansmen had prepared me for this. I was walking in the midst of a barbarous people who found the mountain to be a place where they could perpetuate their primitive practices. Not only were the women naked, but their heads were shaven and their ears were damaged by their heavy necklaces. They wore bracelets and anklets, as well as rings around their arms and necks. Their stylishness couldn't hide how ugly they were with their shaved heads and mutilated ears. And what's more, they were skinny! They all had flat stomachs. Often they had been deformed by childbirth, but they still didn't have the slightest layer of fat on them. Their buttocks were tight, sometimes rounded, but they were as elegant as an adolescent's buttocks, and their legs and arms were muscular. There wasn't one single beautiful woman among all those I met on the way to the market. How shameful it was to display such ugliness without any covering except for a little goatskin around the loins. I thought of Hasmahani. She was then only a skinny adolescent, but she would surely fatten up once she had children. I knew she'd be a great beauty, nice and chubby, with rolls of fat obvious beneath her breasts. And what buttocks! As broad as cushions and even showier. But for these poor woman not favored by nature and degraded by the men, I thought there was nothing to be done. Furthermore, these women didn't seem to be very bright. There was no spark of intelligence in their faces. They stared at me dully and their expressions were almost lifeless.

Of course we mustn't expect too much perceptiveness on the part of a woman. But a woman's possibilities are greater than they first appear. An honest man always acknowledges the intelligence of his mother, because his mother is always superior to other women. An anecdote my older brother Issa told me proves it. In Mombasa, a man must always show his family that he's the true master of his household and that he carefully controls his wife. One of the best ways of doing so is to punish her while the in-laws are present. So from time to time my brother is careful to strike his wife, Aïda, when he has visitors, and especially my aunts, those shrews who keep telling my mother that her sons need to take several wives. My brother goes into the bedroom with Aïda and closes the door. Then she lies down on the bed (or remains standing beside him) and he strikes the mattress with a leather strap while his wife screams in pain. The effect is astounding, and when I'm there I can see an expression of satisfaction in my aunts' eyes, those old shrews. Well, one day when he was performing this ritual, Aïda, lying on the bed, began to take such lascivious positions that my brother became irritated and really struck her.

"Ouch! That really hurts," she cried.

She caught herself immediately and kept pretending to be in pain. That evening, as soon as the visitors had left, my mother called my brother.

"Issa, look at me."

"Yes, mother."

"You surely don't think that you and Aïda have fooled me with your little comedy act! You can stop your playacting. I know you love your wife, you idiot. Just show me the proper respect; that's enough."

Daylight was beginning to fade when Oluti pointed to the summit of a hill we saw rising above the banana trees.

"Behind that hill is Mamtara. We're about there."

Night had already fallen as I walked through the hedge around Oluti's house. The path through the banana grove had led us to four huts grouped around a courtyard where a fire was burning. Oluti had called out to announce his arrival and voices welcomed us.

"Bayu, careful of the dog. He's mean. Be sure not to get too close."

The animal was pulling on his tether and growling. I didn't trust it an inch. We sat down around the fire. A woman threw on some twigs and they flamed up with a crackle.

"Here we are, Bayu. This is where I live. I've got three wives and seven children."

A woman brought us some banana porridge. She served us. Fortunately, the expression on my face was camouflaged by the glimmering flames so Oluti couldn't see the grimace I made when I took the first mouthful. What a taste! Totally bland, with no flavor. There wasn't the slightest trace of any hot pepper to spice it up. I could never have swallowed such cooking if I hadn't been famished from my months of walking.

"We Merus can't live without bananas. If you give a Meru a platter of sorghum or millet, even a platter of taro, as much as he can eat, without bananas he'll say he hasn't eaten." Oluti accompanied his comments with a belch. "Well, Bayu. We can talk tomorrow. You'll sleep in my hut. Just one word of advice. Don't go out at night, because the dog runs free and might bite you. If you need to piss, just piss in the hut."

"There's a place for that inside the hut?"

"Well, yes, kind of."

"Is the dog really dangerous?"

"Yes, he's already bitten two people."

"Had they come inside the hedge?"

"No, they were just walking along outside after dark."

"Didn't they complain to you?"

"Of course they did. I had to pay each of them two goats. Two goats are a lot, you know."

"If the dog is such a danger, why do you keep it?"

"So it can bite people who come by. That way any thieves are forewarned."

"Are there thieves here?"

"Yes. We're rich. Abundance attracts thieves, and even evil spirits."

"So you're rich?"

"Yes, we are rich. How many cows does your father have?"

"He doesn't have any cows. He's not a peasant."

"That's true. As for me, I've got seven cows here, and I've loaned out many others. How many wives does your father have?"

"Two."

"So, you see. I was only a foreigner, but I've acquired three wives by working hard. What do you call that if not wealth?"

A woman came to speak to him, bowing her head slightly, looking down toward the ground as if to avoid his eyes.

"Your water is ready. Go wash."

I washed behind a little fence with a calabash of hot water, and then Oluti led me to his hut. He invited me to step through the narrow doorway. It was too dark to see anything, but the acrid smell of manure invaded my nostrils. I was startled when a cow mooed. Oluti burst out laughing.

"I've got two cows in this hut, you see," and walking past me, he shone his light around. The hut was divided by several openwork partitions. One of the partitions marked off the stable, where the cows were standing near the manger. There were also two sheep and a goat. The stable took up about half the space in the hut. On each side of the door, horizontal racks raised above the ground were used as shelves and could be turned into beds.

"You see, it's easy to piss during the night. You just climb up on the fence and aim for the manure. There's a hole in the wall for removing the manure slurry."

"You keep your animals in your hut?"

"All of our cows stay in our huts. I also used to have a herd down on the plains, but given these troubled times I preferred lending out my animals. We let them out only rarely, even during the day. We bring their food to them."

"Why is that?"

"First of all, so we can collect the manure. And also to prevent the evil eye."

"So you sleep with your cows?"

"Yes, that keeps us warm at night."

I got ready to spend the first night of my life in the company of cows. Barely had I lay down, wrapped in a blanket, when one of the animals gave a long drawn-out moo. Oluti explained to me that cows are sensitive beings, like women, and that my presence made the cow uncomfortable.

I don't remember much about that night other than the cows pissing and the dull plop of their excrement splattering to the ground. And some sheep bleating. As well as the acrid odor of the manure! I had no dreams. But there was strange birdsong during the night, like three whistles, the last of which was accompanied by some buzzing.

Like the day before, the morning was cold and misty. I was torn between the desire to jump up and down to get warm and the wish to maintain a more conventional attitude at the risk of feeling the cold air bite my skin. Oluti had left the hut as I woke up and I waited for him outside. A young woman appeared, naked above the waist and seemingly unaffected by the cold. She motioned for me to come sit in a hut near the fire. She handed me a plate of beans. I have to admit that the woman's beauty was striking in spite of her shaved head and her stretched earlobes. She had fine features, and her face was harmonious even without any hair. She displayed lovely breasts, and their nudity, I must say, shocked me less than they attracted my eyes. Her swollen breasts had nipples that pointed straight out horizontally as if to stretch the smooth skin on the shapely breasts. A fold underscored by a discreet shadow separated her breasts from her torso. Whenever she moved, her breasts seemed to quiver, bathed in waves of light cast by the glimmering fire in the hut.

We know it's always best to try to find something positive in every negative action. Thus I can say that the barbarous custom of leaving women naked has at least one advantage, the advantage of being able to study at one's leisure the shapes that Allah has sculpted on their bodies. During my stay I never failed to observe the breasts and legs of the young women so that I might improve my knowledge of human physiology. Since I was on Mount Meru to learn, no knowledge should be left to chance. And I could never have learned these things in Mombasa, where the women are clothed from head to toe.

So my morning began devoted to the study of the human body. I swallowed the beans while the young woman, some children and an old woman went about their affairs near the huts. Finally Oluti came back and greeted me. Then he said something to the beautiful woman.

"Is she your daughter?" I asked when had finished.

"No, she's my latest wife."

"Oh," I said.

"This afternoon I'll introduce you to the village elders. In the meantime, you can walk around with my son Kialema. He speaks a little Swahili."

Kialema's Swahili was quite rudimentary. Once he got beyond simple formulas, he didn't have enough vocabulary to hold a true conversation. To tell the truth, I didn't really need an interpreter in order to watch Oluti's wife's interesting activities. She cut down a banana stalk and carried it into her hut. The tuft of green leaves disappeared through the doorway as if it had been sucked in. The sound of her machete told me that she was feeding her cows. Then she came back out with a huge platter filled with manure that she put down at the base of the banana tree. Not very noble, if I may say so.

Kialema and I left the woman to her chores and went off to look at the numerous trees that grew in the banana grove. Using gestures, the boy named off for me all the different products the peasants got from the trees. It was an astonishing variety: wood for building and for heating, mulching and fertilizing, fodder, fruits, balms, medicines, ropes, glue. All the trees had either been planted or kept when the forest had been cleared. Kialema couldn't stop telling me all the different species. My sensibility as a woodcarver made me admire all the patient work that had gone into the plantation they had created. The Merus appeared to me in a different light. They were men of wood, friends of trees and guardians of the sap that rises toward the light to build frames for foliage. They were artisans of a rediscovered forest, and they worked in the melancholy of lost woods. I was the sculptor who cuts through the sapwood to expose the heart, there where sap pearls to form beauty spots. Brotherhood brought us together. We were the two extremities of a chain linking man to wood, from its creation to its transformation into a work of art.

The afternoon was nearly over when Oluti announced that we would be meeting the elders of the different Mamtara clans. Mamtara extended from the plains to the forest between two rivers over an area crossed by a chain of hills.

"What will I need to say to the elders, Oluti?"

"Oh, just tell them why you've come to Mount Meru."

"Do they speak Swahili?"

"Some of them do."

"Where did your son Kialema learn Swahili?"

"Oh, that was when he spent a short time in Mombasa, when I sold him to Mazara."

"You sold your son to that Arab?"

"Yes, ha ha!"

"How could you sell your own son to a man who did so much harm to you?"

"Don't worry, Bayu. He didn't stay long. Poor Mazara was killed barely two days after he bought Kialema. Then my son came back to meet me and we returned to Mount Meru."

And Oluti laughed loudly.

I heard a cry and raised my head. There was a strange bird moving around in the branches of a tree. Its unusual beak curved downward and was topped with a growth that looked like a Yemenite dagger. It flew off, followed by four others, their heavy wings whooshing as they beat the air. Were it not for their beaks, the birds would have seemed like ordinary crows, whose color and heavy shape they shared.

"What are those birds, Oluti?"

"They are hornbills. Aren't there any in Mombasa?"

"No. This is the first time I've seen hornbills. What a strange beak. How do they use it?"

"I don't know. There's nothing inside; it's as light as cork. Legend says that the hornbills' ancestor loved the moon. He was so crazy about the moon that he swallowed it. But the crescent moon stuck in his beak, and the hornbill couldn't even see it hidden there in the upper part of his bill above his eyes. Here, when we meet a hornbill, we always say that the moon is walking with its lover. Do you like birds?"

"Yes, I have a great deal of respect for them. They were acquainted with trees before I took wood from them for carving."

Oluti nodded with a smile.

We had arrived at the meeting place, an open area in the middle of a banana grove surrounded by hedges made with shrubs and dracaenas. A huge gnarled tree stood in the center, providing welcome shade. A dozen men, some of them very old, sat waiting for me in a circle on the ground. They were drinking something from a gourd from which wooden handles seemed to extend. The sandy colored liquid came from a cask carved out of a tree trunk. I was less interested in the brew than in the lovely shaped cask, but as soon as I sat down they handed me a container.

"Drink. It's banana beer. It's very good. We mix bananas with millet. Blow on it to remove the foam, just like the old men are doing. Watch them."

On old man with a mischievous look showed me how to do it. With all of them watching, and not daring to tell them that my religion forbade alcohol, I accepted his invitation. I swallowed the brew after pulling out a fly that was swimming in the white foam. It was neither very spicy nor very sweet. The taste was bland for a palate used to Mombasa's spicy cooking.

Oluti asked me to introduce myself and to explain why I had come to Mount Meru. So I spoke about my family, my trip and the three dreams I needed to dream in order to attain manhood. When

I finished, the old men began to speak in no particular order, each beginning to speak whenever he felt like it, even if it mean interrupting his neighbor. All but four of them could communicate in Swahili. Those four asked to have my words translated.

"It's the ancestors who communicate through dreams, Bayu. They might ask you to go back to Mombasa."

"Not necessarily. Sometimes spirits speak through dreams. I myself was once disturbed by a spirit. It would come every night, making a hellish racket in my dreams. I finally had to build an altar and offer a sacrifice to the spirit once a month. Ever since then, it has left me alone."

"Sometimes spirits help us through our dreams. If your wife is cheating on you, the spirits might appear to let you know. When my second wife was cheating on me with my neighbor, I found out through a dream. My wife was beaten mercilessly and the neighbor had to give me a goat in payment. Ha, ha! I did well!"

"You're wrong, my friend. That was just pure chance. My second wife is a real slut, but in my dreams I've never caught her with any of her lovers."

Everyone laughed loudly.

"Your wife isn't any more of a slut than the female cuckoo that lays its eggs in another bird's nest. You're just too old to fulfill your conjugal duties. You're so old you're about to die, and you still choose to marry a little girl!"

"Do you think I'm a novice? Do you think I'm growing erythrina in my fields just so I can admire its lovely flowers?"

I knew that the bark of the erythrina tree could renew an old man's vigor.

"Speaking of trees, some trees induce dreams. Oluti, you must take this boy into the forest to sleep under the great *msadie* tree."

"To get him eaten up by wild animals? Oforo, sometimes the advice you give is really stupid."

"That's where I took my father."

"Yes, and the next day that's where we found him dead."

"The ancestors summoned him. He was very old and death was

slow in coming. The ancestors were beginning to get impatient, and they communicated to me in a dream. Do you think he would have died if the ancestors weren't expecting him?"

"The best thing to do if you want to dream is to get really drunk."

"Absolutely false. Then you'd sleep so soundly you'd spend the night in total oblivion."

"Personally, I don't see anything wrong with what Bayu is doing. I don't see any problem as long as he doesn't dream about killing me! Ha, ha! But he mustn't simply accept the first dream that comes along."

"Our mountain is sacred. People often have dreams on it."

"When we dream, we are with the ancestors. We enter their world. You might as well just die. Then you'd join them directly."

"Stop giving stupid advice to this boy!"

One question they asked led me to tell about the origins of my clan, the story of my ancestor who built the mosque in a tree after moving the tree from the leopard's island. The old men listened attentively. They remained silent after I finished my story. Clearly the adventure with the leopard had impressed them.

"Welcome to Mount Meru. Your clan is made up of brave people."

"The El-Mudi are brave men. Look at this boy. He's barely old enough to be circumcised, and yet he's traveled all by himself to reach our mountain. That's not like all those cheating merchants who come from Mombasa to sell us their cheap junk."

"There are leopards here, too. They live in the forest, and out on the plains as well."

"When my ancestors came to Mount Meru, the mountain was inhabited by little men who lived in harmony with the leopards. The men had tamed leopards like dogs."

"That's not true. Those little men were hunters. They were not afraid to face leopards, but they never tamed them."

"That's not what the traditions of my clan say. Legend has it that those little men lived in caves and talked with leopards. They would hunt together. Our ancestors cleared the mountain forest and killed off all the game that was the life blood of both the little men and leopards. Our ancestors ended up chasing the first inhabitants away from Mount Meru."

"Leopards are formidable creatures. They have a thousand eyes on their coats, and those eyes let them see in all directions."

"You're wrong, my friend. Those round shapes on their fur change into eyes only in certain circumstances."

"Which circumstances?"

"Oh, only the great magicians know that."

"People say that the man who took power in Masangu is allied with a leopard."

The meeting fell silent briefly.

"You claim that magicians have the power to give superior sight to leopards, if I understand you correctly, but do you know any magicians who know how to do that?"

"Yes, and he's right here. Karagwa is such a man."

Everyone turned to look at a man whose wrinkled face was constructed around two big eyes in which all his body's youth was concentrated while everything else was getting old. His beautiful eyes gleamed with intelligence. "Perhaps Losika is telling the truth, my friends. But knowledge is not a leaf that the tree allows the wind to blow where it will. Knowledge lies at the roots of the tree, and the tree never exposes its roots. It would rather just let them rot when its life on earth is finished. When I join my ancestors, I will pass my knowledge on to one of you. It will have to be a brave man. He'll need to have the strength to walk through the bamboo grove and confront the spirits living there. The mystery of the leopard's spots will be revealed to him when he reaches the high meadows."

The silence of those listening to the old man showed me that he was greatly respected, even feared. He continued:

"Bayu is doing the right thing by coming to dream on Mount Meru. Only the men, the animals and the spirits on the mountain will allow him to discover the meaning of dreams. Africa is the country of a dream that other continents know nothing about."

"What is Africa?" an old man asked. He was probably hearing the word "Africa" for the first time. I myself was a little surprised to hear Karagwa use that word, for even in Mombasa it is rarely used. The word designates the continent extending to the west of Mombasa Island, but for the majority of the city's inhabitants, their world revolves around the ocean, with such centers of civilization as Egypt, Arabia, Persia, India and even far-off China.

Karagwa answered cryptically:

"Africa is Bayu's dream."

We talked for along time, and my hosts did the best they could to communicate in Swahili. They questioned me at length about Mombasa. I also had to tell them stories. The story about the Yemenite and the old woman from Kukrani was especially appreciated. The old men laughed at the Arab prince's difficulties. He was the chief of a warlike tribe. His numerous military victories went to his head, and he decided to conquer Sanaa. He needed to cross a desert before he could reach the mountains surrounding Sanaa, and he had to stop in Kurani, the only oasis on the way. In that little town there lived an old black woman who people said was immortal. Every day she would sit on the bridge over a pond on the road leading out of town toward Sanaa. She would smoke her pipe and talk with a carp that lived in the bottom of the pond. Once in a while the fish would leave its hiding place to jump out of the water and talk to the old woman.

According to legend, the woman could keep any army from crossing the bridge and marching on Sanaa. She was able to keep the horses from drinking the water. If the soldiers tried to have the horses drink anyway, the carp would come up from the deep and bite the horses. The Yemenite prince knew that the old woman would resist him tenaciously. So rather than confront her, he sent his falcon to kill the carp. The raptor was a magnificent bird, completely white and prodigiously strong. It could blend in with the sunlight and its prey never saw it until the last moment as it dove out of the sky. The falcon flew over the pond to watch for the carp and grab it as it leaped out of the water. The sky was perfectly blue, and the sunlight shimmered on the water's surface. But the sun's rays couldn't penetrate all the way down to the bottom where the carp remained in the shadows. It saw the bird soaring high in the sky above. The carp left the shadows and came out into the light just for a moment, just long enough to blow a bubble containing its own image. The bubble with the fish's reflection rose to the surface. The falcon saw it rising and assumed the carp was about to jump out of the water. Immediately, it tucked its wings in and dove toward its prey. It reached the water just as the bubble broke the surface.

The victim of an illusion, the bird smashed into the water. It struggled as best it could, trapped in the water, but couldn't fly off. The falcon would have drowned if the old woman hadn't pulled it from the water with a stick. She laid it on the parapet of the bridge to dry out. And that's when the prince arrived with his troops. He was furious about what had happened to his falcon, and he took his fury out on the old woman, accusing her of sorcery. But the woman wasn't intimidated in the least, and she announced to the prince that his army wouldn't cross the bridge and that his horses would never drink even one drop of water. The prince threatened her with death. And he heard her answer:

"You're very black, Prince. Where does your color come from?"

"The sun tanned my skin as I rode across the plains."

"Did you ever know your mother, Prince?"

"Of course. She's still alive and she resides in my tent."

"Did you know your grandmother?"

"Yes. She's no longer in this world, but I knew her perfectly well."

"And how about your great-grandmother? Did you know her?"

"No. She had already departed when I was born."

"That's what people have told you, but it's not the truth. I'm your great-grandmother. Now go back home and tell your mother that her grandmother sends her greetings."

She handed him his falcon. The prince didn't dare say anything and turned back.

All the time I was telling my stories, I made a point of drinking as little as possible, for the calabashes kept circulating from hand to hand. When it came time to leave, some of the men had trouble getting to their feet. I followed Oluti, who without a word started back down the path toward home. He was wobbling, and his frequent stops showed that he was drunk.

"How about just sleeping right here, Bayu? What do you think?"

We were on a narrow path lined on both sides with thorny hedges, the last place on earth I would have wanted to sleep.

"No, Oluti. It'd be better to go home."

"I'm not sure that we can get there before nightfall. Do you remember the way?"

"Uh, no. But you can guide me."

I placed my hands on his shoulders, and though his advice smelled like banana beer, we made it back home.

The next day, I asked Oluti about Karagwa. He had a headache and at first answered sullenly. But then his talkative nature took over and he went into a long explanation.

"Karagwa is one of the three most important men of Mamtara. He's a well-known beekeeper, and he prepares honey for our initiation ceremonies. Karagwa alone is authorized to prepare the mead for these festivals. I drank some of his mead when I moved into my last age group. It's delicious and gives you great strength. The strength comes from supernatural powers that live near the heather. If you climb the mountain, first you go through the forest, then the bamboo groves and finally you get to the high meadows where heather grows. The problem is that you have to get through the bamboos where the spirits live before reaching the heather. The forest itself isn't very dangerous. You might meet an occasional spirit there, and of course animals, elephants, for example, but the forest remains a safe place where we go to gather wood and medicines or to hunt game. But when you get near the bamboos at the edge of the forest, all you have to do is listen and you can hear the spirits moaning. No man will risk his life by going there, except for a few magicians like

Karagwa who have power over occult forces. In Mamtara, he's the only one, along with perhaps a few of his disciples whose identities remain secret, who will venture into the bamboos. The bamboos are always shrouded in fog. It's a dreary world, cold and dark, and filled with moaning spirits. To enter the bamboo groves you need to have immense courage or be crazy.

"Believe me, Bayu. The bamboos are dangerous, it's best not to linger there. But there's something else, and maybe that's what caught your interest yesterday. In addition to the spirits, the bamboos are inhabited by wild animals and in particular by leopards. And people say that leopards are in fact the guardians of the bamboo groves. The bamboos are their domain, you see, and Karagwa surely knows a lot about leopards since he's able to move through the bamboo forest. I'm just an ordinary man, Bayu, and I'm not able to tell you what the leopard really is. Of course it's a ferocious animal, but it's also almost certainly an evil spirit. Whatever the case, it's a dangerous creature and we all fear it.

"Mzui's story will help you understand. One day Mzui was walking through the plains, and he found two baby leopards. Their mother had hidden them, probably so she could hunt. He immediately killed and butchered them. Then he hurried home before the mother could show up. Well, the next day he was discovered in his hut, half-eaten. During the night the leopard had come in through the thatch on the roof and had killed him while he slept and couldn't call out to his neighbors. The calf in the stable had had its throat ripped open as well. And that's what was strange. How could the animal have taken the lives of two creatures without at least one of them sounding the alarm?

"You see, Bayu, out on the plains things are clear. You know which animals to avoid. The buffalo is probably the most dangerous because it's the stupidest. The elephant is less of a danger because you can see an elephant a long way off, and you can be careful not to get too close. As for the lion, shepherds have learned how to deal with it. Lionesses don't normally attack cows, although the herds would be easy prey. Only the old solitary males are aggressive. They are banished by the other lions and become cantankerous and vicious. But the leopard is something else again. It has the gift of remaining invisible. By its fur, the leopard belongs to the sun. But it hunts only at night, when the shadows take over the earth and evil spirits come out of hiding. The leopard is so wild that it avoids even the company of other leopards and lives alone. A leopard is brute force with nothing to restrain it but its survival instinct which requires prudence of it. The leopard is a shadow covered with a golden fleece that's spotted with a thousand evil eyes.

"As I've already told you, Bayu, only one kind of man can confront the leopard. Only magicians who have mastered occult forces."

Oluti grew quiet.

"You've spoken about the three important men. In addition to Karagwa, who are the two others?"

"One is a rainmaker, and the other is the eldest of the Kisanga clan, the first inhabitants of this land. No decision can be made unless all three men are present."

"And how about the other men at the meeting yesterday? Don't they count?"

"Not really. I could have introduced you only to the three really great men. But I had to invite the others."

"Why?"

"Because without them there wouldn't have been any beer. None of the three masters would have had time to make beer. Making beer takes two days. By inviting the other men, one of whom had recently had a meeting and still had some beer left, I was sure to get some."

Chapter five

The people of Mamtara had offered me their hospitality, and now all I needed to do was start dreaming, but my dreams were in no hurry to arrive. Perhaps it was because of the unusual atmosphere inside the hut, the cows whose smell bothered me or the smoke from the fire that irritated my eyes. I would fall asleep, and my sleep would be so deep that I was always surprised the next morning to wake up and see that dawn was already at our door.

I spent my days walking around Mamtara, talking with the people who could understand me, learning greetings in Meru and some other rudiments of the Meru vocabulary. The trip across the plain had stripped away all the pride and arrogance from the Mombasan child I had been. I was able look with an open mind at this new society and its customs, that if not barbarous were at least bizarre. I was surprised there were people who didn't think like us Swahilis from Mombasa and who could still be happy to live as they did.

I made a strange discovery the day one of Oluti's friends showed me around his banana plantation. A dracaena enclosure, as high as hut walls, intrigued me. "That's the sanctuary of my ancestors," the man said, before inviting me in. The dracaenas hid a large wooden chest standing before five posts that had roughly human forms and were carved with geometrical shapes; inverted combs with floral designs and diamond shapes similar to what one might see on doors in Mombasa. Surely these were Arab symbols the Merus had borrowed? But not many Arabs ever came to Mamtara. What was even more astonishing was the three-dimensional bird on top of the central post. It had an enormous head, and its neck was folded upon itself to allow the long curved beak to touch its breast. The wings with their well-formed feathers lay flat against its body. The red beak was the only spot of color in the five white posts. I found that disconcerting. So the Merus had no scruples about representing a living creature. It's true that they didn't know the true faith.

My host raised the lid of the chest and pulled out some human skulls. As I watched incredulously he introduced them with a big smile on his face: his father, his grandfather and an uncle! What a country of savages! My ancestor, Badrani Nyuni el-Mudi, had sculpted a bird on the mufti's door because he had been perverted by these people, I thought, forgetting that he had committed that deed before he made his journey to Mount Meru.

"Who carved these things?" I wondered aloud.

"An artisan."

"Why did he carve a bird?"

"It's not a bird. It's the protective spirit of my clan."

"Why these Arabic motifs?"

"They aren't Arabic designs. We've always made designs like these on our funerary posts."

"But they must come from Arabia. We've got the same shapes in Mombasa."

"Absolutely not. These are Meru symbols."

I didn't know what to say. Disconcerted, I left that strange place.

One night, something happened. It was like a slight quivering in sleep-stirred magma. A boat was gliding across a calm lake, creating little ripples, but I couldn't figure out what it all meant. I got up with the sensation of having had a dream that disappeared when I awakened. All that was left was an impression.

The next night I did dream. The dream made it across my sleep and reached the banks. Here it is:

I come to a house, an old building like we find on the coast, without any inhabitants. Inside there's a little statue representing a person, and against one wall there's a button. I push the button and it activates a trapdoor in the floor, opening up on to an underground hiding place. I think I've finally found the secret hiding place I've been looking for so long, and it's a hiding place that contains numerous books and papers relating to my childhood. I'm getting ready to go down, but at the last moment I change my mind and decide to leave the house. To my surprise, the house is now surrounded by the waters of a lake and the dream doesn't allow me to see the other shore. I meet someone to whom I speak about my discovery, but the person doesn't take me seriously. I go back to try to see the secret hiding place. When I get close, I realize that it has been flooded and is no longer accessible.

It was misty as it was every morning. Wrapped in my blanket and warmed by the fire, I was eating with Oluti and an old man who had come to talk to us.

"Oluti," I asked. "Is there a lake somewhere on the mountain?"

"On the mountain? No."

"There's no lake at all?"

"The only lake I know about is Lake Chana, and it's out on the plain."

"Is it far away?"

"No, but nobody lives there. The lake is inaccessible."

"Why?"

"Because we're at war with the people from Masangu. Or rather to be more exact, they are the ones, since the creation of their so-called chiefdom, who decided to declare war on us. Their soldiers invaded the lowlands that belong to us and chased off the peasant women who used to grow millet there during the rainy season. We've protected ourselves by planting that thorny wall of bushes. We're just waiting, because the elders do not want to send our young men into combat."

"I would like to go to the lake."

"That's impossible. You'd never make it alive."

"But I've dreamed about that lake."

"It must have been a nightmare, Bayu. Wait for another dream and forget that one."

"But it can't be impossible to stay out of the hands of the Masangu warriors."

"Even if you managed to slip through their nets, you'd never reach the shores of the lake."

"Why not?"

"It's a gigantic hole with steep walls."

"There's no way to get down?"

"No."

And then Oluti's friend interrupted him. "Tell him the truth, Oluti."

Oluti began to grumble, muttering incomprehensible words, and then finally admitted reluctantly, "There is a passageway, but it's protected by a spirit. Back in the old days we would go to the lake to fish, but then the spirit chased us away."

"How?"

"He killed the fishermen by breaking their pirogue with one swing of its tail."

"By swinging its tail? It has a tail?"

"Yes, it's a crocodile, an immense crocodile."

"If it's just a crocodile, why don't you organize a hunt to kill it?"

"It has the form of a crocodile but it's really a spirit! You can't kill a spirit because it's already dead! Do you think a real crocodile would be able to reach a lake like that? It's not connected to any river. And what's more, the beast is longer than two pirogues!"

"Why would a spirit go to that lake?"

"Oh, there are probably several reasons. Some people say it's because fishermen stopped offering sacrifices and kept taking without giving anything back. The spirit of the lake may have become a crocodile to punish men for their ingratitude. The elders in Mamtara believe that the spirit of the lake becomes a crocodile once every hundred years, and that's what the clan's oral traditions suggest. If that's true, then what we need to do is offer a particular sacrifice that a few wise men used to know about. Unfortunately, they all died during the big plague epidemic. They took their knowledge with them, and no dreams or divinations have been able to retrieve it. Our great men and our teachers find themselves powerless to find the secret offering demanded by the spirit of the lake."

"Perhaps it's the old Arab who changed into a crocodile to get revenge," Oluti's friend added.

"The old Arab? There was an Arab?" I asked. But Oluti interrupted me.

"To get revenge for what?"

"For the evil the fishermen did to him."

"They didn't do anything to him. That's nonsense."

"There was an Arab?" I asked again.

"Yes. More than ten years ago a man came from the coast with a small caravan and asked if he could settle on the lake shore. He said he wanted to communicate with God, and that seemed like quite an ambitious undertaking. He brought many books with him, including the Koran. But because nobody here knows how to read, we had no use for his books, especially since the people of Mamtara are not acquainted with Islam. Of course we offered him hospitality. So he moved in, living in solitude. What was strange is that he built a stone house at the base of a cliff on a little promontory near water level. No one could believe it! How had he managed to carry the stones down to the base of that cliff? But no matter, we left him in peace, and all the more so because he had supernatural powers."

"We didn't leave him in peace at all! The fishermen were always complaining about him, saying that fish weren't as plentiful since he got there," the old man said.

"Nonsense," Oluti responded. "In any case, finally he just disappeared."

"Just disappeared?" I asked.

"Yes, and that's when the crocodile first appeared."

"Of course," said the old man. "He turned into a crocodile."

"No. It's more like he was eaten by the crocodile. In any case, now all access to the lake is forbidden."

"I could try to reach it anyway."

"Don't count on me to take you there. Besides, I forbid you to go. I don't want to be responsible for your death. I can already hear the elders blaming me when you disappear. Go dream some other dream, Bayu. The nights are full of dreams."

I didn't know how to respond.

"This afternoon I need to go to a hill from which we can see the lake. Come with me if you like, and I can show you how inaccessible the lake is."

I accompanied Oluti to the top of the hill, passing through a maze of hedges woven over dark ground where the peasants had carved out veritable stairways. The banana groves with their panoply of protective trees extended down toward the plain all the way to the thorny barriers. The barrier fence was so distinct that it divided the countryside into two separate zones. One was verdant and joyful, and you could hear human voices and the sounds of domestic animals; the other was dry and soundless, dressed in the pale colors of the lowlands. Out on the plains rose a hill, near a gray-blue spot that shimmered in the sun. That was Lake Chana. In spite of the distance, we could make out the steep cliffs.

"You see, Bayu, back in the old days we used to grow crops all the way out to the lake, and our animals were able to graze over the entire expanse. But since the people of Masangu have become such warmongers, we have had to give up all that."

"Does no one go out on the plains anymore?"

"Yes, and some go out quite often. But the problem is that

growing millet is a woman's work. Women do all the work except preparing the soil. And what the Masangu warriors are especially looking for are women, and cows as well.

"Now look. You see the hill over there. Look carefully. What do you see on the hilltop?"

When I looked carefully I could make out two human forms.

"They are men from Masangu, and from that lookout post they watch over the whole plain. Let me assure you that you would never escape their vigilance."

Oluti had some business to take care of, and he let me start back by myself. A voice stopped me as I walked along. It was the old man who had shared our meal that same morning.

"Young man, if you still wish to go to Lake Chana, I'm willing to help you. In two days I must go out onto the plains, and I'll show you the path."

"How about the guards on the hilltop?"

"Oh, first they need to see us! We can follow little paths where the vegetation will keep us hidden. The true peril isn't so much those warriors but rather the spirit of the lake. What do you want to do at the lake?"

"I want to visit the Arab's house."

"Hum! You've not chosen an easy task. I doubt that you'll make it, but I'm willing to help you. Listen, we'll leave early in the morning after breakfast so that nobody can guess what you're trying to do. You'll come meet me at my house. I'll prepare a bag of food for you, enough for several days."

"Thank you, *mzee*," I said, using the appropriate term to address an old man. "I'm infinitely grateful. How about you? What will you be doing out on the plains?"

"I'm going to see my wife."

"Your wife lives on the plains?"

"Yes. And in two or three days, she'll be in blossom again. Well, now I've got things to do. We'll meet the day after tomorrow. Don't say a word to Oluti. I'll see you soon."

I wasn't able to learn anything more about his mysterious flowering wife. Now I needed to wait until our departure day. On the appointed morning, after stuffing myself with beans and yams, I went to meet the old man. We reached the enormous living barrier that protects Mamtara from outside dangers. The hedge is composed of an impressive tangle of thorny trees, bushes and shrubs, and the natural defenses seem impenetrable. A tiny door a boy was guarding allowed us to slip out through a passageway carved through the thorny mass.

"When you come back, Bayu, you can use that big silk-cotton tree as a landmark. That's where the entrance is."

The entrance would have been impossible to see without the big silk-cotton tree standing there like a lighthouse.

We crossed a succession of millet fields in which the tiny grains had grown reddish because of the drought, and then we traversed parcels of land that clearly had been abandoned or left fallow. The rows of trees looked like rosaries that the peasants had planted as prayer offerings to the land. The trees growing along the dry riverbeds kept us out of sight. Ancient trees, draped in vines and covered with epiphytes, soared upward on both banks, and their branches met, often forming a vault that gave shade to the dry river's sandy bed. There was nothing to fear, and we were able to talk as loudly as we wanted, frightening off the bands of little gray monkeys that often barred our path.

"I'll leave you halfway to Lake Chana, Bayu. But I'll show you another dry river that'll lead you nearly there. All you'll need to do then is head for the hill beside the lake. As for getting down to the shore, don't ask me how. The only practicable path leads down to the place where the crocodile likes to hang out. So needless to say we never stay there very long. Everywhere else there are steep cliffs. Of course there may be tunnels leading down to the lake shore, formed by torrential currents during the rainy season. There are certainly caves at the foot of the escarpments. In fact, I suspect the Arab used one of those tunnels to get down to where he built his house."

We left the shadows of the huge trees and walked out onto the grassy savannah.

"Here we are," the old man said, pointing to a large tree.

There was no indication of any human presence.

"This is where your wife lives?"

"Yes."

"I don't see her."

"Do you see that tree?"

"Yes."

"Well, then you can see my wife."

The tree stretched out like a parasol of small green leaves. Its roots ran over the soil, forming a star with the gray, white-marbled trunk at the center. Thus created, the trunk divided into several parts. I wasn't sure how to understand the tree. I was attracted by its beauty but disappointed by its knotty wood that would be useless for sculpture. We sat down on a large root a few feet away from a circle of stones, a sign that fires had been built there. I took the gourd from my bag.

"Oh, there's no reason to use your water gourd. There's plenty of water in the baobab over there. Let me go get some. I'll be back right away."

"I can come with you."

"No. The baobab is protected by a swarm of particularly aggressive bees. They would sting you."

"And how about you? Won't they sting you?"

"No. They leave me alone. They are grateful to me because this tree blossoms every year at this time, giving them access to a rare variety of pollen. Most flowers are no longer blooming. So, wait for me here."

I was skeptical, but let him go. I watched a flock of sparrows that were using the tree as their perch. The birds were dancing like acrobats to catch and eat larva hatching in a termite mound.

"Here, drink some of this water. It's as pure as the heavens. A bee did sting me, some foolish young bee born just this year that didn't know who I was."

The water, lightly perfumed by the baobab wood, was delightfully cool.

"Have you ever loved a woman, Bayu?"

"Yes, *mzee*. I love my fiancée."

"Oh, you're a lucky man! How fortunate, and you're still so young! Let me tell you my story and you'll understand why I'm willing to help you today. During my lifetime I've had two wives. The first was chosen for me by my family. She was neither ugly nor beautiful nor intelligent, but she could make babies and take care of my cows, and I couldn't ask for anything more. The second one I found almost by myself. Her father, a friend of mine, offered her to me, and I accepted so that I could expand my family and fulfill my manly duties to procreate and insure the clan's prosperity. She wasn't particularly beautiful, but she was nicely plump, and that's unusual around here, because our women have to work hard from dawn till dusk. And then too there was something attractive about her, a certain indefinable quality that made her stand out. In short, I built a hut for her and gave her some cows and a parcel of ground. I paid off all my obligations to her family, and then to finish things off, or rather to start things off, I got her pregnant. Things could have gone on like that if, after the child was born, something strange, something almost enigmatic hadn't happened. I started loving her! I know that might seem ridiculous, but the fact is that I loved her. I loved her with that juvenile feeling that sometimes inflames newly-circumcised youth, but a responsible adult man owes it to himself to avoid such feelings. And what's more, the woman responded to my love. She too fell in love. Our passion brought us happiness like I never could have imagined.

"We lived happily together. It goes without saying that we hid from everyone around us how we really felt. I couldn't risk being the laughing-stock of my clan or being called a weakling by my neighbors. For several years I experienced intense happiness, and no one but my first wife knew anything about it. Alas, what life can hide, death uncovers. An unknown epidemic ravaged Mamtara, killing at least twenty people in a month. It was a horrible disease, covering its victims with pustules and then smothering them in bouts of fever. A horrible curse had fallen upon our land. We had probably offended the mountain and it was taking revenge. We offered up numerous sacrifices to the mountain, and finally the curse subsided, but not without carrying off one last victim. That last victim was unfortunately my wife. My wife, Bayu, the source of my happiness! I couldn't hide my pain. Soon the rumor spread that instead of burning her hut and abandoning her body in the forest I was still grieving and shedding tears. My clan was furious. They sent a group of men to take the body and throw it in a mountain chasm. That's the customary practice when someone dies from an unknown disease. We throw them from a precipice a half-day's walk away in the forest. The men came to get the body, but I wouldn't let them have it. They gave me a night to change my mind, and then they were going to burn her hut and me along with it if I wouldn't give in. When night came, I took the body, wrapped it in a shroud and left Mamtara. I ran through the banana plantations to reach the plain. Nobody saw me and I could easily find my way because the moon was full. I walked a long way, not knowing where I should go. I came upon this tree. It was dead, fleshless, without any leaves. But, in the raw moonlight, it was reaching its long thin branches up toward the sky as if it hadn't given up on life, as if it were filled with the hope of blossoming again. It wasn't so much imploring the sky as it was affirming its own beauty and eternal presence. Its grace touched me and I decided to bury my wife's body among its roots. For her to rest forever at the base of this noble tree was my desire. I remained to watch over her grave, in no hurry to return to Mamtara and face my clan's anger. And then a miracle happened! The tree turned green and blossomed once more. In just a few weeks new growth appeared on its branches. The tree's silvery foliage returned. And the buds formed, bringing to life magnificent flowers. If you only knew how happy I became when I saw the spectacle. It was all the more amazing because the normal time for blossoms was two moons earlier. My pain was lessened, because I knew that my wife had not gone to be with evil spirits deep within the earth, but rather to the cosmos. She had gone back to the universe while remaining near me. I was happy.

"I returned fearlessly to Mamtara to face my clan and its

contemptible traditions. I held my own against the elders. The unique spot of color on the colorless plain at the end of the dry season, the blossoming tree, was there to give me strength and prove that I had made the right decision. That's why I'm helping you, Bayu. Oluti is trying to protect you from the risks you are running by going to Lake Chana. He would like to see you settle in Mamtara, and the elders of his clan are ready to give you a wife and a parcel of ground. But they forget that a man's destiny is to accomplish his dreams.

"You see, Bayu, the flowers always blossom again at the same time every year, just when the moon is full. Every year I came to pay homage to my wife."

We spent the night at the base of the tree, contemplating the design of its branches against the vault of the sky. The tree hooked several stars on its branches.

"That must be what the tree's new blossoms really are," I thought as I fell asleep.

When I awoke, an astonishing sight was in store for me. The tree had blossomed during the night. It was wearing a profusion of flowers with lanceolate petals; red flowers with white spots. The lower branches, heavily loaded, were crowned with a vermilion crest. The flowers gave off a heady perfume, and the bees were already gathering their pollen. The old man was sitting back against the tree, chanting softly. He was talking to his wife, a smile on his face. I didn't want to disturb him. The evening before, he had shown me the dry valley that would lead me toward Lake Chana, advising me to leave early in the morning. I said goodbye and walked away. He called out to me.

"Bayu, my wife sends her greetings."

"Thank you, *mzee*. Give her my greetings as well."

And I set off to accomplish my dream.

The river currents had dug a shallow channel, lined with thorn bushes, African hemp and a few large trees. There were few signs of life except for a few flocks of francolins that would run away when I approached, heads held high like proud girls when boys tease them. A warthog scampered off with its young, and the undulating flight of some small hornbills with red beaks gave some life to the austere countryside. After a few meanders, the river spread out and sank into a small hollow at the foot of some enormous rock formations. The hollow was surrounded by thick vegetation. I climbed up on one of the rocks. On top there were some agama lizards with their orange heads and blue-gray bodies. One of them had caught a beautiful, brilliantly colored butterfly, and its wings were beating furiously. The lizard was in no hurry to swallow its prey and sat there motionless, as if the life had been sucked out of its body to be concentrated in the last glimmers of light that the butterfly, near death, was casting around it.

Standing on top of the rock, I surveyed the plains. The butte that hid the lake rose up not far away. I could take in the entire countryside with a glance: The plain's dry expanse, the armor formed by the trees and bananas to protect the foothills of Mount Meru, a little further on the slopes conquered by forests, and then finally the high peaks that had nothing but clouds to hide their nakedness. My eyes swept across the foothills and back to the plains, stopping to look at the last hill, the Masangu warriors' observation post. I hadn't given much thought to them as long as I was still with the old man. There had been no sign of them. I wouldn't have worried at all if the wind hadn't suddenly carried to me the sound of a voice. Without thought, I dropped down on the rock. How imprudent to stand up on an outcropping in the middle of the plain! I had been watching the horizon out across the plain, but that wasn't where I should have been looking. Down below the rocks, three men armed with shields and lances were moving in my direction. One of them looked particularly fearsome. His face was framed with long white and black feathers.

In one bound I leaped down from the rock and plunged into the thick vegetation, hoping to escape back through the river valley, but I tripped on a stone and fell into a cavity hidden under some bushes. I could hear steps on the rocks. The men were coming down the escarpment. They must have stopped. They began to strike the bushes with their lances. The crevasse I had landed in extended on horizontally through the rock. I followed it on my hands and knees. My shelter kept me out of the trackers' reach. I couldn't hear them any longer. Suddenly there was a sharp crack, followed by some crackling and then more crackling still. They had started a fire! They were trying to flush me out using flames! If I didn't get out, the fire would roast me alive. I was panic-stricken, and my first reaction was to leap backward, but then I noticed that the crevasse opened up onto a tunnel. Bent over, I entered without hesitating. With my flint stone, I lit the resin-coated stick the old man had put in my bag so I wouldn't get lost at night. And then I continued down the tunnel, going deeper and deeper into the gallery that had been carved out through the rock.

Even though bats frightened me as they suddenly flew off, I felt safe in the tunnel, far from hostile men. I had the strange feeling that I was moving outside of time. Impossible to tell how much time had elapsed since I had started down the tunnel. I came to another shaft that seemed to lead upward, and not knowing which direction was best, I decided to continue down the first one. It opened out onto four hollowed-out pockets in the rock, one after the other, separated by thresholds or linked by narrow openings. They were true caves, high enough for me to stand upright. The air seemed pure, and only the unpleasant smell of the torch's burning resin bothered me a little.

When I entered the second cave, I noticed some red marks on the wall. They were simple vertical marks, not natural, surely drawn by the hand of man. I carefully examined the walls of the first two caves but didn't find any other marks. It was in the third cave that I discovered the paintings. The word "paintings" may be a slight exaggeration, because they were only rough sketches and looked more like scribbling than the work of a real artist. And yet they showed a certain grace, no doubt because of the unusual place they had been drawn. In total silence, my torch projected its glow on the wall, giving life to strange creatures: people depicted with just a few strokes, and some animals, among which I could easily recognize antelopes and gazelles. The drawings were hunting scenes. A man was drawing his bow, aiming at some gazelles. One had been struck by an arrow and another was lying on its side. My heart began to pound furiously when my torch lit up a new painting showing a spotted animal. A leopard! Human beings without weapons were running along beside it. A little further, another leopard held in its fangs a monkey that I would have taken for a child had it not been for the tail. Some men were seated expectantly below the animal. On the opposite wall, two huge leopards were shown with two tiny men, and one of the men seemed to be sleeping. The circles on the leopards' skins were like eyes, and their fangs were bared.

And I hadn't reached the end of the surprises. The last cave didn't have any decorations, but on the floor there was a perfectly preserved animal skeleton. At first I thought it was a big dog, but the head was that of a cat with large canines. It was surely a leopard. The skeleton worried me, because the animal certainly hadn't come of its own accord to die in this narrow underground cavity. It must have been sacrificed and then the body deposited in this place. No doubt I had discovered the site of some pagan ceremony that was as old as it was incomprehensible.

The animal's head was turned toward the opening, and that's where I went immediately, eager to leave a place where the forces of evil were surely active.

I had no idea how long I had been walking in those subterranean galleries. Finally I noticed some light off in the distance. I extinguished my torch so I could see the light more clearly. The light was a dull yellow, so it didn't seem to be daylight. A thousand thoughts invaded my mind, each more pessimistic than the others. If the glow was the light of a fire, then I was condemned to meet the devil, for who else would have a fire underground? A cry rang out, freezing me with fright. Evil genies must be dancing in one of the caves along the tunnel. In my fear, I started back up the tunnel and then stopped, determined to go confront the devil. After all, I belonged to the race of the El-Mudi clan! I inched along quietly on my elbows, flat on my stomach. I hardly dared breathe, so afraid I was of drawing attention to myself. The glow grew brighter, and as I rounded a curve in the tunnel, it shone on every wall. The tunnel fell away, and from the opening poured the strange glow. Horrible cries rang out again, like monkeys screaming. They made my blood freeze. In the silence that followed, I heard some dull pounding. Was the devil using a mortar and pestle? I had come to the womb of the earth, where the devil holds sway, and I had found his lair. I started to move back, but then something held me there. Bravely, I inched toward the hole, and then against the gray luminous background a star appeared. A star! Quickly I crept closer to the opening and discovered Lake Chana there below, reflecting the full moon shining up above me in the night sky.

The cave opening pierced through cliffs that formed a nearly perfect circle around the water of the lake. It was a beautiful escarpment capped with a crown of trees. Up above, the immense vault of the sky displayed its starry armada. A few massive clouds dragged themselves nonchalantly along. The moon, the true master of the place, ruled clothed in its diffuse halo. In the moonlight, the glassy waters of the lake glittered. Hidden away in a hollow in the earth, protected by the thick forest surrounding it, the lake seemed to be dozing. The silence was troubled only by some baboons barking and owls calling. All was calm. I wish I could have said the same thing about me. From my vantage point on the shore, I contemplated the dark waters worriedly for a long time.

The steep cliff face was an impossible obstacle, unless I dove into the lake, running the risk of crushing myself if the water wasn't deep enough. On my left, an enormous rockslide had cut into the escarpment. An entire section of the cliff had broken apart and lay in big chunks all the way down to the water's edge. That seemed to be the only way down to the lake, and it was supposedly guarded by the crocodile. But however much I stared down at the shore near where the rocks had slid into the water, I didn't see the spirit of the lake.

On the opposite bank, an enormous block of stone had broken away from the cliff and fallen into the water, forming a tiny island. A lovely tree was growing on the rock.

Slowly the moon moved across the sky, its reflection appearing on the lake's surface. A yellow disk like a gigantic water lily was floating on the lake. When it reached the center of the circle formed by the lake, an eddy appeared, the water began to swirl and a body broke through the lunar orb. A long animal had surged up from the depths and was dividing the moon's reflection in two, forming an eye like that of a wild animal. The animal began to pivot, swimming around the golden circle. I realized it was the spirit of the lake, the crocodile that had come to remind men that we can't get away with breaking our pact with nature. It was the guardian of the waters and held the secret of the place. Its size was impressive, longer than three times a man's height. Its legs seemed short, but its head was enormous and flattened out as if by blows from a club that had spared only the eyes and nostrils. Its lips didn't fit together perfectly, and displayed a row of teeth. Rows of bumps, pointed excrescences, ran the length of its body, converging on the huge, powerful tail. Just seeing the animal move its tail was enough to make me realize it was a formidable weapon. Its totally black carapace was an assemblage of solid plaques that no assegai could ever pierce. I remembered Oluti's warnings. How could one confront such an animal, endowed as it was with supernatural strength and possessed by a spirit's intelligence?

Legs tight against its body, the crocodile swam by swinging its tail back and forth. It kept circling around the moon's reflection. Sometimes it would lift its tail and slap it down violently on the water's surface. It was an amazing spectacle to see the immense tail rise out of the water and then slam down with a huge foamy splash. Then the monster would lift its head out of the water and open wide its jaws. It would remain like that for a few moments and then plunge its head back in the water. And then it would begin circling around the moon again, sometimes snapping at the yellow spot as if to seize the moon in its jaws. It would call out, and the cries sounded like drum rolls. The dance the animal was displaying for the moon resembled a nuptial parade. It lasted part of the night, until the moon's reflection left the lake. Then the monster's slender shape melted into the shadow of the cliffs. Until then I had had no trouble staying awake, but at that point my attention began to wane. I could feel my strength leaving me, and I was invaded by great lassitude. Sleep delivered me from the spirit of the lake and its terrifying embodiment.

The water reflected a cloudless sky. From the top of the cliff fish eagles were taking flight. I could hear them calling before I saw their black shapes crowned with the immaculate feathers on their white heads. The eagles would rise, carried by updrafts. No doubt they had seen before I did what seemed like an enormous tree trunk washed up on the lake's only beach. The crocodile lay motionless on the pebbly shore extending down from the rocks scattered by the slide, its jaws open. The enthusiasm inspired by my dream had crumbled away in one night. My ardor to reach the lake had disappeared! Even motionless, the crocodile displayed worrisome strength. Its deep black body had surely been scorched in the devil's lair. An evil spirit possessed it, and its threat weighed heavily on the watery expanse.

I looked away from the crocodile, which looked like a charred piece of wood in which savage fire still burned, and I tried to find the Arab's house. Impossible to see it. There was no building built back against the cliff as Oluti and the old man had described it. I doubted they had told me the truth. However much I focused on examining every part of the cliff, there was no trace of any ruins. Perhaps the water level had risen? But surely the Arab would have built his house beyond the reach of high waters, and besides, now was the dry season. Since there wasn't any house, perhaps I could give up trying to get down to the lake. That idea gave me a certain satisfaction. Still, my intuition told me that the house really did exist but that something within me prevented me from seeing it so I wouldn't have to combat the spirit. Suddenly I realized what the problem was. Might the house be behind the island, even though the island hid only an infinitesimal portion of the cliff? I needed to find out. First, I had to get out of the cave. I found small handholds on the rock and pulled myself out of the opening. Clinging to similar rough places on the rock face, I started climbing. The rock was hard and didn't crumble away, giving me a good grip. At one point my foot slipped, and as I was trying to find a better hold, the sight of the water lapping at the base of the cliff made me dizzy.

I began to climb again. Already I could see the treetops outlined against the sky. Soon some roots made it easier for me to make progress. Eventually I managed to stand up in one of the small depressions, covered with dirt and grass, that cut into the top of the escarpment. I walked into the shadows of a wood covering the slope. This slope was not that of a hill carved out by the lake, but rather of a crater; the outside wall of the crater sloped gently down toward the plain. I didn't venture down in that direction for fear of meeting the Masangu warriors. I slipped between the trees, staying close to the edge of the cliff, stopping now and then to listen and even to sniff the air like a wild animal that finds its way by smell. The forest edges were inhabited by small colonies of monkeys and by groups of baboons whose shapes I could see on the opposite bank. Warthogs ran off, and several of those little antelopes called dikdiks looked at me with their big eyes before bounding off into the bushes. My intention was to walk around the lake so I could see what was behind the island. I started toward the rock extending out of the water with its single tree.

There were few sounds in the forest aside from birdsong. And then I heard the echo of a saw blended in with the birdsong. I was astonished, and started listening carefully. Were some men cutting wood? The place didn't seem at all likely for woodcutting because the trees were small and would yield little wood for construction. Plus the place was isolated, and there was always the danger of meeting armed Masangu bands. And yet I could hear clearly the sound of a saw or a rasp on wood, coming from a thicket covering the crest of a hill. I crept closer silently, afraid that a branch would snap under my feet. The sound ceased and then began again. I crawled under some bushes, and finally reached the top of the little hill that was weighted down with a multitude of trees. The sound disappeared again. And then I saw a huge tree. On one of its branches, hanging out over the lake, hung a baboon corpse. Flies were swarming around a huge bite on its neck. It was a strange sight that I couldn't avoid linking with the unusual cave painting I had seen in the tunnel: A leopard holding a monkey in its jaws. This baboon must have been killed and dragged up into the tree by a huge cat. Prudently, I pulled back, fearing that the animal might be prowling about. I made a big detour to find a place from which I could look out over the island. Seen from that angle, the little island seemed to have drifted out on the waters of the lake. It was further away from the cliff than I had first thought. And I hadn't been wrong in my guess. Attached to the cliff, a wall of rough stones formed a modest house. The only part visible was one wall with a door and a window. It was troglodytic, which confirmed the old man's idea that the Arab had reached the lake through a tunnel.

My discovery brought me face to face with a fait accompli: The house did indeed exist, and thus the combat with the crocodile was inevitable, unless I was willing to give up my dream and fail on my journey to Mount Meru. I considered going back to Mamtara, hoping to dream another dream, but the cowardliness of such a decision was an affront to my sense of honor. Decency dictated that I continue my undertaking. I needed to combat the crocodile, not necessarily to kill it, but at least to prevent its attacks, for it surely would not fail to attack me if I crossed the lake. And that was the problem: How could I reach the house? Had it not been for the Masangu warriors, I might have been tempted to look for the opening to the tunnel leading down to the house. But only sheer luck could crown such a difficult venture with success. The warriors were probably doing me a service by eliminating that possibility. Using my bare hands alone, it was out of the question to climb down the rock face with its overhang. I might have been able to imagine climbing down if I had had a long rope. But since there were no vines in the forest that option too was impossible. As for diving from the top of the cliff, I didn't give that much thought because the water near the house didn't seem to be very deep. Diving might be possible elsewhere, but then I'd need to swim across part of the lake. And how would I then be able to avoid the crocodile?

I spent the whole day reflecting as I examined the lake shore. When the setting sun reached the horizon, my plans were set. I had noticed that the crocodile sometimes left the pebbly beach and dove back into the lake, probably looking for fish. So the beach was accessible for a few hours. My plan was to tie up a live animal on the beach for bait. Then I would hurry up to the top of the escarpment, halfway between the beach and the house, to a place where the color of the water indicated that the lake was deeper. Then I would dive in and swim over to the Arab's house while the crocodile was devouring the animal I had sacrificed. Once the animal was eaten, the crocodile would doze off as it digested its prey. It would have no great desire to try to catch up with a good swimmer like me.

I made some snares with string I had. It wasn't difficult to make slipknots and place the snares judiciously on a game path. I placed snares in several places and then went to sleep for the night.

The next morning there were no animals caught in my snares. I was disappointed, but reset the snares where I saw traces of other paths in the grass. I spent the day trying to explore the crater, but at one point a group of baboons blocked my path, forcing me to turn back. I must have encroached upon their territory, because two huge males faced up to me and started jumping up and down and screaming. Their mouths were open wide, and they curled back their lips, displaying powerful jaws. I didn't risk continuing. There were plenty of other areas to explore. The crater edge was thick, especially on the south face, where the roll of earth was as heavy as the stomach of mature Mombasa men.

I moved quietly, for fear that the Masangu warriors might spot me there in the woods, because they could easily be hiding in some of the thickets. A shadow passed over the ground. I raised my head and saw the silhouette of a large wading bird. A flock of birds was resting in a grove of trees. They were perched at the top of trees whose trunks were covered with droppings, making it look as though white sap was seeping out. They didn't fly off when I approached. They hardly even looked at me. Two ibis did fly up from out of the grass to join the flock in the tops of the trees. The foliage was speckled with balls of feathers from which beaks emerged. Behind the beaks I could make out their heads and their necks tucked back. Long legs held up their bodies like the stems of fruit defying the laws of gravity, turning up toward the sky. There were many ibis, some hammerkops with their long, hammer-shaped heads attached to stubby bodies, and a multitude of herons, colored like cinders and coal. There were also egrets dressed in white robes like students on the way to their madrassi schools, and unimaginably ugly marabou storks. And a little distance away, to my great joy, there was a flock of black storks. What amazing birds! They were standing upright on five or six trees that had pale foliage, from which hung long pods streaked with indentations. They carried themselves with such grace. The harmony of their black and white feathers, the bright red color of their feet and beaks; everything breathed perfection. I moved closer, and they weren't at all disturbed. They watched me coming and didn't move even when I sat down at the base of one of their trees. They remained serene, resting with the customary self-confidence of great migratory birds that have completed their journey. What admirable celestial sailors, linking the continents by crossing seas, defying bad weather, enduring hail, fighting the winds!

To my mind, storks are messengers from bygone days, days when I was living in the depths of things, not totally happy, although all my senses were alert. Storks are the dream portion of my being, as if they come from hidden layers within my soul and not from some far-off land. Perhaps that's why they welcomed me with such benevolence. I had the impression that I was discovering them but that they already knew who I was. Spread out among the branches, they formed a rough circle around an old tree with a powerful, gnarled trunk, in whose branches a shoebill had built its gigantic nest. Their nests are almost as big as huts, and other birds also go there to nest. During the nesting period, it becomes the Noah's Ark of numerous winged folk. A variety of birds set up housekeeping inside, or raise their young on top. This particular shoebill's nest was attached solidly to some big branches and was empty, so I didn't hesitate to climb the tree to examine it. What skillful architecture, putting together branches, twigs and grass to form such a mammoth structure! A man could crouch down inside it. I crept inside, knowing the tree would support my weight, and after I had removed the wall of one room, the idea came to me that I could prepare a good bed for myself. And indeed, it was possible for me to sleep either in the fetal position or with my legs extending out through the back wall. So I decided to spend the night in this cocoon nest surrounded by birds.

Evening came, announced by the clouds' purple tinge. The sky appeared to burst into flames for a brief moment. The light faded, and slowly shadows drowned the underbrush. And then from the ground rose unbroken chirping; the chirping of locusts releasing all the passion they had held in during the day. Other insects picked up the song, and whispering leaves joined the insect symphony. Pods hanging from the branches rubbed against each other, tinkling softly. Soon the entire forest rang out with uninterrupted melodies, and birds took turns as soloists.

The moon rose. It bathed the forest in its yellow light, giving new form to the trees, carving out enigmatic shapes in the mass of branches and painting tree trunks with henna. That was the moment the storks chose to begin to sing. They started by clacking their beaks. They opened and closed them forcefully, making the sound of a cracking whip, and whistling. They accompanied those sounds by stretching their necks out and pulling them back, then raising their beaks toward the moon. Their whole bodies joined in. They bent their legs and then straightened them again. They spread their wings, displaying the white under-feathers that contrasted so vividly with their black flight feathers. They seemed to be doing their dance for the moon, because their song, as well as their movements, seemed to be lifted up toward it. Several storks took flight. They flew higher and higher in concentric circles. So it wasn't only the crocodile that danced in the moonlight. The birds in this paradise also paid homage to the moon's power.

I fell asleep happy, tucked in my bed, like a bird on the world's first morning.

During the night some guttural sounds woke me. The storks were nervous. They were clacking their beaks and flapping their wings. Their cries tore through the silence. This time it wasn't the prelude to a dance or a serenade to the stars. Their agitation indicated that some danger was lurking. My senses alert, I stuck my head through the opening in the nest. I could see how agitated the storks were. They would fly up and then land back down on the same tree, and egrets were flying around nervously. I could hear the sound of a saw, much like the sound I had heard the day before. At first I couldn't identify it in the midst of all the noise the birds were making. But then between two heron calls I made out the sound again. I didn't have to search long for an answer to why the birds were so upset. I could see the outline of a big cat against the bushes. The animal came out of a thicket and walked out into the clearing.

I was paralyzed with fear. I could see it was a leopard. It was edging forward. The branch's shadows slipped over its supple body, and the splashes of moonlight on its fur called attention to its spotted tattoos. It passed beneath my tree as I watched. I thought it hadn't spotted me, but suddenly it turned its head toward me and grimaced, showing off long whiskers illuminated by the moon rays. And then it continued on its way, while my heart was almost exploding and the horrible racket in the treetops grew louder and louder. When the birds finally stopped their ruckus, I realized that the leopard had gone. I couldn't remember anything about the look it gave me except that it had stared at me. All I could remember was the cat's face, its whiskers and its gaping jaws. As for its fur and those eyes that supposedly covered its fur, all I noticed was their lashes lined with kohl. On the other hand, there remained a precise image of its powerful, muscular back legs and its long tail with a curl at the tip. It was an impressive animal, created by nature to be a killer. How brave my ancestor Badrani Nyuni el-Mudi must have been to face the leopard living on the island where the fig tree was! I would need no less courage to confront the crocodile.

At dawn I ate some of the food from my bag and went to check my snares. A dikdik had been caught in one. The dikdik was jerking violently, trying to get its leg out of the slip knot. It was a male with short ringed horns and a thin head with a long muffle. Its big eyes looked feverish and its ears were lying back. The skinny body and thin legs gave an impression of great fragility. Meager prey for a crocodile, but it would keep the beast's attention and perhaps give me enough time to swim over to the house. I couldn't ask for more.

I hoped to be able to leave the house through the tunnel, though there was no proof the tunnel even existed.

After hiding my bag in a hole in a tree trunk, I started off, carrying the little antelope. I could sense something behind me. The female dikdik was following its mate. "You have no idea what's in store for him," I thought.

The crocodile had returned to the water, and the sandy beach was now free. With the dikdik in my arms, I clambered down over the rockslide and reached the shore. I made certain the crocodile wasn't hiding at the lake's edge, masked by half-submerged rocks, ready to lunge at me. And then, using some string, I tied the dikdik up to a heavy rock. There was no way it could escape. I hurried back up as fast as I could, through the huge boulders, to get to the perch I could dive from. My first reflex was to look down at the beach. The crocodile still hadn't come out of the water. I wouldn't have had to hurry so much and get so out of breath! There was no sign of it at the lake's surface. The only ripples I saw were caused by the breeze. The dikdik had given up tugging at its rope and stood with head high, ears raised, watching first the lake's surface and then the rocks. It sniffed the air, trying to pick out some smell that might suggest how its end would come.

The morning flowed by. I was beginning to get impatient. Suddenly the dikdik began to get nervous, jumping up and down and trying its best to break the rope. A black arrow shot across the lake. Propelled by the breaking wave its massive tail was creating, the crocodile swam to the shore. Once on the ground, it moved awkwardly, so different from its grace in the water. I didn't wait to watch the kill. Besides, I had no time to spare. I leaped into the lake without waiting another moment.

The shock was brutal. I felt a short moment of panic, submerged in the freezing water, before I finally rose back up to the surface and regained my composure, as when I would swim in the sea near Mombasa. I swam like a fish toward the place the house stood. The island was my landmark. I moved rapidly. The beach where the crocodile was eating the dikdik began to recede, and the island grew larger. I thought I was out of danger and I didn't even go to the trouble of looking back to see what the crocodile was doing there on the shore. I could almost have enjoyed swimming in the lake, warmed by the vigorous activity, though I was a little surprised by the taste of the water and by its smell, so different from sea water.

I reached the little island. It was nothing but bare rock on which the one tree was growing. I walked around the island and the Arab's house came into view. The wall set into the cliff had evidently been built at the entrance to a cave. The house's foundations extended down into the water. I dove in to see how deep the water was there. And that's when, as I was making a turn, I noticed an underwater shadow heading in my direction. The shadow was too far away for me to identify it, but close enough to be worrisome. All I could make out was a dark undulating shape. I took my knife out of its leather holster, ready to strike, and began to swim rapidly toward the nearby house. Anxiety overwhelmed me though I didn't know exactly why. Suddenly the evidence hit me like lightning. I was being hunted by the crocodile! It was too late. The monster was almost upon me. I could hear the furious thrashing of its long tail. No way to escape. I would have to fight. I got ready for the combat, raising my weapon to strike the crocodile hurtling toward me. I was about to plant the knife in its head when the crocodile pivoted, and swinging its enormous tail, struck a violent blow to my hips. The knife slipped out of my hand. My only chance of survival was to flee. I tried to swim away, but actually I was just flailing the water with my arms and legs. The crocodile seized my right leg in its jaws and began to drag me down toward the bottom to drown me. I struggled violently but was helpless in the monster's jaws. The pressure of its teeth on my leg became stronger. I was beginning to run out of air. I opened my mouth in spite of myself and some water rushed into my lungs. I was just about to lose consciousness when I discovered that my head was above water, and I was coughing out the water. The crocodile still had me in its mouth, and its teeth had cut into my flesh. It was content to drag me along at the water's surface with my leg jammed between its jaws. The monster made for the island, passed by on the less steep side, and there, it opened its mouth and turned me loose. Instinctively, I climbed quickly out onto the rock, hurrying to the top as if I had freed myself. But it was clearly the crocodile that had granted me my freedom.

It pulled itself out of the water and lay there on the bare rock. I felt as if I had just awakened from some horrible nightmare. Had I not been dreaming? Had I not been sleeping there on that rock? My dripping body and clothes as well as the wounds on my leg proved the contrary. When I got my breath back, I looked at the crocodile. Lying there in the welcome warmth of the rock's surface, it opened its mouth. Sharp teeth were awaiting the signal to enjoy a feast. What was the crocodile waiting for? It could sweep the summit of the island with its tail, throw me into the water and devour me. Unless I climbed up into the tree, I would never be able to avoid its tail. But that didn't seem to be its intention. It simply lay there, content with having captured me, its partially open jaws breaking into a smile. The creature was watching me. Its eyelids with their grayish lashes opened to display yellow eyes with brown almond-shaped slits. As it watched me, its glassy stare seemed to be asking: "Why are you surprised, manchild? How did you think you could fool me with that ridiculous bait, that pitiful dikdik, me, the spirit of the lake?"

I had no doubt that I was dealing with the spirit of the lake. However, why it decided to save me remained an enigma. Why did it want to keep me prisoner on that little island instead of devouring me? Only a small part of the rock surface was submerged. Nothing grew but the lovely tree, its existence miraculous on such bare rock. I didn't know what species it was. Its branches held a cluster of light green leaves. One fat, cone-shaped fruit, about the size of a man's head, was hanging all by itself at the end of a branch. Hornbills must have eaten the rest of the fruit. I had nothing to hope for from the tree except perhaps that its shade could protect me from the sun.

I began to pay more attention to the lake shore. The cliff dropped straight down to where the house stood. The door was just an open rectangular breech in the wall, and the water was about two cubits deep at the entrance. The stone had been nicely shaped and carefully set, a witness to the Arab's skill. On the other hand, the roof, if it had ever existed, was gone. Beside the cliff the rock face was steep, but on the other side, where the crocodile was dozing, the slope was gradual. I could easily have dived in and made it to the house had it not been for my reptilian watch dog. If I dove into the water it would come after me and drag me back by force to the island.

I remained seated against the tree while the crocodile lazed on his rock like an indolent lizard. It was truly immense, its tail extending all the way down to the water. Just by looking at it, I grew more and more anxious. As the sun set, the crocodile still hadn't moved. I spent my first night in captivity shivering in the cold wind coming off the lake. The next day, my guard swam around the island, striking the water violently with its tail, creating huge splashes and soaking me with water. Then it went back to its place and again opened its jaws with their ivory points. The day was long and difficult, even though the cool wind and the clouds that hid the sun put an end to the unbearable heat. The change in the weather announced the first rains of the long rainy season. I wouldn't have been surprised if it were already raining on the mountain.

My second night on the island. Dawn found me tired and famished and my stomach ached. I got dizzy when I tried to stand up. The atmosphere of the lake had changed. It took me a moment to realize that the water level had risen. The island had shrunk, but the crocodile was still there on the shore. In exasperation, I decided to try to swim across to the cliff. I was just readying myself to dive when the one fruit hanging on the tree caught my attention. I had forgotten all about it, hidden as it was by the foliage. I couldn't climb the tree as fast as I wanted to, because I was dizzy from hunger. Once I was up in the tree, I slowly and carefully climbed from branch to branch to reach the fruit. To my great satisfaction, it was ripe and came off easily. When I pulled it off, the crocodile suddenly raised itself up on its tail, lifting its open mouth high in my direction. Its mouth snapped open and shut several times, and then it fell back in a thud to the ground.

The black monster dove into the water, then immediately

returned to the surface. It leaped into the air, clamping its jaws down on some invisible prey and then fell back again into the water. I was climbing down the tree very slowly because the fruit was heavy. A wave washed over me when my feet were once again on the ground. The crocodile gave a long grunt and then snapped its jaws together once more. Disconcerted, I watched it, the precious fruit held tightly against my body. What did this sudden activity mean? Did the crocodile want the fruit its nose was pointing toward? Was it trying to deprive me of the food so I would die of hunger, or did the crocodile need the fruit itself? I had no idea what kind of fruit it was. Was its thin tender skin protecting tasty flesh?

I pushed my finger into the pulp, but a horrible grunt stopped me, and the hideous face of the monster reared up in front of me. In fright, I tossed the fruit toward the crocodile without thinking. I acted out of instinctive fear. It immediately grabbed the fruit and turned away. Keeping its head at the water's surface, the enormous animal swam peacefully away, the mysterious fruit in its mouth. I watched the crocodile until it reached the middle of the lake. There, it raised its jaws as if to show me the fruit, and then it dove under and didn't reappear.

The crocodile never came back to the surface. Although I looked around at the whole expanse of the lake and studied the shore carefully, watching for some time, the spirit of the lake had disappeared, swallowed up in the depths.

I was so surprised that it was hard for me to realize that I was really free. The crocodile must have captured me so that I would gather the fruit that it could never have reached otherwise. Even today I have no idea what was in that fruit. Did it hide a treasure? Did eating its flesh confer some supernatural power? I don't know. I've never seen fruit like that again, nor any trees like the tree that bore it. At least I understand that the fruit was an offering to the spirit of the lake. Once satisfied, the crocodile had granted the lake its freedom for a long time, liberating me at the same time. I was free to leave the little island and go to the Arab's house.

I leaped into the water to get over to the house. Alas, the water level had risen, covering the door and the window, so I couldn't see inside. I dove down and went through the window under water. The cave wasn't as deep as I would have thought. Perhaps it opened onto a second cavity. The ceiling sloped down progressively and disappeared in the darkness. Of the Arab's former presence there was no sign at all. No furniture, not even a board that might have floated to the surface. It was impossible for me to find the secret cache. If it existed, it remained drowned in water. I was disappointed. Who knows what I might have discovered?

Although my situation wasn't very comfortable since I couldn't touch the bottom, I stayed in the cave for a while. After the anxiety-filled confrontation with the spirit of the lake, the peaceful water in the cave was restful. It formed a tiny internal lake, its surface quiet and smooth. The cave muffled all outside sounds. The little lake seemed to doze serenely, imitating the larger lake outside that had to confront life's tumults. My forced fast had made me lighter. I began to float, contemplating the rock lit up by a beam of light high up on the wall. Thus my eyes wandered between night and day, separated by the barrier the Arab had built.

I would have gladly remained there longer had it not been for the hunger that was beginning to gnaw at me. I left the flooded house and swam back to the beach. The dikdik was still there at the end of its rope. So the crocodile had spared it. I could have taken it back to Mamtara as a gift to Oluti but it seemed better to release it. It dashed off immediately, leaping from stone to stone until it reached the top of the rockslide. Scarcely had it disappeared when another dikdik came out of the grasses and hurried after it. Evidently the female had been waiting. I climbed back up, eager to find my bag, hoping the monkeys hadn't discovered my supply of bananas. Obsessed by my desire to eat, I never saw the rope carefully camouflaged in the grass. When it stretched taut, there was no way I could avoid it. Four strapping fellows leaped out of the bushes and fell upon me.

Chapter six

The warriors kept very close to me. I don't see how I could have escaped, since my hands were tied behind my back and my ankles were tied together with a leather strap. One of the men had ostrich feathers around his head, reaching down to his chin. The others were wearing feathers like collars around their necks and on the skins they had thrown over their shoulders. They all wore anklets and bracelets made of fur. Their battle paraphernalia included lances with short iron heads, large shields painted with geometrical designs, swords in their scabbards, and little knives attached to their left arms. Lastly, one warrior was hefting a formidable dogshead club. All four of the soldiers were dressed in ochre leather tunics. Their closely-shaven skulls made their deformed ears stand out. Their ears were decorated with little sticks driven into the edges and wooden pegs plugging the distended lobes.

They didn't speak to each other during our march, except when I fainted. I refused to get back up even when they struck me. Then they agreed to let me eat the last bananas in my bag. In spite of their roughness, their attitudes showed me that they considered me an important prisoner. They were probably hoping to make a nice profit by selling me as a slave or be honored for capturing a Swahili, because there weren't many around. I assumed that the Masangu chiefdom was our destination. We walked all day long across a wooded savannah, sometimes meeting groups of warriors and more often shepherds and herds of zebus with their large humps. We stopped for the night. The light began to fade. The summit of Mount Meru emerged above a sea of clouds. We were submerged in the shadow the mountain threw at our feet.

The next morning, a shepherd gave us some cow's milk. We swallowed a few bananas and started off again on our endless journey. At about noon, some millet fields appeared among the trees, the first sign of farming activity. Women were bent over, weeding the cereal using sickles. They would stand up as we drew near and turn their heads to look at us. I thought I spotted a small stream meandering between the millet patches and then flowing into a field. Some men were working around it. We stepped across it, and I realized that it wasn't a stream but a real canal they had dug. At one end, two men were in the process of irrigating their millet field. I hadn't expected to find such skill in these lands.

The canal, shaded by bushes, guided our steps. We approached a valley, given away by the mass of green trees, where the canal disappeared. We didn't try to follow it because before us stood a wall of thorns like the one protecting Mamtara from the plains. A few moments later, we were walking through banana groves. We came to a wall built with large stones and an entrance guarded by two soldiers. Behind it there were more bananas, but also many huts and enclosures for animals. A wooden stockade, guarded by an armed man, brought us to a stop. They made me sit down on a log that was lying there. From time to time men would go through the stockade. They would remove their sandals before entering and put them back on when they came out. Preceded by two men, no doubt servants, an Arab came out. Speechless with surprise, I watched him gather his things together without noticing me. I couldn't fail to notice his white tunic and kofia and his light face decorated with a gray beard.

He would have left if I hadn't called out a greeting to him from under my guards' disapproving stares.

"*Salaam aleikum.*"

"*Aleikum salaam.*"

"*Shikamoo, mzee,*" I said, using the appropriate Swahili words to greet an older man respectfully.

"*Marahaba,*" he responded, giving the standard response.

"I'm Bin Safwani Ibrahim el-Mudi from Mombasa, *mzee.*"

"May your soul have peace. I'm Mohammed Yasser el-Kakuri from Kilwa. What are you doing here with your arms tied together?"

"I was captured yesterday in Mamtara by some soldiers."

"Ha! Allah alone knows what a man's destiny is. What were you doing in Mamtara?"

"I was exploring the region."

"Alone?"

"Yes."

"You were very foolish. Where is the caravan you came with?"

"I didn't come with a caravan."

"You're not only foolish, you're crazy."

"Perhaps, but not crazy enough not to wonder what's behind this stockade."

"The king of Masangu and his court."

"So we are indeed in Masangu."

"You truly are a little bird fallen from its nest."

"You don't know how right you are, *mzee*. And how about you, what are you doing here?"

"I'm a merchant, and I've come to arrange to sell my products. My caravan is waiting in Ngurto."

"In Ngurto?"

"Yes, the fort out on the plain."

He kept talking. "Perhaps I could buy you as a slave."

"Do you think the king will sell me as a slave?"

"I don't know. Masangu is at war with its neighbors and it's never easy to guess the king's intentions."

"What's the king like?"

"He's a formidable man. For me, he's a magician and I wouldn't dare meet him if I were not Allah's protégé. But he pays well, and that's the important thing. You see, he speaks Swahili perfectly. He's not like all these blacks."

The Arab spoke to his servants and began making ready to leave. "Son of Safwani el-Mudi, I wish you courage. Allah has willed that you be captive, and your fate is in his hands. I'll be back in several days and will check on your situation. You would make a good slave. Goodbye."

"Goodbye, *mzee*."

As he was walking away, he called out: "You'll see, the king keeps a fiendish animal as his friend."

A guard led me inside the stockade. There was a round construction with a porch, opening back into a cone-shaped hut, and on each side, the thatched roof came all the way down to the ground. We crossed the porch, which opened onto a round space. A row of warriors stood at the side of the courtyard. In their left hands they held long oval shields that rested on the soil, and in their right hands they held lances. Their lances were different from the ones my captors had. The blades came to a very sharp point and the sides were also sharpened. At one end there was a socket in which the handle was set, and the handle too was partially covered with metal. It must have been an effective weapon in the hands of skillful warriors. The soldiers looked fierce, and their expressions, indifferent at best, displayed the intransigence of men used to dealing with death. The line of soldiers was broken where a large house opened onto the courtyard. It was an immense thatched roof supported by a multitude of wooden columns. In the shade one could make out shapes seated on stools or directly on the ground. I couldn't see them very well because the sun was beating down on the earthen courtyard. Its reflection dazzled me.

The only man sitting on a chair, no doubt the king, dominated the others. The guard pushed me forward, and he tripped me so I would fall flat on my face. Lying there on the ground, all I had to do was raise my head, for it wouldn't have been seemly to get back to my feet. A man stepped forward. His hat was made of a goat stomach, and he was carrying little bells. In a threatening tone, he addressed me:

"Stranger, greet King Shina of Masangu, our benefactor. His eyes are like the eagle's; he can see everything. His ears are like the elephant's; he can hear everything. And his claws are like the leopard's..."

I stammered out a greeting, turning toward the king, whose head I could see was crowned with a long feather. On his left, I could also make out the shape of an animal whose eyes were glowing in the dim light, probably a big dog. In Mamtara, there were some huge dogs used for hunting and sometimes in war. The man with the bells kept speaking in his pompous way, asking me to give my identity and then to explain why I had come to Mount Meru. I decided not to tell them about my dreams, describing myself as someone looking for rare woods for carved doors in Mombasa. Better that I be taken for a merchant who might be able to negotiate trades between the coast and Masangu if I were freed. After each of my answers, the spokesman went back to his place beside the king. The king would whisper something to him, often questions that the man with the little bells would in turn ask me. I picked up a few of the king's words and realized that he wasn't speaking Swahili as the Arab had claimed, but rather in Meru. They asked about my caravan. Taken by surprise, I decided to tell the truth: the caravan left Kobekobe without waiting for me and I had been unable to catch up with it.

"The king would like to know how you managed to reach Mount Meru all by yourself."

"I was guided by a lion."

My answer had a noticeable effect. Up until then the audience had been quiet, but now a murmur ran through it.

"The king would like to have some explanation about the lion. Why did you follow it?"

"It took me under its protection after I got lost."

"The king wonders if you spoke to the lion."

"No."

"The king asks the question: do you know the language of wild beasts?"

Somewhat astonished, I said no. And then I had to give details about my stay in Mamtara. One question I couldn't answer was about Mamtara's forges. I didn't even know there were any forges.

"The king wonders what you were doing at Lake Chana?"

I couldn't answer because at that moment the animal hidden in the shadows got up. It came out of the darkness and lay down in the sun not far from me. Its musky scent spread through the air. I was shocked. It wasn't a dog, but a leopard.

It was about three cubits long and nothing but muscle. Under its fur, the supple shapes of its muscles moved like shadows playing on the surface of a sculpture standing in the sun. Its yellow coat took on a golden hue, especially its back, with the sun glistening on it, though the belly area was almost white. The cat had dipped its fleece in desert dunes and desert roses had stuck to its coat, their prints embroidering the leopard's eyelike markings. Dark corollas opened wide on its belly and haunches and grew smaller on its front legs and the nape of its neck. They extended out onto the leopard's head, down between the large ears. At its body's other extremity, the eyelike markings covered the long thick tail that was turned up and white at the end. Magnificent whiskers spread like fans around its nose. There was a line of dark spots rising from each side of its mouth toward its eyes, and in the sunlight, its pupils were nothing but vertical slits. The animal seemed very supple. It must have been able to pounce with lightning speed. Its sharp claws, whose dark tips I could see, were surely terrible weapons. Its jaws were just as formidable. Sharp canines, rivaling those of the crocodile in Lake Chana, extended from its partially open mouth. It was a born killer.

Without even a glance at me, the animal lay down on its side, its head resting on the ground, warming itself in the sun like a cat.

"The king asks you to justify your presence at Lake Chana. He is not accustomed to waiting."

"I was exploring the lake shore looking for good trees."

"The king would like to know what you were doing with the crocodile."

So the warriors had seen the spirit of the lake. I certainly hadn't gone unnoticed as the crocodile's prisoner on the island.

"I was hoping to study a rare tree growing on a little island. A crocodile tried to kill me but I managed to find safety on a rock on the island. It kept me there for two days, watching beneath the rock, and then finally it disappeared and I was able to swim to shore."

My answer seemed to satisfy the assembly. The men began to talk among themselves, and the king did not intervene. They must have been debating my fate. I began to recite the *shahada* and prayed to Allah that he might keep me from slavery. An exchange between the king and the men ended the debate. The spokesman listened to instructions from the king.

"The king declares that you will stay in Masangu as long as the war continues. You will not be sold as a slave. Because you rubbed shoulders with the lion and fought the crocodile, you are a brave man. You are not a captive, nor are you completely free. You must not leave our territory. However, the king gives you authorization to visit the forest to look for rare wood. You will live with old Kabero, a man of honey who knows the forest. He speaks Swahili well."

After a pause, the spokesman continued: "The king has one last question. Is looking for wood the only purpose for your journey to Mount Meru?"

"Yes," I answered.

The spokesman listened to his sovereign. "The king says that you are lying, and he gives you this warning: if ever you try to escape, you'll meet the leopard's claws on your path. At present, salute Masangu's king, for he is…"

And the man with the bells recited a litany of praise.

The king's words surprised me. The guards lifted me up, or rather they ripped me from the ground and carried me off like a prisoner, in spite of what their sovereign had decided. It was only when the soldiers untied me, once we were on the other side of the wall, that I thought the king must have spies in Mamtara. He had already been informed of the real purpose of my journey.

Mzee Kabero lived in Masangu's higher elevations, not far from the edge of the forest. He was an affable man, and I had no difficulty becoming his friend. He was respected throughout Masangu, known to be an honest man and a skillful beekeeper. Whenever I told peasants I was living with *Mzee* Kabero they would ask me what his first name was, in order to know who I was talking about, since I had only given them the name of his clan. And then they would say "oh yes, *mzee wa msituni* (the old man of the forest)." Indeed, Kabero was a forest regular. That's where he placed his hives. His knowledge of the woods, where spirits and wild animals lived, conferred on him quite a reputation. He was old enough to have great-grandchildren, but that didn't keep him from leaping about like a kid on the steep forest paths.

He had gotten wind of the crocodile story and asked me to tell it to him. I related my adventure without mentioning my dream about the house, but I didn't omit the story about the fruit, for Kabero seemed trustworthy.

"You don't lack courage, Bayu. I'll admit I was surprised at the king's clemency. Other prisoners are either sold as slaves or used as forced laborers. Instead of that, he's almost given you freedom. True, you can't leave Masangu, but you are free to move about as you wish. Of course, if you try to slip away from me when we go into the forest, wild animals will devour you. Or at best we'll find you dead from hunger. Because you're a foreigner, you'll get lost in the forest. Even if you managed to escape, you'd expose yourself to some horrible death. Don't take King Shina's threat lightly. His leopard will kill you if he orders it to. It's all quite strange. He seems to want to keep you captive and yet offer you protection at the same time. Perhaps he was impressed by your relationship with the lion. It's rare to be guided by a lion, even if it's not totally unheard of. Some hunters make a pact with the lions on whose territory they hunt. What's different in your case is that you're a Swahili, an ignoramus."

He pronounced that last sentence so seriously that I was a little vexed.

"As you could see, King Shina is allied with the leopard. That's where he gets his strength. However, the leopard's primary predator is the lion. That's surely why Shina respects you. I don't think he's afraid of you. Otherwise he would have killed you."

Time passed in Masangu. When each day ended, it blended in with the weight of the past. My memories of the day would fade as my spirit turned toward the coming dawn. I waited for nighttime hoping for a new dream, while the farmers were keeping their eyes open for signs of the long rainy season. I enjoyed ample freedom, although Kabero's grandson always went wherever I did. Masangu's territory extended from the plains in the south to the high mountain forests in the north, between two deep valleys that bordered the neighboring countries. To the west there was Uru, a region allied with Shina, but it butted up against Kibosho, a rival chiefdom. To the east, the gorge met a country at peace with Masangu, but further to the east there were enemy regions such as Mamtara. Whenever I reached the limits of where people lived on the high mountain, Kabero's grandson would signal that we couldn't go any further. My presence and status were known all over Masangu, even though many of the peasants still had not met me. It wasn't necessary to guard me carefully, because the way I looked made me stand out. Had I tried to flee, some peasant would have noticed me, recognized me and denounced me. A squad of soldiers would then have set out to look for me, and they would have quickly caught me in that country, whose geography I didn't know very well. Once, however, I did manage to escape the peasants' vigilance. In a way, the experience was unfortunate.

They had constructed a complex network of canals to bring water to the banana groves and even all the way down to the lower slopes where they grew millet. The canals ran along the valley of the Mrusangu River. The valley was magnificent. Nature had worked the volcanic material in the same way a Mombasa cabinet maker works wood. It had carved into the mountain's flesh, cut out a maze of streams, embroidered it with flourishes of isolated rocks and given form to the damask forest slopes. Although the trees were no longer in bloom, their foliage provided elegant contrasts. Colorful mosaics were formed by green and yellow leaves, by branches, some empty and some loaded with fruit, and by streamers of vines. Against the opposite slope the tree trunks stood out in white, gray, and ochre lines between the silvery strips of waterfalls. The Masangu highlands offered simply magnificent views. I had plenty of opportunity to observe hornbills in flight and admire their beauty, deriving not from the majesty we normally associate with large birds, but rather from their strangely shaped bodies. Thus the valley became one of my favorite places to walk, and discovering the canals added to my pleasure and passion for the place.

The way they had laid out and built the canals was brilliant. Water had been diverted into the canal by a dike made of stone, and it then wound across the slope while the river continued to plunge straight down the mountain. The canal had to run a long way before it reached inhabited areas. What technical prowess! I was amazed. Just think about the difficulty of building an earthen canal along a steep slope in such a way that its walls do not yield to the water pressure or other physical forces. And the peasants even built aqueducts. Hollowed out tree trunks are suspended by ropes or built on wooden pillars. Thus the water can cross chasms. I've heard about magnificent irrigated gardens in Baghdad. The black slaves who took care of them must have come from Mount Meru.

Frequently columns of ants follow the dike or the path along the canal. Their bites are painful. When I complained about the ants to Kabero's grandson, he answered:

"Don't forget that they are the ones who built the canal we're walking along."

"What do you mean?"

"The ants permitted the canal's construction by showing the elders where they needed to build."

"I don't understand."

"Well, our ancestors, when they built the canal, looked to the ants to lay out the canal's path, because ant columns always march on level paths and thus they are ideally suited for canals. So our ancestors made certain that the ground was level by following the ants. They always come out in great numbers just after the rain, and that's proof that they know the water's secrets. They understand on what ground water is happy to flow."

The way the canals were built fascinated me. I often sat for hours watching the water in the canals, catching crabs—greatly surprised to find crustaceans in the mountains—and playing with tadpoles and insects. I followed the water back up to the dam that diverts it from the river. After Mamtara's tree artists, I discovered Masangu's skilled water workers, men who became allies of the river so that it would give up part of its flow. And there lay the problem, in that covenant with natural forces.

One day, as we were walking, my guide, Kabero's grandson, led me to the last banana groves near the edge of the forest. When I saw the smile on the face of the girl who came to meet him, I realized that our destination hadn't been chosen by accident. And when, offering his awkward excuses, he asked me if I could get home by myself, I agreed immediately. But instead of going back the way we had come, I couldn't resist following the last canal that disappeared into the ravine, although it meant I had to follow a forest path and disobey the rules. My curiosity got the better of me; truly I had no plans to try to escape.

I started down the narrow path created by the dike along the canal, leading back under the shadows of huge trees. I could sense the presence of the highland forest through the silence, especially because of the chill and humidity in the gorge. In places, the vegetation was so thick that it formed a tunnel overhanging the canal. The forest canopy plunged the path into a mysterious atmosphere, which I found captivating. I let my imagination run free. Sometimes the canal ran along an escarpment. Waterfalls crashed against the stones. I pretended that there were enemies besieged in their fort, pouring down boiling oil. I would skillfully sidestep it and then hug the wall to keep from being hit by the stones they were throwing at me. Whenever clusters of vines reached the canal, my army of faithful soldiers would storm the wall. I could hear the villains screaming as my men slit their throats. Their bodies would crash down on the dike. The impact would break the backs of any of those poor creatures who were still alive. I would kick them off the dike and they would tumble down the slope, sometimes getting caught in the gnarled roots of the huge trees. If one of the hollowed logs lay crossing a ravine above a raging torrent, I would start across as if I were climbing the mast of a ship on a raging sea, and with a leap I would land on the deck of the enemy ship. Little monkeys were playing in branches that were puffed out like sails in the wind. The pirates who had tried to steal my load of spices from Yemen would flee.

All my senses were oriented toward listening to the forest sounds and picking up the strange forest scents. I didn't meet anyone along the canal until I got to where it met the river. Well, almost no one. I'm not talking about the flocks of gray monkeys or colobus monkeys, those housewives who dust the tree leaves with their long tails. No, I'm talking about real human beings who brutally put an end to my childish games of the imagination.

Human forms appeared on the slope opposite me, on a rock outcropping that jutted out into the river. There were some men standing above a zone of rapids. The river was struggling to move forward, fighting with huge swirls. A little further down, a canal's stone dam was visible. The men on the rock were visible from the river, whereas I was hidden by the forest. There were four of them, facing the river and talking loudly. They were singing, holding out their arms as if in prayer. Their words were masked by the rushing water, and I couldn't make them out. Then they grew silent. One of them opened a bag and poured its contents into the river. They seemed to be just ordinary plants. Another poured out some brown liquid from a bucket. Their chanting began again. And then suddenly it ceased, when three men I hadn't seen before came out from under some foliage. Actually, there were only two men. The third person was a girl of about twelve years old, surely not more, dressed only in a loincloth. Strangely, she seemed to be half-asleep, or maybe she was sick, because her head was unsteady and kept flopping over. Two men were holding her up. And then I realized that her hands were tied together and that her feet were shackled. A strange way to take care of a sick person! What's more, at that point one of the men tightened the rope around her calves. I had vaguely realized what the men were planning to do, but my mind wouldn't let me admit the truth. Everything happened very quickly. The two guards grabbed the girl by the shoulders, picked her up and tossed her over the precipice into the swirling water. She fell like an inanimate mass, struck the water and sank, as if she had been swallowed up by the river. The men disappeared, all except one old man who spoke to the river in a loud voice. But already I was rushing away.

"*Mzee*, a peasant told me that people offer sacrifices to the river."

Kabero was hollowing out a log about four cubits long to make a beehive.

"Yes, that's right."

"What do you sacrifice?"

"I'm not sure. The masters of the canals are the ones who perform the appropriate ceremonies. They give offerings of honey, beer and goats. Some say that from time to time they sacrifice a young girl as well, every three years I believe."

"Why a girl? That's a waste of a human being."

"It's better to lose a branch than the entire tree. Do you think the river gives us its water freely? It demands compensation for the good it brings to us."

"Yes, but even so, a woman is a lot."

"Yes. Man must make sacrifices to nature. He must give nature part of himself."

"And how about the girl? Where do you get her?"

"She is stolen either from some poor family or from a neighboring country. I had a cousin who disappeared that way when I was a kid. And now with the war, it's easier than ever to find a girl. But she does have to be a virgin."

He turned the log over and kept hollowing it out to make a cylinder. The hive would be ready once he plugged the ends back up, leaving only some small openings for the bees to fly in and out.

"And how about war, *mzee*? For whom is war a sacrifice?"

"Oh, war is men's business."

"Why are you at war?"

"For trade, Bayu, for trade with the caravans. Before caravans came to Mount Meru to buy our products, we all grew crops on our own lands, brides were chosen from neighboring countries and we had contact with the people living on the plains and near Kilimanjaro. We had no reason to fight. But now we all want the profits from the caravan trade for ourselves, especially since they've begun bringing weapons. Back in my father's day we didn't have kings or chiefs. They appeared about twenty years ago, as did slaves. Before that time, Merus didn't practice slavery. Back in the old days we were governed by the elders. And then some agitators began to gain power. They claimed it was necessary to unite around one man in order to confront our enemies, and they were able to take over. Sometimes, they've been people who weren't even born here. Foreigners, just like Shina."

"Isn't Shina from Masangu?"

"No. He used to live in Uru. His origins aren't very clear, but we know he was sold as a slave to our first king, Kilesia."

"Shina was a slave?"

"Yes, but it wasn't long before he took the place of the master. Our king was very fond of him because he was intelligent, he could speak Swahili perfectly and his mind for strategy was helpful in defeating the army from Lyamuna, a rival chiefdom. The king gave him more and more responsibilities. And for a slave, his situation wasn't bad at all! The servant always knows his master's weaknesses, but from there to try to take the throne.... There was an altercation between the two men. King Kilesia accused Shina of sorcery. Shina managed to escape and find refuge in the forest. Kilesia himself led the expedition to track him down. The fugitive had been spotted in an area where hunters often went because there was so much game. The dogs found Shina's trail. He was backed up against a precipice. Our king was a man of great strength. He went on ahead of the others so he could kill Shina himself. Scarcely had he drawn near when a leopard suddenly appeared from out of a thicket and ripped his throat open. The dogs, though they were massive hunting dogs, were all killed or wounded in a few moments. In panic, the soldiers fled. That's how our first king Kilesia died.

"The news of his death was still fresh when Shina, accompanied by the leopard, came through the banana plantations and entered the palace. He proclaimed himself king and invited the inhabitants and Kilesia's family to recognize him as sovereign. Everyone agreed. Times were troubled. War was threatening at Masangu's gates. Whether Shina was a usurper or not mattered little, as long as he could protect Masangu from its greedy neighbors, especially from Kibosho, a chiefdom with which we are always at war. Shina managed to impose himself by his extraordinary move. Only Shauku, Kilesia's brother, wouldn't accept Shina as king. He went off with his brothers to look for Kilesia's remains so he could give them proper burial. He also wanted to bring back the gold diadem that Kilesia wore as a symbol of his position. Once back, he planned to kill Shina and his leopard and take over the kingdom himself, keeping it in the family.

"The following day, while the elders of all the different clans in Masangu were pledging their allegiance to Shina, who was establishing his court, the new king gave a bag to one of Shauku's cousins. Inside was Shauku's head. The claw marks left no doubt as to the cause of his death. As for Shauku's sons, they were never seen again. Finally, Shina executed Kilesia's sons and put out the eyes of his grandsons.

"Even though Shina has raised a powerful army, his power rests above all on the fear the leopard inspires. I get along fine with Shina. I give him honey, and he leaves me alone. But I'm like everyone else; I'm afraid of his leopard. The pact he's made with the animal makes us all fearful. Nobody knows how Shina was able to tame it. His reputation as a man in league with a leopard has spread far and wide over the whole mountain.

"There, Bayu, now you know Shina's story."

"Who are you at war with now?"

"We're fighting the king of Kibosho. He's allied with the herdsmen from the plains, savages who don't even bury their dead."

"They don't bury their dead?!"

"No. They just leave them to decompose in the bush. The war is limited to a few skirmishes on the plains. Plus we keep an eye on each other from both sides of the valley separating Uru from Kibosho. Things could be worse. True wealth is made up of men, well, of men, women and cows. With this war, the king has delayed the initiation of the class of adult men so as to keep the warriors in the army. After all, our young people need to procreate. Of course, we old fellows, that's a task we're still pretty good at, too, ha, ha!"

"So you have different classes, warriors and adult men?"

"Yes, there are the circumcised, the warriors, adult men—that is, those who get married and have children—and then there are mature men like me."

"You haven't told me anything about Mamtara, *mzee.* And yet you're at war with Mamtara, though there aren't many caravans that come to this region."

"Mamtara owns the only iron deposit on Mount Meru available to the people of Masangu. But the elders in Mamtara are afraid of Shina, and they have blocked the sale of all weapons and all iron to Masangu. They know that Shina is not to be trusted."

"Does anyone know where Shina found his leopard?"

"No. Shina may have captured it as a cub and raised it, but nobody had ever seen the animal before Kilesia was killed. How could Shina have trained a leopard without anyone ever seeing it? That's the great mystery. What we do know is that he's a *mganga*, not a sorcerer, but a very great *mganga* who understands nature, who is able to get close to the leopard and establish contact with its spirit."

"Is the leopard a male or a female?"

"It's a male."

"Does it always stay close to Shina?"

"No. Some days at court the leopard is gone. And I'd be willing to bet that it goes hunting in the forest at night. Often, it spends its days sleeping inside Shina's house."

"You must sometimes see it leave when it goes to the forest."

"Oh, it's hard to see a leopard! The leopard is the most secretive of animals. It can even rub up against you without you knowing it's there. Just now as we speak, perhaps it's right here listening to us. It will slip away and we'll never know anything about it."

"Have you ever seen the leopard in the forest?"

"Yes. Recently I happened upon it as it was pulling a dead antelope up into its tree."

"Its tree?"

"Yes. Panthers drag their prey up into the branches of some tree and come back later to eat them. That, in fact, is what happened to King Kilesia. In Masangu, there's a famous hunter named Ndeshiwona. The day Kilesia disappeared, he was hunting in the forest with his sons and brother, unaware of the conflict between Kilesia and Shina. The men were walking along when Ndeshiwona saw something shiny up on a tree branch hanging out over a precipice. The men recognized King Kilesia's body hooked on a branch, with the gold diadem still on his head. They fled in fright. The leopard had placed the body there. After Shauku disappeared, nobody would ever go get the body, and so today his soul must still be wandering through the forest."

In Kabero's banana plantation there was a dracaena enclosure protecting the bones of his ancestors. I never tried to enter for fear of seeing offensive sculptures. But then Kabero himself took me to make a libation to his ancestors in my honor. Embedded in the earth were two posts, rough-hewn logs taking on human forms, and a chest containing his family's bones. He poured some banana beer out on the ground while invoking the shades of his ancestors.

"There are no carvings on your posts?" I asked.

"Only rich men do that."

"Do they carve birds or animals?"

"Yes, they carve animal shapes."

"It's strange that you can sculpt animals. My religion doesn't allow that."

"Why is that?"

"When the sculptor dies, Allah, our God, asks him to give life to the creature he has just sculpted. The man fails and goes to hell. Only God can create."

"Your religion is astonishing. Of course, here we never sculpt human faces for fear of being accused of sorcery."

"But these posts have human shapes."

"Yes, but that's just so the shades can come live in them. Our ancestors live underground. We carve their shapes in wood in order to attract them. But we never imitate Creation, because it's impossible to reproduce any animal exactly."

"In Mamtara I saw a very realistic bird sculpture on a funeral post."

"We do that to please the spirit of the tree. It is able to see itself in an animal that used to come to the tree before it was cut down. If you were to carve living beings, you would make contact with forest forces. What do you do in Mombasa to appease the spirit of the wood you carve?"

"We always use dead wood."

"You use 'dead wood!'" There surely are some strange Swahili expressions! Wood never really dies. Even when it's dry, the force of the tree still lives within it."

Days passed. I stopped measuring the Merus with my own measuring stick. I had become a discreet observer of their society. The more I grew accustomed to their unusual ways of doing things, the more I modified my opinions. I myself was changing, and that transformation was changing the way I saw other people.

One morning, I looked at my face in the little mirror I had carried with me from Mombasa. I hadn't used it since I got to Mount Meru. The image the mirror reflected surprised me. My appearance had changed. I still saw a boy's features, but some small thing gave my face a new expression. Finally I realized what it was. My eyes were different. They no longer expressed the innocence of childhood; now they reflected the harsh, real world. My pupils were even darker than before. But there was a gleam that filtered through, lighting them up from the inside, the first signs of something yet to come. The metamorphosis of my body toward adulthood had begun, but I could see merely its interior manifestation.

That particular day I was called to King Shina's court. I hadn't seen the sovereign since our first meeting, and I had no idea why he had summoned me. I wasn't displeased, because I hoped to glean information about some explosions I had heard that morning. They had come from the palace and caused great commotion among the peasants, who wondered what the devilish Shina could be up to. I walked through the first two barriers and entered the courtyard following normal procedures. This time, I lay face down before the guards could force me to prostrate myself. But they pulled me back to my feet, proof that my status had changed.

Shina was seated on his throne, his leopard beside him. It was panting, its mouth open, eyes squinting even though there was no sun, and its magnificent whiskers stuck out on both sides of its face. A daddy-long-legs dropped awkwardly down beside it. The leopard jerked its head around and snapped up the spider. Then it resumed its earlier position, nonchalant and proud. It could read the fear on the men's faces whenever it looked at one of them. The king's comportment wasn't much different from the big cat's. He was sitting upright on the throne, and he held his head high, an eagle's feather attached to the nape of his neck. His face looked like the face of sultans, taught never to let their emotions be seen in public. Big rings hung in his ears, although the lobes weren't stretched out. His straight nose was slightly flattened, his pupils were very dark and his gaze straightforward. I would have thought him a Swahili if the Merus hadn't gotten me accustomed to the great diversity of their appearance.

Near the king stood the Arab merchant I had met when I arrived. Twenty or so harquebuses lay on the ground along with ammunition for them. So the Arab wanted to sell those extraordinary weapons. They could provide Shina with a true trump card in his struggle against Kibosho if his men knew how to use them. But they weren't easy to use, as I well knew, because I had tried them in Mombasa. In fact my family had carved stocks for some harquebus barrels the sultan had purchased in Cairo. In recompense for our work we had been allowed to be present when they practiced shooting and even to try them ourselves. I remember that day with pride, because I was the best shot, and the sultan took the opportunity to praise me and call his soldiers useless. Those weapons, although they are useful for protecting a fort like Mombasa, are very heavy and don't seem appropriate for Meru country, where the fighting is usually composed of quick strikes and rapid movements. On the other hand, they are unbeatable for holding walled places like Ngurto or the king's palace. The horrible noise and the clouds of smoke they make would be quite enough to frighten off attackers who would be seeing firearms for the first time. It was a daring act for the Arab to bring harquebuses to the interior of the continent when all the coastal cities were fighting greedily for them.

The man with the bells took the floor: "The king has summoned you, Bayu, because the eagle enjoys seeing up close the chick it could rip to pieces with its talons at any moment. The foreigner we welcome today belongs to the El-Kakuri family, prosperous merchants in the city of Kilwa, the great port on the Indian Ocean. Kilwa and Masangu are like seeds of the same fruit. El-Kakuri wishes to participate in our kingdom's greatness and has proposed to the king these weapons that spit fire and sow terror. The king has accepted his offer and bought the weapons. However he has rejected our guest's request to purchase you as a slave. Our guest wanted you to be included in the price of the weapons. The king categorically refused. The merchant insisted, but in vain. You will remain in Masangu, for such is the will of the king."

For a moment he was silent, probably so that I could fully appreciate his sovereign's magnanimity.

"Our guest asked one last favor, the opportunity to meet with you before starting back to Kilwa, because he has something to say to you."

After a signal from the spokesman, the merchant spoke to me in Arabic so nobody else could understand. It was surely quite improbable that anyone at the court understood Arabic.

"Bayu, before leaving this country, I wanted to give you a present. I would have liked to purchase you, not as a slave, but rather to give you freedom. You would have become my associate, and I would have given you my daughter in marriage. The kindness I wanted to show to you might seem surprising, but you will understand when I tell you that you look very much like one of my sons, the one my fourth wife, a black woman, gave to me. I loved that boy very much, but, alas, he has already been summoned by the All-Powerful. I know that my son is at his side, and so I have no reason to be sad that he is gone. But how can I not remember the happy times we spent together when chance, which is always only the will of Allah, puts me on the path of his double? Remember, Bayu, that you will always be welcome in Kilwa. I'll welcome you like a son. As a pledge of my consideration, I've given you a gift. One of my men took it to your host's house as you were on the way here to the palace. I'll let my gift be a surprise."

I went back home to Kabero's house. My host and I opened our eyes in astonishment when we unwrapped the gift. It was a gun! Not a harquebus, but a beautifully made rifle, much lighter and easier to handle. My hands grabbed the weapon to feel its weight and to rub the smooth stock.

"It's inexplicable, Bayu. The king's comportment is a riddle. He allows you to live and also gives you freedom to move about. And then he permits a foreigner to give you a weapon so valuable that to own it himself he wouldn't hesitate to wipe out all of Masangu!"

"But he doesn't know about it."

"Yes, that's possible. If he doesn't confiscate your weapon in the next few days, then he must not realize you have it. All the same, the king's attitude surprises me. Sometimes I wonder who you really are. You must be hiding something from me."

"I'm just a Swahili from the coast. I belong to the El-Mudi clan. We are woodcarvers, from father to son, and have been for generations, *mzee*. There's nothing else."

"Then how can you explain why the king takes such precautions with you? He has managed to tame a leopard, and he allows an unmarried child, with no children, to live here as he pleases!"

"I'm not living just as I please, *mzee*. I'm a prisoner here in Masangu."

"But less than a moon ago you were in chains, and now you receive presents from foreigners!"

"Yes, but that wasn't my choice."

"Come on now. When you're an old man and your judgment has the strength of heartwood, you'll realize that we are able to choose more often than we know."

"But also sometimes we are chosen."

"Yes, that is true. In the meantime, I've got only one piece of advice for you. Hide that weapon before Shina's men take it from you. Tomorrow we'll go into the forest. The first rains are almost upon us, and I must begin to gather honey."

I was thoughtful as I went to bed, preoccupied by the complex web linking me to King Shina and to the Arab. I doubted that Shina was as interested in my fate as Kabero seemed to believe. Far from me, the wish to judge Shina or the Arab, and surely not Kabero. The immature boy who had left Mombasa with his set opinions no longer existed. Now I was seeking discernment.

During the night I had a dream, a very small dream, just a drop of water in the ocean of subterranean thoughts. But the part that made it all the way to me impressed me greatly:

I go down to the banks of a river. On the opposite bank I notice a horse. I swim across the river with the intention of capturing it. The horse catches fire, but that doesn't keep me from mounting it. I spur on my mount, gallop off on my flaming horse. A huge bird follows me. It tries to peck at the horse's neck.

The next day I was following Kabero through banana plantations on a path leading to the forest.

"*Mzee,* have you ever seen horses on Mount Meru?"

"Once, at Ngurto. Sometimes the Arabs are on horseback at the head of their caravans."

"And on the mountain?"

"We don't raise that kind of animal."

"Aren't there some wild horses in the forest?"

"No, there have never been horses on the mountain. I've been told that those animals come from Arabia."

"Runaway horses could have reached Mount Meru."

"They would have been killed by lions."

"Yes, that's true. But they might have flown here."

"Flown? Do horses have wings?"

"I don't know. After all, it might be possible."

"Have you ever seen horses with wings in Mombasa?"

"No, but I know that the Arabs have winged mammals."

"They must be spirits, not animals."

"In any case, I know a Yemenite in Mombasa who saw an animal like that. It had four legs and wings."

"How about that! You've got to tell me that story!"

"It's a long story. It's not only about a monster, but also about a jewel and a magpie."

We had reached a hilltop at the edge of the forest. Kabero asked a child to go get one of his sons who lived down below. While we waited, I was able to tell my story, in which a winged animal appeared to a man. Although the original events had happened in an Arab country, an encounter in Mombasa was at the root of a curious misadventure that remained puzzling for a long time until finally chance allowed me to understand it.

As I was walking once in the woods on Mombasa Island, I noticed a shiny object in a magpie's nest. It was yellow and sparkled like a jewel. I couldn't help climbing up to see it up close. And it was indeed a jewel, a gold brooch. It depicted a strange animal that had an eagle's head and the body of a lion, with a pair of wings attached to its back. A carved block of gold formed the body, while the wings were made of fine strips that looked amazingly like feathers. The gold's brilliance conferred on the beast a beauty that far surpassed its monstrosity. The brooch lit up in the light. As it glistened, a shiver seemed to run through the animal's body, giving it life. Its body, shimmering with fire, seemed to quiver. A shock ran through its torso, and the wings began to beat. The lion was roaring, the eagle ready to take flight. The illusion took hold of me, and I opened my fingers as if I were liberating an insect.

As I contemplated the gold brooch, in my heart I felt a slight twinge that quickly turned to joy. I knew the origin of that astonishing jewel a magpie had deposited in its nest. Discovering it gave me the key to a mystery that was painful to a Mombasa man and gave joy to more than one of his friends. The man in question, a Yemenite, was a jeweler by trade. His name is Hasan and he still lives in Mombasa. Hasan loved a certain woman, but he would never say who it was. Hearing him talk, we understood that she was a member of a wealthy family and that she couldn't display her passion in public. Although being a jeweler requires great skill, a jeweler doesn't enjoy great social prestige. Whether the woman was beyond his reach or not, Hasan longed to win the beauty over, for she was tormenting his soul. He courted her with jewelry he had created with his own hands. One day he gave her a golden brooch shaped like a butterfly. The insect would have landed on a blossom if the woman had accepted it. She said that the butterfly's body was too thick, that it looked like the torso of a lion. Although Hasan was cut to the quick, he reacted tactfully, telling the woman a story he had told us previously.

Hasan had spent his youth in Baghdad, with an uncle, a goldsmith in the Al-Karh market. The two men left by boat to join a cousin in Mosul when the Tigris was in flood, and they got lost in the maze of the river's channels. The next morning, while mist was still covering the swamps, they came upon the remains of a city. Solid buildings with windowless walls and rectangular shapes stood out in the mist. Intrigued, Hasan and his uncle turned their boat toward the city. They pulled ashore and walked toward a breech in a wall.

Just then the sun's rays burst through the fog and like a long golden sword broke over the buildings' facades. Originally the bricks had been varnished, and where varnish still remained it reflected back the light. The two men were entering a courtyard just as the sunlight struck a nearby wall. The men's eyes followed the sun's rays. Imagine their fright when they saw a monster standing against the wall, staring at them! It had the body of a lion, a pair of wings and the head of an eagle. Its beak seemed to open. Terror-stricken, the two men rushed away and left the city forever.

Hasan didn't dare talk about his misadventure before moving to Mombasa, as if he needed to put a certain distance between himself and the beast. But when the woman he was courting criticized the butterfly brooch, he seized the opportunity to recount his strange meeting. He probably hoped to show himself off to advantage, but the woman remained skeptical and mistrusted the storyteller. When Hasan saw her reaction, he answered proudly.

"Since you don't believe me, I'll make a brooch that will look like that animal, and I'll give it to you."

"You want to give me a brooch shaped like a monster?"

"A monster touched by an artist's hand becomes more graceful. You'll be surprised by how noble the jewel will be. It will have subtle beauty, superior to the beauty of all the jewels you've ever adorned your charming body with, my queen."

"Including all those you've already given me?"

"I made all that jewelry under the influence of love that listens to itself alone. I worked the gold without detecting the thoughts of the object about to be born. Now, my beloved, the flame of love consuming me is incandescent blue, so pure that I can see through it. It's no longer a veil between the jewel and me. I can feel its desire taking shape in my hands. I'm ready to listen to it. You surely can understand that, because God created you to adorn the earth. You'll wear the brooch on your breast. Each breath you take will make its wings beat. When my hands clasp your waist, O my queen, emotion will fill your breast and the brooch will take flight."

The woman kept silent. When Hasan finished and looked quietly at her, she lowered her eyes, pulled her veil back over her hair and walked away without a word.

Hasan returned home elated. He jumped up and down, flapping his arms like a bird taking flight. His sister asked him why he was so happy.

"You can't understand," he answered.

"Nor does the young rooster in the chicken yard understand much."

"God gave birds wings so they could rise above human mediocrity."

"And he made men mediocre so they wouldn't fly away."

"Men, perhaps, but not their art."

And with those words, Hasan stopped flying.

He worked carefully to make the jewel. The first three tries he rejected; they ended up smashed to bits. On the fourth attempt, inspiration was revealed, and dexterity followed. The animal had journeyed from distant antiquity all the way to Hasan's workshop. Hasan gave life to the metal, and metal's life brought light to the Yemenite's fingers. The workman managed to complete in three days what previously four weeks of hard labor had not allowed him to produce.

The brooch was ready. Hasan couldn't stop admiring it. It was an object as noble as his love. He had accomplished the task that would allow him to win over his beauty.

He invited the young woman to his workshop on Friday at the time for prayers. The workshop had a sun-drenched terrace hidden away from the neighbors' view. Hasan placed a stool decorated with a piece of black satin in the center of the room, and then he lay the jewel on the pedestal. The object glittered in the sunshine.

The woman discreetly entered the workshop and greeted Hasan. He bade her go up to the next floor so that he could give her the jewel. She climbed the steps and started out onto the terrace. She saw the stool covered with the black cloth. She turned around toward Hasan, who was following her. Surprised that she didn't seem more attracted to the jewel, Hasan moved past the young woman who was blocking his vision.

"Where is the jewel?" he cried out.

"What jewel?"

"The jewel, right there!" Hasan shouted, pointing at the stool.

"I don't see anything."

"That's impossible!"

Hasan inspected the terrace and then looked over the walls.

It wasn't conceivable that a thief had come over the roof and stolen the jewel.

"That's impossible, impossible!"

"What's impossible?" wondered the woman, not understanding.

"The jewel. It's not here any more. I put it on the stool, and now it's gone!"

The woman reflected a moment.

"It must have flown away."

Hasan, busy looking everywhere, paid no attention to her. When he finally realized the woman had left, he knew he'd never see her again.

"You see, it's possible to depict animals in spite of your religion," Kabero said to me when I had finished my tale.

"That's not the same thing. Hasan's goal was profane rather than sacred."

The look in Kabero's eyes showed me that he didn't understand the meaning of my words. His limited mastery of Swahili didn't let him follow a polished conversation. The way he looked at me seemed to be telling me: "You are truly strange."

"What did you do with the jewel?" he asked me.

"I didn't want to take it back to Hasan. I lay it on the ground and walked away. A magpie that had been watching me constantly flew down to the jewel and carried it back up to its nest."

"Who knows if it hasn't flown all the way to Mount Meru. Perhaps we'll find the brooch in one of the forest trees."

And with that, we entered the forest on Mount Meru.

Chapter seven

The forest is always a marriage of green and shadow, an everlasting union of verdant color with nuanced light that filters through the foliage. The dominant clan is the plant clan. The wood and leaves are the progenitors of a prosperous lineage that is constantly replacing its children. The leaves fall, but the trunk remains. And even where the clan extols its dead, nature doesn't linger. The leaves are buried in the humus they themselves create and the wood slowly rots away alone, discreetly and quietly.

Sometimes, as we walked, our feet sank into the ground, desecrating tombs where there had been no mourners. Very little grass or plants on the carpet of fallen leaves. Shrubs form bouquets of large leaves among tall trees that rise to prodigious heights. Their trunks soar up toward the light, and at the tips of their branches it looks as if the tiny leaves must be gathering light as bees gather pollen. Things are quite different for the bushes. They must be content with the crumbs of light their condescending older brothers let drop.

They are like a band of rowdy children whose mischief leads them to assume acrobatic poses. Their multiple woody stems twist about and their branches shoot off in all directions, elbowing others, grabbing their adversaries in a raucous free-for-all. The thoughtful attitude of the tall ascetic trees is nothing like the little ones' turbulence. They don't have their place in the sun, but they are happy with the freedom allowed by the darkness of the undergrowth. Vines fill some parts of the forest, long wooden ropes covered with moss mooring dhows with their loads of leaves. The crevasses drowned in shadow and overflowing with such supple wooden stems resemble graveyards where ships lie wrecked. Their hulls rot away, covered with algae. Along with the moss there's a strange lichen, a mass of tangled white threads, hanging in garlands. Some of the trees are totally cloaked in this frayed cloth. As we were coming out of the shadows into a large cove infested with black moss, seeing the trees covered with those ragged white strips in the diffuse light, I could imagine huge ships with tattered sails moving toward their doom.

I was particularly attracted to the cedar trees, those kings of the forest that can grow to amazing heights and can have girths the size of a hut. According to Kabero and his sons, these trees were several centuries old. The cedar's base is protected by enormous buttresses, and where those buttresses meet they often form a cavity like a walled porch. Honey men and hunters sometimes take shelter there at night when they need to spend several days in the forest. They also store branches there to dry, protected from the rain, so they can burn them later when they're gathering honey. Kabero pointed out that cedar was the best wood for building, along with the yew pine, another majestic tree with sickle-shaped leaves, and the juniper, an immense conifer growing on the mountain's eastern slope. Majestic is indeed the word that fits such trees. Not only does the cedar rise toward the sky, it also develops gigantic branches along its trunk. They spread pitilessly, disregarding any trees that might have been trying to grow under their tutelage. Whenever I pulled bark off these trees from under their shrouds of moss, I would disturb cockroaches and millipedes. It's a strange world in which life proliferates on earth composed of what has died. One tree caught my attention with its tawny cork, and I couldn't keep myself from cutting off some shavings, as if such despoliation was going to show me some unique sapwood, the wood's quintessence that Mombasa woodcarvers have so often dreamed of in their childhood dreams.

"This tree is dangerous for our animals. If cows or goats eat its leaves or chew its bark, they die. The tree is poisonous," Kabero told me.

"And how about that one," I asked, pointing to another tree covered with cork.

"That's the *irahana*. It contains a healing sap. Say, Ngotiko, I wonder what has happened to Masumboko? He should have caught up with us by now."

Ngotiko, one of Kabero's sons, grabbed his machete and struck a tree with it. Four blows echoed through the forest. Immediately afterward, four other blows answered. He struck again. One long sound, two short ones, and then another long one. Like an echo, the same rhythm answered, and this time I was able to identify it.

"He's getting near."

Kabero had put his things down on the ground and was examining some trees of medium height standing near the edge of a clearing filled with flowers and buzzing with bees. He exchanged a few words with his two sons and then looked at me with a smile.

"Oh yes, we should be speaking Swahili, or you won't understand anything. I'm looking for a good place to put a hive, and this tree should do the job. It has perfect exposure. You see, the hive has to be facing an open area, and it has to be protected from the wind and correctly oriented toward the sun. Bees have their own paths through the forest, and we honey men are able to recognize them. We set our hives along the paths the bees follow. Otherwise, the hives could go for years without attracting a swarm. This tree would be absolutely perfect if there weren't so many ants. They must have a nest up there. These ants have nasty bites. That's why I'm sending up one of my sons. We'll get a good laugh! Look here, here's their old nest."

"Why do they change nests?"

"The nest finally drops, because the ants devour the leaves and the bark and end up destroying the branch the nest is hanging in. So finally the branch just breaks."

"Some animals destroy what they build," the son noted. "Consider the praying mantis that eats its mate. And the chameleon, that kills itself to give life."

"That's just a fable," the father said.

"What, about the chameleon?"

"It is said that to give birth to its young the chameleon throws itself from the top of a tree and crashes to the ground. The crash splits open its stomach, and then the babies are able to leave the mother's body. That's not true. In fact, the chameleon lays eggs and keeps on living in peace."

Masumboko, Kabero's second son, caught up with us. His father asked him to climb the tree to see if there was an ants' nest. He quickly scampered up toward the top.

"Ouch, ow! Yes, *mzee*, there are plenty of ants!" he shouted down.

"Can you see their nest?"

"Ouch! It's right here. Send me up a machete."

They attached the long knife to a rope Masumboko dropped down. He swung ferociously at the branches on which the nest was attached. Dry leaves, twigs and pieces of bark began dropping down around us. And then the lower branches bent, slowing down a black mass as it fell. The nest, a ball the size of a man's head, dropped to the ground. A multitude of ants were rushing around on the compact clay surface.

"Masumboko, you go burn the nest. We'll get the hive."

I followed Kabero and his son while Masumboko, back down on the ground, had stripped off his clothes and was slapping at his body to dislodge the ferocious ants.

Kabero planned to get a hive that had no bees because it had been poorly placed. He climbed the tree with surprising agility for a man his age.

"Oh, it's not surprising that there aren't any bees! An aye-aye had a brood in the hive. Nasty critter! It chewed away the cover."

"What's an aye-aye?" I asked the son.

"Haven't you ever heard them in the banana plantations? You can hear them at dusk when they began to call shrilly, 'ay, ay'! They've got pointed ears like a cat, a nose like a rat and big eyes that shine like balls of fire in the sunlight. The people in Uru claim that aye-ayes are their ancestors, their dead fathers and grandfathers who've come back to eat their share of food, because they live on bananas and other fruits. But in Masangu we don't believe any of that. We chase them off with our slingshots."

"Ancestors or not," added Kabero, climbing down from the tree, "I can assure you that it's best not to happen upon an aye-aye in a hive with its young. The nasty creature could rip your eyes out with its claws."

The two brothers picked up the hive. Kabero guided them as they hoisted it into the tree so they would position it correctly. And then we started off toward an apiary where the old man hoped to gather a first crop of honey. We crossed some small treeless valleys. There were flowers everywhere, and bees were working busily. Wild animals had beaten down paths through the tall grass. Piles of elephant manure were strewn over the ground. Kabero showed me a trap Shina's men had dug. It was a long hole at the bottom of a valley. In fact, it was made up of two holes separated by a wall that was slightly lower than ground level.

"They'll camouflage the holes with light branches. The elephant falls into the trap, its front legs in the first hole and its back legs in the second one. There's no way it can get out. We too hunt elephants so we can sell the ivory to caravans. There is so much hunting that there are fewer and fewer elephants on the mountain. That's not such a bad thing, because sometimes the elephants go down to our villages and destroy our crops."

"Is this where old Mashauri comes to milk elephants?" one son asked.

"No, that's still further on."

"Who is Mashauri?"

"He's a famous *mganga* from Masangu. He's a doctor who knows which medicines can protect against the evil eye. Elephant milk is one of the most effective ones. Mashauri knows how to cajole an elephant cow so that he can milk it and not risk being killed. My family owes him a great deal, because he saved us from a curse that had fallen upon the clan. My uncle and my brother were dead in less than a week. We called Mashauri to combat the evil eye. He went into the forest to get some elephant milk. It was a long time before he came back, because it wasn't the best season for calving. In the meantime, my cousin got sick and was very near death. Fortunately, then Mashauri came back. He had us all drink a brew made with milk."

Kabero grew quiet as if he had finished his story.

"Did that work?"

"Of course it worked. My cousin got better, and you can see that we're all still alive."

As we were walking along, Kabero stopped at the foot of a tree where there was a hive. "Do you see these marks?"

Brown scratches zigzagged up the tree to the height of a man and then disappeared. "They were made by the little leopard's claws."

"The little leopard?"

"Yes. It's not a real leopard, but it looks a lot like it, though it's much smaller. I don't know its Swahili name. In Meru we call it *nzana*."

"I think I know the animal. In Swahili, the word is *ngawa*, the serval. Does the serval even eat bees?"

"It destroys everything, all the honey and all the bees. It can kill the queen. Once a swarm is attacked, it leaves the hive for good. The serval is a plague, but around here it's quite rare. Otherwise we'd need to plant sharp stakes around all the trees."

"And does the leopard eat honey?"

"No."

"Never?"

"No," Kabero repeated.

"Well, not in the beginning," Ngotiko said before his father cut him off.

"The leopard never eats honey," the old man said angrily.

We came to the apiary. Kabero scowled when he saw one hive with the cover missing. The men looked all around the tree.

"The cover has been stolen, as unbelievable as that may seem."

"Why is that unbelievable?"

"Because stealing a hive is a very serious crime. Thieves are always punished."

"Punished by whom?"

"Punished by the spirits of the forest, of course! Forest spirits never allow thievery. Sometimes people think they're smart and can disregard the laws of the forest, but those people never remain alive very long."

"What happens to them?"

"Nothing. We just find them dead. Well, Masumboko, go get the wood I put to dry in the cedar trunk. And Ngotiko, you clear a place for the fire. You see, Bayu, we have to build our fire some distance away from the hive because bees are very sensitive. If the fire is too close, the bees swarm out and attack us. Look here. Someone tried to cut down that dead tree. He must have run away, because the bees attacked him when he started chopping."

Ngotiko had sliced away a layer of humus, a crust made up of a multitude of roots entwined around dry leaves. He pulled it back like a prayer rug, and then on the bare ground he built a small pile of leaves and dry twigs. They caught fire quickly. Masumboko threw on some dry sticks. Smoke began to rise and then spread out like the pale specter of a mushroom. Kabero moved some of the burning logs to ferns he had laid out on the ground. He wrapped the thick ferns around the logs and tied them up with vines. Then he climbed up in the tree, holding a rope so that he could pull up a calabash, a knife and the smoking bundle. We moved away from the tree, for dark drops were already pouring out of the hive. The bees, spurred by the smoke, were leaving their den. The buzzing got even louder when Kabero placed his bundle of smoking ferns just under the hive.

"Ouch, ow!" we heard.

"They're starting to sting the old man," one of his sons said.

Kabero put the ferns on his shoulders and removed the cover at the back of the hive, while in front the smoked bees kept pouring out. Then he cut out the combs, placed them in the calabash and lowered it so that one of his sons could reach it. Then he hurried back down to escape the bees' wrath. There followed a honey tasting. We pulled off pieces of comb and chewed avidly on the translucent substance, spitting out the wax. The honey melted in our mouths and slipped deliciously down our throats. It was dense and sweet, almost cloying. The flavor reminded me of the cakes, the Turkish delights and all the other sweets we eat at weddings and religious celebrations along the coast.

We started toward home. We came to a pond, a mass of mud covered with plants where elephants had stamped around, and started making slower progress.

"*Mzee*, perhaps you can tell Bayu about your misadventure with the python."

"Oh, yes. You'll enjoy this, Bayu. In those days I was still young, though I was already married and the father of my first son, who unfortunately did not survive. I had followed some elephants deep into the forest. I had reached the bamboo groves and was practically lost. Dusk fell as I was on my way back down to Masangu. It was already dark when I reached this pond that we are at now. And then I saw a pair of eyes glowing in the darkness. Yes, two big luminous eyes with no pupils, shining brightly. I was terrified. I thought a spirit must have followed me from the bamboo groves, because the groves are full of spirits. You can hear them moan whenever you get close. I ran as fast as I could until I reached our houses, and the spirit didn't follow me. When I told the clan elders my story, they burst out laughing. What I thought were eyes were really just python eggs, which have phosphorescent qualities. Well, I thought, I'll go and see for myself. And so I came back here to the pond. It was daylight, but the eggs were still shining brightly. Actually, it's not the eggs themselves but some substance the python spits up that produces the light.

The python coats its eggs with it. The temptation to steal them was great. But instead I quickly ran away, because scarcely had I made a movement toward the eggs when a huge python started down out of the branches above the nest. I ran home as fast as I could…."

Clearly it was one of the Kabero family's favorite stories, for the sons laughed heartily.

"Are there many pythons in the forest?"

"Yes, but it's hard to see them."

"Do you know where they live?"

"No, except for in the abyss of evil spirits, I'm not sure where they live."

"The abyss of evil spirits? What's that?"

"It's an immense chasm in the mountain, a deep pit, and it goes down into the earth so far that you can't see the bottom. There are evil spirits living there along with pythons."

"Where is the abyss?"

"Above Uru, near the 'cedar with a door.' Have you heard about that cedar? It's an unusual tree, because there's an enormous opening that goes all the way through it, forming a kind of entrance. They say that the top of the tree hides a treasure, protected by its thick branches. Any men who've climbed the tree have simply disappeared. The cedar tree is guarded by a spirit, a hornbill, to which people used to take offerings. Nobody goes there anymore since King Kilesia died. That's where the hunters found his body, hanging from a branch above the precipice."

I went back to the forest with Kabero and his sons almost daily. At dawn, Kabero would cut some fodder for the goats and sheep, and then he was free for the rest of the day. Every day our long walk would take us on a different path. Sometimes the men would stop to study a tree trunk or place a hive. Whenever a tree seemed like a good place for a swarm of bees, Kabero would make a mark on the trunk. By that simple act he claimed use of the tree for himself. There were many signs in the forest; axe marks, knotted ropes or cloths, symbols carved into a trunk. It was no longer a wilderness, the virgin forest

I had discovered several weeks before, but rather a space men were acquainted with and used frequently, as proven by the many paths we followed. I was beginning to learn to find my way, to identify trees, to interpret the sounds that filled the silence. One day, I was the first to notice a swarm of bees in a knot-hole on a cedar, and that gave me a great deal of satisfaction. Finding wild swarms or the nest of a variety of bee that doesn't sting was almost a game. Of course, the fun ended whenever we had to get honey from trees that were difficult to climb, but at least our game kept alive that old predatory instinct that slumbers in men.

We would gather the honey from each hive. When the beekeepers climbed back down their arms were barely swollen from bee stings. They didn't even bother to take out the stingers. Rarely did more than five or six bees sting them when they stole the honey, for as Kabero said: "Bees are our friends."

Following Kabero's advice, I constructed some hives myself, although it was too late for any swarms to take them over and produce honey before the end of the season, now almost over. I enjoyed carving a hive from a log. You had to dig out the inside of the log and polish the outside to give it a surface on which rain would have no purchase. The roof of a hive demands similar work. In spite of having only rudimentary tools, I quickly rediscovered the old movements that had been my daily routine back in Mombasa when I carved doors and furniture in my father's workshop. My dexterity with the tools amazed Kabero and his sons. Pride pushed me to aim for perfection, and I even went so far as to sign my hives with Arabic letters. I worked more easily than I had in Mombasa. My body had grown bigger during my journey over the plains and it had become stronger and more agile in its contact with the forest. My senses were sharper. New vigor gave force to my arms and legs. Sap was rising toward the branches of adulthood.

When he saw my name carved into the wood, Kabero, who couldn't read or write, had a curious reaction.

"You've carved some birds."

"They aren't birds, but rather letters, *mzee*."

"They look like swallows. If your religion forbids depicting birds, all you have to do is write. Your letters are like a flock of birds."

The day came when Kabero invited me to gather the honey myself. His request took me by surprise. I couldn't refuse, although I wasn't very comfortable with the idea of confronting those little monsters high up in a tree in some awkward position. For someone who has fought with a crocodile, that might seem strange, I realize, but I had become quite accustomed to relaxing in the shady undergrowth, waiting for my ration of honey as I watched butterflies, looked for rare birds or wandered through the trees. Hearing the old man or his sons scream in pain up in the trees didn't bother me at all, as long as a few minutes later their calloused fingers would hand me a chunk of honey dripping down out of its waxy case. Getting the honey myself was a painful experience, what with the ferns burning my back, the smoke irritating my throat and eyes and especially the bee stings that caused my arms and one cheek to swell up. Not to mention the embarrassing fall I had. And what was worse, Kabero announced that from then on I would gather the honey from one out of every three hives. Nostalgia washed over me, and memories of Mombasa filled my mind. Truly, I was beginning to miss my native city. I was longing to go home. But I still needed to have my two other dreams before I could start back, and my dream life couldn't have been poorer. All I had managed to dream about was a horse, and such an animal didn't even exist on Mount Meru. Other dreams would trouble my nights, but then they too would disappear before I woke up. When I got up, I would always have the vague feeling that I had forgotten something.

Although the Merus' was an oral culture that was unfamiliar with writing, the forest was an open book to them. I would have gladly compared it to the Koran were it not that such an idea would be blasphemous. Kabero and his sons never failed to read the signs scattered in the woods. It was as if the bark of the trees, the veins in the leaves, the earth and its vegetative carpet, the streams and the ponds, and the animals and their tracks made up a language to be deciphered. Under the forest's dictations, the honey men learned a great deal. They composed the letters of an alphabet. They created a Holy Book that speaks about the unity of men, of animals and of plants.

The forest passed its knowledge on to me through Kabero and his sons. The way I looked at other people was now profoundly different. I tried to forget about myself and be more attentive to the words of others. In Mombasa, only my amorous desire for Hasmahani had led me to do that. On the slopes of Mount Meru, knowing how to listen had become an end unto itself and the means to learn. I craved learning new things. I realized the scope of my ignorance. The forest was full of paths.

Often we walked along an escarpment made up of rocks mixed with clay. One evening I noticed the shape of an animal drawn in the clay. A leopard! The head was formed by a shaped rock while marks in the clay formed the impression of a body. Without the three-dimensional stone head, I would have assumed it was simply a chance occurrence, for the big cat's legs were nothing more than simple lines.

"Who made this?"

There was an awkward silence. Masumboko and Ngotiko said nothing, but finally their father answered. "It was Mpemsaba, an apprentice to the craftsman who carves our funeral posts. Mpemsaba has gone crazy; he is possessed by the spirit of a tree he cut down without performing the proper rituals. He's probably the person who sculpted that leopard image. At least the head. The marks are natural. Running water made them."

"Are you sure he's the sculptor?"

"He was found dead, killed by some wild animal." Kabero didn't need to explain any further. I understood. The leopard had killed the man who had depicted its face. "You see how dangerous it is to draw an animal, *mzee*."

"I don't think so."

"Let me tell you a story, *mzee*. As I was traveling from Mombasa to Mount Meru, I heard a bird singing in a rock. It was imprisoned in the stone. I wanted to set it free, and I managed to break the rock.

But it was only a bird fossil. The song stopped immediately. That's surely proof that the bird was happier hidden inside the stone."

Kabero didn't answer right away. He thought for a moment. "You're wrong, Bayu. I too have a story to tell you, a story about Kimandi, a wise man I accompanied to his final resting place. He lived in Masangu, although he was an Arusha. The Arushas live on the west side of the volcano. They have frequent contact with the herdsmen who live on the plain and speak their language. Some even still venerate Mount Ol Donyo Dorok, situated a few days' journey from here. They don't pray as we do, facing Mount Meru's summit."

Indeed, Kabero addressed his prayers every morning toward the mountain peak. The Merus, who have not been touched by the true faith, think that God the Most High lives there.

"One day Kimandi announced that he was leaving Masangu and that he would never return. He was going to Mount Ol Donyo Dorok. We knew that we would never see him again and so decided to go with him, wondering if we would survive the journey, for one doesn't lightly venture onto a mountain where God lives. We went through the forest and came to a rocky escarpment. There was a ravine cutting through the barricade. We were about to go down into the ravine when a bird appeared, fluttering before us as if barring our passage. Finally it landed on a stone and spoke to us. Here, on Mount Meru, birds don't speak human language, but on Mount Ol Donyo Dorok, they do. The bird said to us:

"'I'm the guardian of the gate that leads to the Dwelling. Only birds can enter.'

"'We too are birds, for our words take wing,' Kimandi answered. The bird seemed to think for a moment and then responded. 'In that case I'll let anyone pass who can answer this question: Why do you not have wings?'

"You'll never imagine what Kimandi answered. He began to sing like a bird! A long, melodious bird song. The bird, the real bird, flew off. Kimandi followed it and disappeared."

Kabero looked straight ahead for a moment, then continued. "I don't think the song you heard came from the bird fossil. The song was coming from your own person. It was guiding you toward your vocation. For, there in that image of a bird, that is where your being must surely reside."

One day as we were resting in the forest, Kabero said to me:

"Do you remember you asked me once if the leopard eats honey?"

"Yes, *mzee.*"

"I told you it doesn't. Well, that's not totally true. At the beginning of humanity's time, just once, the leopard ate some honey. It's a story our forefathers have passed on to us, a secret story. You must never tell it, especially not to any woman or man who is not a bee keeper. Promise me."

"I swear, *mzee.*"

"Well then, listen. Humanity began when God created two identical beings so they could populate the earth. They were neither male nor female but combined both sexes and could reproduce. God placed them at the center of the universe, which means on Mount Meru. They were happy, and lived on honey, for the bees were their friends. They dallied madly with each other, and even did a little more than dally, but they didn't have any children. God was disappointed, wondering if he had created imperfect creatures. So he sent a leopard down to earth. It wasn't a true leopard. It was shaped like a leopard, but its coat was smooth and had no spots. The animal came upon the two beings as they were gathering honey from a tree trunk, and it swallowed them whole. And then it leaped onto the tree trunk that housed the bees and tried to steal the honey, but the bees were furious, and they attacked, stinging the leopard all over its body. The pain from all the stings made the leopard spit the two beings back up, and they were still alive. Under the bees' assault, the leopard had to retreat and hide in thick brush, its body covered with huge bumps caused by the bees' stings. The bumps swelled up and burst, forming tiny craters whose edges grew dark. The scars made the swellings disappear, but the black marks remained, creating the leopard's spots. Thus was the leopard created. As for the other two beings, they noticed that they too had changed. Their short stay in the leopard's stomach had changed their bodies. One lost its feminine attributes and the other its masculine attributes. They had become man and woman. Not satisfied, they tried to recover their original state and they went looking for the leopard to see if it would give them back their missing parts. They found the leopard and offered it honey in exchange. But the leopard swallowed the honey, declared that it would give nothing back, and disappeared. To get their revenge, the man and woman asked the bees never to give one more drop of honey to a leopard. And that's why the leopard has never again eaten honey. And that's how humanity was born."

"Hmmm!" I said.

"What do you mean, hmmm?"

"The story is hard to believe. Man and woman were created directly by God. There was no intermediary."

"That's what you say."

"No, that's what's written in the Koran."

"The Koran? I don't know anything about the Koran. I'm telling you what our elders have always taught us."

"And how about the leopard's eyes? Has anyone told you about them?"

"No. It's true that some people say the leopard can change its spots to eyes, but that's all I know about leopards."

Chapter eight

Time passed, to the rhythm of honey gathering. Kabero had adopted me. His words indicated that he wasn't expecting me to leave his home. Events were to decide otherwise.

One morning Kabero informed me that there was a horse on Mount Meru. I was immediately reminded of the dream in which I rode a horse of fire. It seemed possible I could find out what my dream meant. I didn't know that I'd be living the most troubled days of my existence.

As I entered King Shina's court, I was thinking about my dream and Kabero's words: "An Arab has just given a horse to the king of Kibosho. Those Arabs really know what to bring to appeal to the Merus! And do you know what fate the king of Kibosho has reserved for the horse? He's going to sacrifice it during the initiation ceremony for the young men attaining warrior status! They'll be circumcising the young men in the next few days, and the ritual demands animal sacrifices. The horse is among the animals to be sacrificed."

At King Shina's court, his spokesman said to me:

"The king agrees to listen to you. You may speak."

"I've come to ask permission to leave Masangu so that I might go to Kibosho. I intend to steal the king's horse and bring it back to Masangu."

Laughter rippled through the assembly. Even the warriors, normally expressionless, couldn't keep from smiling. In the shadow of the shelter under which the court was assembled, the two ears of a feline perked up to listen. Shina was not laughing. He kept his eyes on me, and the look in his eyes was hard, almost painful. The spokesman asked me:

"And how do you think you'll be able to manage such a feat?"

"I've got my ideas, but first I wish to have the king's agreement. I've never broken the order not to leave Masangu. If the king removes the ban, I'll talk."

The spokesman was speechless, visibly surprised by my audacity. It wasn't common to hear words like that from the mouth of a foreigner who had escaped from slavery only a short time earlier.

One of the men of the court interjected: "Tell that impudent fellow that the king never wastes his time with a child!"

"Often a child can inspire those who are mature, old man," I retorted.

"He's crazy," someone said.

"And sometimes the old man cuts off the young shoot that irritates his feet," the courtier responded.

"It's easy to attach that shoot to a supportive stake. I promise to bring an end to the conflict with Kibosho if I am allowed to take their king's horse," I proclaimed solemnly.

The spokesman looked dismayed, people in the assembly started laughing and the warriors looked at me haughtily. They were probably expecting the order to seize me and throw me in prison. Then the king began to speak.

"Fine, Bayu. I grant you this favor. Now, explain yourself."

"Tell me, spokesman. Do your spies know whether the horse will be sacrificed before or after the circumcision?"

"After."

"Then you can wait. You'll make a surprise attack on the newly circumcised. They won't have the strength to defend themselves and will surrender. You'll make them prisoners and bring them back here. After a move like that, the king of Kibosho will have no choice but to sue for peace."

A heavy silence hung over the court as if my words had severed everyone's tongues. The king sat up straight, adjusting himself on his throne, staring at me solemnly all the while. He spoke:

"That's a good idea. But we won't take any prisoners. It's better to kill them all."

"That's not what I said!" I protested.

"No, but you gave me the idea, and it's an excellent one. I'm surprised I didn't think of it earlier myself. What does the assembly think?"

Silence. Death was stalking. Was the fate of the newly circumcised already sealed in the palace court?

"The idea is utter blasphemy. It's against all our laws," an old man threw out.

"When the warriors from Kibosho burn your house and rape your daughters, you'll still be talking about laws. As for me, I find the idea, although not very respectable, quite a good one," another old man answered.

"They will be armed only lightly or not at all, and the ceremony will take place on the island where the river forks. It'll be easy to surround it. I don't see how they could escape. Let's take them prisoner," the first old man continued.

The other men gave him no support. One of the courtiers did introduce a nuance.

"The idea is excellent, I agree, but we shouldn't kill them after the circumcision. For then they'll already be men."

"So?" another man wondered. "What difference does it make if they're already men when we kill them?"

"We'd need to have a burial ceremony for them so their souls won't wander all over Masangu."

"And maybe you'd like us to take their bodies back to their parents and say we're sorry, too?"

"Oh, stop trying to show off. If we kill unarmed men, their souls will haunt Masangu. It's preferable to kill them before the circumcision ceremony."

I was alarmed by such words and tried to intervene. "It'd be better to take them prisoner..."

But nobody would listen to me.

"As long as they haven't been cut yet, they'll be able to defend themselves, or at least flee. But circumcision will weaken them so much that they'll barely be able to walk. Once they've been bled down low, they'll let themselves be bled up high, like chickens."

"It's shameful for us to kill the newly circumcised men. They are innocent!" I shouted.

"Shut up! You don't have the floor anymore."

"I think it's better to kill them after they're circumcised, given the effect we expect. If we kill only children, the families will mourn their death and then think about vengeance. But if we massacre adults, the clans will be hit where it hurts the most."

"That's right. Kill the children and only the women mourn. Kill the adults and you'll be destroying future generations. Plus you'll be giving a permanent wound to all the generations that came before, their elders and their ancestors."

"That's exactly why we need to kill them before they are circumcised. We are human beings. It's better to kill children."

The old man who was opposed to the massacre spoke once more. "We cannot kill human beings during a rite of passage. That would be an offense to God. And what's got into you, talking about Kibosho as if it's a country we should destroy?! Have you forgotten that in our fathers' days we used to live together harmoniously and that the men from Kibosho were our brothers?"

"You're still living in the past. Those days are long gone."

"There's a solution to the concern about the souls of the dead men. Let's throw their bodies into the abyss of evil spirits. That way we'd be rid of their souls forever."

"A very good idea! The abyss is about an hour's march from the island. It'll be easy to carry their bodies that far."

"So we've come to a decision, my friends," the king said. "We'll kill the men after they're circumcised and throw their bodies into the abyss of evil spirits. Bayu, you can keep the horse as a reward for your idea. We need to act quickly. The initiation ceremonies have already begun. The circumcision ceremony will take place in three or four days. I'm calling the army together this evening. Not one word of our discussion must leave this place. You, Bayu, you'll stay near the palace until you leave for the attack. After our victory you'll be free."

The king stopped speaking. The session ended. And then the leopard came out of the shadows and sat down in the middle of the court. Turning toward the assembly, it bared its teeth and growled.

Shina's decision filled me with dismay, the more so because he dared give me the credit for the idea about the massacre. I was not at all pleased to be deprived of my freedom and even less happy about having to join the expedition. I was embarrassed with regard to Kabero, for I had left him that morning without saying a word about my intentions. He didn't even know that I had gone to see the king.

They housed me in a camp behind the palace. In one day it filled up with warriors, mostly young men, placid and taciturn, almost resigned, although I could sense a certain excitement. They knew that a battle was in preparation and that they would spearhead the attack. Nothing had been mentioned about the trick the king was planning. The possibility of someone leaking the information to the king of Kibosho was too great. A drummer could have beat out a message to someone posted on the other side of the ramparts. Perhaps that's why none of my companions could speak Swahili. I was unable to talk with them except for a few words I had learned from Kabero. Clearly Shina didn't trust me. The next day, as he was reviewing his troops, I saw him talking to one of the adult men soldiers who had joined the young warriors and pointing to me. I don't know what Shina was saying to the man, but I'm sure they were talking about me. Before the king left the square, I hurried over to him.

"King, I do not want to go kill the circumcised men."

The man with the bells who was walking beside him was furious that I would dare address the sovereign directly.

"Do you wish to capture the horse?"

"Yes, but—"

"Then you'll go to the island. Nothing is forcing you to participate in the attack."

And Shina walked away.

Some goats were brought into the camp and divided up among the different units. The order was given to kill them. We didn't slit their throats. Killing them required turning the animal over on its back and holding its legs up. One man smothered it while another plunged a knife directly into its heart. Death was quick. The thorax was cut open and the blood emptied into a calabash, and then the stomach was opened and the vital organs were pulled out to be distributed according to the warriors' ranks. Finally the rest of the animal was cut up for cooking, surrounded by flies excited by all the blood. The camp roared with all the buzzing insects that had come to join the feast.

I stayed off to one side, because the tasks associated with butchering are not considered noble by my clan. We ate the meat and soup mixed with raw blood. Islam forbids consuming fresh blood, but although I tried to explain that to the elder who held out a calabash to me, he wouldn't listen and forced me to drink. I felt that I was committing a grave sin, but I did it anyway.

In the middle of the night they woke us up. Songs were rising up all over camp, accompanied by hoarse exhaling that reminded me of an orgasm. Some of the men had prepared a brew from different tree barks. Each of the warriors present had to drink some, while others were leading in a bull with big curved horns. The drink caused a slight numbing effect in us, and then our legs and arms began to tremble. The bull was frightened by the torches and all the excitement in the camp, and it needed several men to hold it tightly. A warrior shot an arrow into its jugular vein, and blood spurted out. The blood was collected in a calabash, and then the vein was bandaged up so that the animal would not die from loss of blood. Next we were lined up and made to drink the raw blood. In spite of my revulsion I swallowed the horrible liquid. The taste rose up into my head and I had to repress the urge to vomit.

We formed a circle. Spurred on by the beating drum, the dance began. The dance was nothing like our Mombasa dances, where the movements of our feet are in harmony with the swaying of our hips and the gestures of our hands. All we did was jump up and down, as high as possible, exhaling noisily. The dance accelerated the action of the bark drink. The liquid reached our bloodstream and rose to our brains. It purified our minds, enabling them to welcome the flood of energy the dancing created. Our leaping increased our strength and gave vigor to our bodies. Our muscles relaxed, our reflexes grew sharper. The bull's blood coursing through our arteries gave us a bull's power. When my feet touched the ground, a force entered my body and it sprang high. A flood of energy carried me along with it. My legs could no longer feel what they were doing. All pain evaporated. Our bodies became light, supple, and agile, ready for battle. The warriors formed a circle, and as we danced, at times we would all rush toward the center, shouting hoarsely. I could see their bloodshot eyes, their gleaming pupils, dilated by the drug. In the flickering torchlight, unsettling shadows danced over faces that appeared to be covered by angry masks. In the middle of the circle a ball of energy was forming, radiating out from our bodies. We were stripped to the waist, our lances standing upright beside our bodies like sexual emblems. Soon, those lances would enter our victims' stomachs and would rip open their guts as if in a symbolic rape, despicable though it was. I could feel violence rising within me, a death wish I had always been able to hold back before, and now it was loosened, like the horse of fire in my dream. My being turned away from its feminine side, and like the moon in its last quarter, let itself be taken over by its shadowy elements, its evil face. I was ready to kill.

We left the camp in single file, running through the banana plantation. Our feet pounding on the ground must have terrified any peasants who happened to be awake. We heard nothing, except for some isolated aye-ayes greeting the warriors. The drug in our bark drink must have given us a sixth sense, because we were running in the darkness without torches and didn't fall once. All I could see was the banana plants, their leaves standing out against the darkness of the moonless night. We slowed to a walk when we reached a path through the first trees of the forest. In spite of our sixth sense, sometimes we bumped into one another or tripped over roots in the darkness. Likewise, there was no way we could avoid sometimes stepping on anthills. When that happened, the unfortunate ones would call back quietly to warn those following. All reference points had disappeared along with the light.

I thought I knew the forest, but I realized it was completely foreign to me once night fell. The birds had grown silent. From time to time monkeys called out, and we could hear insects buzzing in the forest background. We walked for a long time under the vaulted trees, crossing several gorges. Now that we were getting used to the darkness, our eyes could make out some hills and plant forms, as well as the path we were following. Our column came to a ravine leading south, and we followed it. I knew we were starting toward the slopes where people lived. A large wooded hill appeared in the middle of the river that flowed like a silvery ribbon on our right. We drew closer. It was an island formed by a tributary isolating a rocky outcropping. Its banks were steep, and a thick wood covered the summit. Our column paused. The order was circulated to keep silent and get ready for battle. We were going to surround the island and then move into the woods to look for the clearing where the circumcised were to be found. At the first signal, we would light our torches, and when we heard the second we would launch our assault. Our orders were clear: We were to kill every human being. No prisoner would be tolerated. On the other hand, we were to protect all the animals. That last order reassured me that the horse would be spared. But it couldn't make me forget the gravity of the crime we were planning in the forest shadows.

Moving down toward the island, we needed to slip between huge rocks. I turned my head briefly and saw the silhouette of a big cat running across the rock. I shivered, looking ahead again so as not to lose my balance. The leopard had already disappeared the next time I turned my head.

The water in the river was freezing cold and about knee-deep. Two columns of men advanced awkwardly over the stones carpeting the river bed. We moved around the island on both sides and met up on the far side. Then we climbed the rocky banks with the help of tree roots that extended their long arms out toward us. It was more difficult to make progress in the thick vegetation. We didn't dare chop our way through for fear of wakening our victims. However, the clearing where the huts stood didn't appear to be guarded. We could barely see the huts' thatched roofs rising above the palisade in the night. Dawn was still a long way off.

I thought about the young men sleeping in the huts, their hands probably resting on penises still sore from the cut, pain still coursing through their entire bodies. Perhaps they were dreaming of their manly roles, of sexual pleasure and of fecundity in the service of future prosperity for the clan.

We heard a sword striking a tree trunk twice, which was the sign we should light our torches. Flintstones striking iron began to produce sparks, and soon a series of bright flames lit up the area around the barrier hedge. Then the silence, scarcely troubled by the torches' spluttering resin, was broken by three blows. A clamor arose, taking over the clearing. The warriors poured out of the woods like huge devils armed with swords and lances. They threw their torches on the thatched roofs. Two men, elders dressed in spotted skins, probably the initiation masters, appeared in the courtyard between the houses. They were greeted by no fewer than five lances that ran them through and through, as if the warriors could not restrain themselves at the sight of their victims. The two men collapsed with a moan. The straw crackled as it burned but couldn't cover up the first frightened cries from the newly circumcised men. They rushed out in panic, skins around their loins and strips of colobus fur wrapped around their arms and legs.

The massacre began. The warriors threw their lances at their targets as if it were a training exercise. But now the targets were alive, though not very mobile. Some of the young men tried to flee, running grotesquely. The poor fellows simply dropped to the ground, putting their hands to their circumcision wounds or clasping the lances embedded in their bodies. In just a few strides, the soldiers were able to catch up with them and administer the final blow. The warriors were swinging their deadly clubs with agility. I could hear the sinister sound of skulls being crushed. There were many young men; if they had not been hampered by their wounds, perhaps they would have been able to resist. Instead, they begged for mercy with pitiful cries. When they weren't asking for pity, they called out for their mothers, hoping that invoking their mothers might save them, that the miracle of their births would happen again, that like plants they could grow back from their roots. Their tears and groans only incited their assailants' murderous craze further. The devil had taken possession of Shina's army. The warriors' faces, lit up by the flames rising from the burning huts, glowed with satanic ardor. They were celebrating heathen nuptials in which desire turns to death and gives birth to blood.

Violence threatened to take over in me as well, but I managed to resist. I clung to my lance instead of throwing it at some victim. But the harder I clung to it, the more I was filled with malaise. I saw a boy crouching by the door of one of the huts that wasn't burning, his hands on his head. I ran toward him, not really knowing why. He raised his head. He was only a child, with fine features and very light skin, probably younger than I was, surely the youngest of that age class. I thought I could hear a voice saying: "Kill him." I refused. "Kill him," the voice repeated, but my own voice drowned it out. "No," I shouted. The boy looked strangely like me, although he had lighter skin. He was so white that I thought he must be an Arab. "Mommy, mommy!" I heard him cry. His eyes rolled back in his head and a stream of blood poured out of his open mouth. A lance from one of our warriors had just pierced his chest. He twisted in pain. I hardly knew where I was anymore. The warrior walked up and swung his sword down on his victim, ripping open his face from forehead to chin. The young man stopped moving. Blood gushed from the wound and I was struck by its smell. A violent dizziness overcame me, and I stumbled backward. One man was on fire, a living torch. He brushed past me, collapsing not far away, impaled on a lance. On the other side of the clearing, between two blazing huts, there was a small corral. In the midst of the swirling smoke stood a horse. The horse was alarmed by the noise and fire, and it was rearing up and kicking. I could hear it whinnying through the noise of the massacre that had reached its peak. Some of the circumcised had tried to cross the hedge and run off into the forest, but they didn't make it far for the warriors' lances had wounded them mortally. In the clearing, Shina's warriors were executing the last survivors and the wounded. I tried to move toward the horse. All the huts were on fire, thick smoke was rising from the thatched roofs and the wooden frames were crashing down in sparks. Flies were beginning to fill the air. They had taken over, excited by all the blood. Crazed, they were flying in all directions, throwing themselves blindly into the fire or striking us in the face like little projectiles. Near one of the huts, a dwarf with a twisted face was standing motionless on a post. His torso was covered with scars. Between his tiny legs hung an enormous penis. At the base of the post lay some dead chickens. The flames shining on the little statue gave it the expression of a terrified man. Its eyes, simple oval shapes without pupils, stared at me. I turned away. In the corral, the horse was frantic. I walked up to the wooden fence. I was able to touch the horse's neck and take its head in my hands. It calmed down at my touch. Its body was quivering intermittently, and it kept whinnying loudly. Slowly, it began to relax. My presence was reassuring. As for me, immense fatigue washed over me. All my strength had left me. I would have liked to climb on the horse's back, but instead I slid down beside its neck, clung for a moment to its chest and then fell pitifully. I found myself on the ground, my back against a horse's leg, and the leg didn't move. I blacked out.

I dreamed that I was riding the horse across the ravaged, burning clearing and that I was fleeing along the river. But this time, no bird followed us.

"Bayu! Bayu! What's the matter? Do you feel all right? Come on, get up."

I pulled myself to my feet. The man speaking to me was the adult I had seen with Shina when the king pointed at me.

"Come, we're leaving. It's all over. We must throw the bodies into the abyss of evil spirits. You have to help me carry one of the victims."

"But what about the horse?"

"It'll follow us into the forest. We'll tie it to a tree and you can get it again when we start back down toward Masangu."

We picked up the body of the boy who had been killed before my very eyes. He was horrible to look at. His head was bloody and covered with flies, as was the lance wound gaping in his chest. I took his arms so I wouldn't have to look at the body as we walked along. A shiver ran through me as I grabbed him by the wrists. A column formed, and we left the clearing by the main gate facing the mountain peak. All the bodies had been picked up except for the corpse of one of the elders, which had been left near the entrance to the clearing. Shina's young soldiers were strangely calm for criminals who had just killed dozens of innocent people. They had regained the same impassive expressions I had seen back in the camp. We started off. Soon day would be breaking, unfolding disaster to the inhabitants of Kibosho, surely alarmed by all the smoke. They would find nothing but traces of blood, the huts reduced to ashes, and the body of one of the masters of the initiation ceremony, totally naked and castrated, a wooden stake driven into his mouth. We crossed the river and climbed up the other side of the ravine, followed by swarms of flies. Sometimes they would land on my sweaty back, and I would jerk my shoulder to chase them off.

"Why do you keep jerking around, Bayu? They're just flies," said the man who was holding the dead boy's legs. Our cortege moved silently through the forest. Once we had passed the gorge, walking was easier. The forest was quiet. The smell of blood had frightened off all the mammals and the buzzing of all those flies had warned the birds that something unusual was happening. The forest was in mourning even before Kibosho began to mourn its dead. The huge trees took solemn stances and the shrubs stopped swaying, like children intimidated by some solemn ceremony. In spite of my malaise, I asked the warrior about the dwarf that had been carved at the top of the post.

"It wasn't a dwarf, but the spirit of circumcision. The initiates offer up chickens and their foreskins to it."

"Why?"

"So that it will capture the negative forces that circumcision sets loose. If they were to be left free in the world, such forces would be very dangerous."

"And if there is no statue?"

"Then violence breaks out."

The man laughed. I remained silent, disgusted. The horizon had until then been blocked by thick undergrowth, but now it opened up, and behind the trees emptiness appeared. We had arrived at the abyss of evil spirits. A chasm opened up on the mountainside, large enough to contain the island we had overrun. It was funnel shaped, and we couldn't see the bottom. Huge trees captivated by light threw their branches out into the opening where waterfalls plummeted down. I was afraid I'd get dizzy as I followed the men along the trail. The path ran along the escarpment, leading up to a promontory suspended above the void. The porters took advantage of the rocky promontory, where a fig tree towered over them, to unload their cumbersome burdens. They swung the bodies of the dead circumcised men from left to right and then released them. The body would rise and then begin its descent, leaving the cloud of insects behind. A dull sound would sometimes indicate that the body had scraped the side of the funnel, and I thought I could hear laughter. I was in a hurry to get it over with, but we had to wait for the others to get rid of the bodies they were carrying. When our turn finally came, I nearly fainted at the sight of the void. One step more and the abyss would open beneath my feet. The man holding the boy's feet told me to turn around so that I could swing the body out into the chasm. I managed to do it without looking out over the void. But then there I was face to face with the dead boy and his black-crusted wounds covered with flies. I couldn't stand the sight. His head was drooping. It seemed to me that death itself was watching me. We began the swinging motion so we could throw him over the precipice. I looked up so as not to see the victim's face. What a shock! The fig tree's thick branches were spread wide, and on one of them the leopard was sprawled, looking right at me! I jumped in surprise just as the man pushed the body in my direction, bumping me out over the edge.

I owed my salvation to the wild banana trees and bushes that broke my fall. Screaming, I crawled through the branches, then slid headfirst down onto a carpet of tall grass. I was about to fall into the chasm when a root snagged me. I hung on tightly, my legs hanging out over the void. In terror I called for help.

Up above me, Shina's men didn't even look down. On the contrary, another body crashed into the bushes. The warriors had no intention of throwing a rope down to me. The root began to crack, and fear of falling made me try the movement that saved me. I threw one arm out and was able to grab a rock and pull myself up. Then I crept forward until I came to a tree trunk. Up on the summit, the warriors were finishing their sinister work. The last bodies were being tipped one after the other into the abyss. One body, totally naked, bounced against a banana tree, turning over several times before landing on its back right beside me. After it fell I heard a splash. So there was water down there. And something else. For an echo came back up, and the "splash" turned into a joyous "ah!" The echo repeated the same sound several times. In fact, there were so many bodies falling that it was as if I could hear someone laughing. An evil spirit was laughing deep down in the earth, chuckling with pleasure at the sight of so many mutilated bodies. One body fell into a bush and rolled up against a huge root that looked like a snake. That man was among the rare dead who would escape the spirits. Small consolation. It wouldn't keep those few from the shame of rotting away out in the open in a place where their families would never dare to come look for them. The dead man began to move, and horror seized me—but it was the root moving. An enormous python, disturbed by the commotion, began to drag itself out of a clump of leafy plants. It wrapped itself around the body as if trying to smother the man. Anxiously, I looked around me. I carefully examined the cliff wall that was covered with vegetation, and my horror increased. There were about ten huge pythons moving along the chasm, heading toward the spot that was piled high with corpses! They moved very quickly, their bodies winding and slipping through the grass, unhindered by the steep slope. They drew closer to the bodies lying every which way on the ground. Two snakes began to fight over one of the bodies. My fear reached its zenith when a python, twice as long as a man, loomed up out of the bushes and started toward me. Without any weapon I could defend myself with, I moved away as fast as I could, bending over to hold on to the grass and plants so I would not lose my balance. The python started after me. In my panic, I tried to leap across a stream fed by a small waterfall. I missed, slipping on the wet rock and nearly falling into the chasm. I tried to grab a root sticking out of the vegetation, but the root reached out to me. It wasn't a root, but the arm of one of the dead bodies. I used the body for leverage and took refuge in the thick brush—but the serpent was already there. The scales that covered its brown body were spotted with geometrical violet marks.

It raised its pointed head in my direction. Two little black eyes stared at me, and its tongue fluttered like a ribbon in the wind. I was sure it was going to suddenly strike and wrap itself around me. Instead, it turned toward the body lying there face down in the water. It slowly wrapped around the man and pulled him back onto the grass. The dead man's head fell back and looked at me. His face had a huge gash down the middle. It was the boy I had carried to the abyss. And truly he did look like me: the shape of his face, the high forehead, the nose (all his other physical features were distorted by the mask of death). The serpent opened its jaws and swallowed the boy's head. I thought it was going to chew it, but it just continued to swallow the body, opening its mouth still wider. The shoulders disappeared. Two bumps preceded by a huge ball appeared beneath the scaly skin. Incredible to see how the serpent absorbed its prey, turning into an enormous stuffed caterpillar. For the whole body followed. The snake was stuffed like a wine gourd. Slowly the legs too disappeared into the monster's jaws.

With so much food in its stomach, the python ought to have remained still, but it began to move across the stream. It coiled its long tail and tried to drag along its huge stomach, but its body slipped on the sheet of water. The stream was flowing fast enough to pull along the scaly mass of flesh, and in an instant the python was plunging into the abyss. I expected it to scream, forgetting it was just a reptile. There was a heavy thud, followed by a diabolical laugh. The laugh echoed back and forth between the silent chasm walls for a long time.

The other pythons had swallowed their own share of human flesh, and, tired from the work, were lying deep in torpor. I looked at the wall, checkered with cracks and plastered with vines that seemed solidly anchored in the stone. It seemed possible to climb up. I decided to wait for dusk, because Shina's warriors—I didn't trust them at all—could still be lurking around. The abyss was plunged in absolute stillness. Suddenly I heard whinnying coming from up above, attenuated by the distance. A whistle tore the air. A mass of flesh crashed down to the rocks in front of me, with a sound of breaking bones. My horse had just fallen past me! Shina's men had thrown it into the abyss! The loud cackling from deep down in the chasm was distressing. It was clear that Shina wanted to eliminate me completely.

I spent the day waiting and didn't even look at the pythons busy digesting their food. The events had shaken me. I could easily have become a criminal if I had yielded to the violence of the massacre. Evil lived within me and was awaiting the proper time to appear. That's where my dreams had led me!

The light began to fade. After the heat of the day, coolness rose from the bottom of the abyss. Before starting my climb, I would have liked to see the bottom to find out if the evil spirit who so enjoyed human misery would dare to show itself. But the pit was drowned in darkness. Impossible to know how far down the water was. However, as I was readying myself to leave the precipice, something began to shine at the base of the chasm. A white light cut through the layers of darkness and made it to the top. I thought of the phosphorescent python eggs Kabero had told me about, or maybe it was just the light in the demons' den.

I began to climb. The sun had disappeared behind the mountain, but there was still enough light left in the sky to guide me forward. Vines and protruding rocks helped me climb. As I moved upward, I felt like I was freeing myself from something. I was leaving the circumcised dead men in the abyss. I was leaving forever the boy who resembled me.

Chapter nine

The sun rose. I wasn't sure if I should return to Masangu and risk confronting Shina or bypass Masangu and go back through the forest to Mamtara instead. Hunger gnawed at me, so I made straight for the first houses in Uru just outside the forest, where I could ask for some food. From a hilltop near the forest edge I looked out over Kibosho and could see smoke still rising here and there. That made me realize that Shina must have sent his troops to attack the rival chiefdom after the massacre of the newly circumcised men, taking advantage of the confusion. I slipped into a banana grove, making my way toward some huts huddled in the protective shadows of a *mfumu* tree. The *mfumu* is a tree whose main trunk is composed of huge vines twisting around each other. A multitude of air roots connected the ground to the branches high above. The roots are about as thick as a man's arm or even thicker, and they form arches around the tree trunk. Under the wooden vestibule they formed stood a woman with her child. I greeted her and introduced myself. I stammered out a few words in Meru, explaining that I had been in the forest and that I was hungry. She cut off my clumsy efforts and answered me in Swahili. It was rare on Mount Meru to meet a woman who knew Swahili, for the men are the ones who travel. The women do too, but only as slaves. Which means that they never come home.

"I've heard about you. King Shina invited you to Masangu and you live under his protection. What are you doing in the forest?"

I could have told her that I was gathering honey. But without a bag, dressed as I was like a warrior and with all the scrapes from my fall, my lie wouldn't have held up.

"I was part of the expeditionary force that killed the recently circumcised men in Kibosho."

"Oh, so it is true, you did massacre them. During the night, just before dawn, the Masangu warriors came through here. They were heading toward Kibosho. Why didn't you go with them?"

"I'm a foreigner. I've got no reason to join in their war."

"You're right. What madness there is in the hearts of men! What women give from their wombs, men take away with the sword."

She brought me some mashed corn and peas. She was a beautiful woman, still quite young. Her name was Aeling Otholo, but, she added, "by matrilineal lineage, I belong to the clan of the Irienie women."

"The Irienie women? Who are they?"

"It's a matrilineal clan. That means that our lineage passes down through the females."

"I didn't know you had matrilineal clans on Mount Meru."

"Ours is perhaps the only one. Our clan isn't very well known here because we live in Kilia, a country two days walk from Uru. The Irienies venerate the *irié* bird, the spirit of fertility. Our ancestor, a woman called Mkanusa, was the *irié*'s mother. You must have seen the bird in the forest, it's quite common."

"Is the *irié* that bird with the black body, bright red wings and a little crest on its head?"

"Yes. Wait, there are always two couples in that tree. We should be able to spot them."

We moved to one side so that we could see the top of the tree. An *irié* spread its magnificent wings as if to greet me, as it hopped from branch to branch. In Swahili, we call it the *shorobo,* our word for the turaco.

"There are always a few *iriés* in this tree. At least two couples make their nests here every year. But five years ago, just before I got married, after the leopard had stolen their eggs, they made no nest."

"The leopard? Which leopard?"

"Don't be so edgy! Are you afraid of Shina's leopard? I don't fear it at all. In fact, once I went searching for a leopard."

"Tell me the story, daughter of the Irienies. I'm listening."

She began to laugh.

"You're a strange fellow. Before telling you the end, I need to start at the beginning. The ancestor of my clan was Mkanusa. She was an infertile woman the *mgangas*, our doctors, hadn't been able to help. Mkanusa went off into the forest and ran across a herd of elephants with many babies. She asked a mother elephant what the secret of her fertility was and what advice she might give to someone who wanted to have children. The mother elephant answered: "Take a bird the color of your skin, dip its wings in your menstrual blood and mate with it. You'll bring forth the bird of fertility. If the bird survives and mates with other birds, you can be certain that you'll become a mother." Mkanusa was very black and very beautiful. She seduced a bird the color of jade and dipped its wings in some of her menstrual blood she had collected in a calabash." Aeling stopped and began to laugh. "Why such a face?"

"Women are impure when they bleed."

"Of course. But you must realize that for a long time you yourself were nothing but a drop of that blood until an ancestor finally decided to come back to earth. But let me continue. Mkanusa and the bird with red wings mated and she gave birth to an egg."

"An egg," I repeated, somewhat skeptical.

"Yes, yes. An egg."

"That's strange."

"That's exactly what we call the feminine mystery. Let me go on. Mkanusa put the egg in a warm place to hatch. The next day, the egg cracked open and a little bird came out. Mkanusa fed it until it was big enough to fly. It left Kilia, and with Mkanusa following, flew to Uru. It perched on this very *mfumu* tree and built its nest. It was an *irié* with a black body and red wings. It mated with a black bird and begat all the *iriés* of Mount Meru. The *irié* is the bird of fertility. It keeps my clan from being sterile. Obviously, Mkanusa gave birth to many children, but only to girls!"

(Aeling seemed pleased about that.)

"This place has become the sanctuary of the Irienies clan and we women take turns working in the banana plantation. All the Irienie women are noted for their fertility and are much sought after by young males. They never have any trouble finding a husband, especially since they are beautiful."

"Of that I have no doubt, Aeling, when I look at you."

"Thank you."

"You still haven't told me about the leopard."

"It was a female leopard, and I encountered it five years ago. I hadn't yet become a woman, though I was already nubile. I was late in developing. My breasts had already formed, but my period wouldn't come. Time passed, and it looked as if some evil was upon me. At first we thought it was a curse, but then we noticed that the *irié* birds nesting in the *mfumu* had left the tree. The old woman of the clan consulted the oracle. It revealed that a leopard had stolen their eggs. I asked the old women for permission to get the eggs back from the leopard, for intuition told me that it hadn't eaten them. The absence of broken shells was proof. The old women agreed, but it was harder to convince the hunters. One hunter did tell me that the animal lived near the king's leopard's den, near the precipice where King Kilesia lost his life. The precipice is like a cliff. It's near the 'cedar with a door' and it's crowned with a dead tree where Shina's animal has often been seen with its prey, and on rare occasions with a female leopard. At the tip of the precipice, there's a huge rock sticking up out of the vegetation. That was the leopard's resting place, so that's where I went."

"Why did you think that leopard, and not Shina's, had stolen the eggs?"

"There were no broken shells, and that meant that the eggs had been stolen without being eaten. Only a female could do that."

"Why?"

My question made Aeling smile. "You still don't understand? When I got there, the leopard was lying on its rock. It looked like your cousin Shina's leopard." (Aeling used the word "cousin," assuming I was related to Shina by blood). "The leopard raised its head as I approached. It backed up and leaped from its rock to find protection at the entrance to a cave where it could defend itself. I realized that it had hidden the eggs in the cave. Do you get it now?"

"Not really."

"The leopard was sterile. It had stolen the bird eggs hoping they would pass their fecundity on. I explained carefully to the leopard that it needed to give the eggs back so that our clan could be fertile again. I promised to make the leopard fertile again as soon as my own period started. It agreed to the pact. I came back home with the eggs, followed by the *iriés* that had been watching from the trees above the cave. The birds settled back into their nest. A week later, some bumps on my upper lip announced my period. I stayed inside for several days to collect my blood in a calabash filled with cow's milk, and then I took it to the leopard.

"Several months passed. I was pregnant and was resting in the shade of the *mfumu* tree, listening to the *iriés* chattering in the branches, when the leopard appeared. Two little ones were with her. We spent the afternoon together, watching over the two little cubs that kept getting into mischief. Then we parted and I never saw them again. No hunters ever saw the female again. Of course nobody ever goes to the precipice anymore since that's where King Kilesia died."

"And how about Shina's leopard? How did he manage to tame it?"

"I think that would be impossible."

"But you yourself did speak to a leopard."

"Yes, but that was because the female wished to listen to me, and then too we're both women. For a man to tame a male leopard, that would be totally different."

"How long ago did he tame it?"

"I don't know. Probably after he left Kilia."

"He used to live in Kilia? I heard that he came from Uru."

"What do you mean, you heard? If there's anyone who ought to know about Shina's life, it's you. After Kilia, he did indeed live in Uru before he was called to King Kilesia's court. The king of Kilia had quarreled with Shina and sold him as a slave to a rich Uru man who then sold him to the king of Masangu."

"In Kilia, did you often cross paths?"

"Of course. I was living with my parents at the palace. Shina was the king's Swahili interpreter, and my father was the one who dealt with foreigners, keeping them in his home and working out trade agreements. That's how I learned Swahili, by contact with those foreigners."

"So Shina was first an interpreter."

"Stop trying to fool me, Bayu. You came all the way from Mombasa to find your cousin and you don't even know what he does!"

"My cousin? Shina is not part of my family."

"He's not part of your family? Are there several El-Mudi families in Mombasa?"

"What do you mean, several El-Mudi families? There's only one clan with the name El-Mudi all over the Indian Ocean and along its coasts, and that's my family!"

"Well, it's Shina's, too. Because his name is Nasser Jefar el-Mudi."

I stared dumbly at Aeling. Flames seemed to be burning my entrails, moving up toward my heart, and my ears were ringing. I closed my eyes and put my hands on my stomach.

"What's wrong, Bayu? Are you ill?"

When I opened my eyes, the world was swaying. I placed one hand to the ground so as not to collapse.

"Do you feel faint? Would you like to lie down?"

I didn't answer. Aeling had me lie down on a mat in the shade of the *mfumu* tree and brought me some water.

I lay there for a long time in a state of great lethargy. A variety of thoughts developed and moved over the surface of my mind like clouds in the sky not sure which direction they should be taking. Shina's face kept coming to mind; his actions and attitude were much clearer now.

The clan is like the chain in a well, a chain the artisan has carefully crafted. If one weak link happens to break, he either repairs it or discards it so that he can weld the chain back together. And then the chain continues its endless task, tirelessly pulling up water for thirsty clan members. Shina had left the chain, and that was his real crime. And now he had to destroy other links so that the clan elders couldn't learn about his crime. Such outrage was unpardonable.

I fell asleep, totally exhausted and overwhelmed. When I woke up again, my confusion of the evening before had yielded to great anger. The loathsome Shina was its cause. I knew what I needed to do. Aeling had fixed me a plate of food. When I finished eating, I thanked her sincerely and expressed my wish to leave. As I left the sanctuary of the turacos, walking out through the opening in the fence, she said:

"You asked me how Shina had managed to tame his leopard. I'm not sure, but if I were trying to cajole a leopard, I would give it something that was the same color as its hide."

"Thank you for your opinion, Aeling. Perhaps it will enlighten me some day."

"Yes, Bayu, enlighten is the right word, because the leopard is indeed the color of sunlight."

"Probably so. However your own skin is black, and yet how radiant it is."

Aeling's eyes shone. I walked quickly away.

I took the path toward Masangu and then walked around the banana plantation, starting back up into the forest. My goal was to find the golden diadem King Kilesia had been wearing before he died. Some hunters had seen his body hanging in a tree above the precipice. I was hoping I could be carrying the diadem when I entered

Shina's palace. Because a confrontation was inevitable. The honor of the clan was at stake. It takes fire to fight fire.

I began to reflect on how much I had changed since leaving Mombasa. I was accepting things as they came without rebelling too much, but still ready to stand up against them if they were in opposition to my clan's values. The clan seemed to be the locus of blossoming par excellence, both the point of departure and the destination of the long journey each human being must undertake. Our human condition is to live in perpetual movement, and the clan alone can provide some expression of permanence for our being.

I slept in the forest. The next morning I started off to look for the precipice. The explanations Kabero and Aeling had given about its location enabled me to find it, as well as the "cedar with a door," the gigantic tree whose base formed an arch through which three horses could have passed, walking side by side. All morning long I dug around under the thick bushes at the edge of the precipice. I managed to identify the tree on which the leopard hung its prey. A long bare branch with lots of claw marks extended out over the void. Clinging to a vine that I had tied to the branch, I ventured down over the edge. There was a tree growing at the bottom of the escarpment whose top branches made it hard for me to move horizontally. Still, I managed to inch my way across it, and then, hidden under some foliage, I spotted the diadem caught in the branches of a small tree! It was a lovely gold crown, composed of one semicircular piece that was carved with geometrical shapes. The leather strap had already been eaten away by insects. I let myself down to the ground, holding tightly to the vine. I heard something crunch under my feet, and then they bumped against something round. It was a human skull! When I pulled back the layer of humus and decaying leaves I discovered a pile of bones. Many were animal bones, but there were also three human skulls. Kilesia hadn't been the only person to perish by the leopard's fangs.

As I was looking at the bones a hornbill landed on the branch where I had hung the diadem. It grabbed the jewel and flew off. In an instant my treasure had been stolen out from under my nose! I was furious. A few beats of a wing had wiped out my great fortune at having found the jewel. The bird flew from tree to tree, and all the while I screaming a flood of curses at it. It could have outdistanced me with just a few wing beats, but it seemed to be taking its time, happy to show off the diadem. And that's how we made it back to the "cedar with a door." When the hornbill landed on a branch near the trunk, I realized that it must be the spirit of the tree that Kabero had told me about. It flew off toward the intertwined branches that hid the tree's summit, and disappeared. I was filled with great apprehension, because I knew that the cedar was a magic tree. Everyone knew that any man who tried to reach its summit would be lost. Its arched base plunged immense supporting pillars into the ground, covered with a grainy bark. The tree exuded unsettling strength. Stunned, I stood there before the forest giant. It seemed to be saying: "I'm the forest." But my desire to confront Shina was just too strong. I had to retrieve the diadem at all costs. So I started up the huge tree, pulling myself up through the vines and finally reaching the leafy ceiling. I was able to move through the thick foliage with little difficulty. There was nothing extraordinary on the other side except for the impressive tree top that continued stretching up toward the sky, dominating the forest. But there was very little light. The hornbill was perched on a very high branch, showing the diadem off to its companions. I kept climbing up toward the birds, leaving the topmost branches of the neighboring trees far behind. Strangely, the further I moved from their shade the more feeble the light seemed to be getting. For late morning, that was quite surprising. The half-light was like dusk when I finally touched the hornbill's branch. The bird hadn't moved, but that worried me less than the strange light phenomenon. Where had the sun gone?

Shadows invaded the great forest. Myriads of swallows surged forth, surrounding the tree like a dome of meteors. The branches were covered with their white, black and red tufts. The atmosphere was very bizarre, and the darkness was getting deeper and deeper. It must have been the cedar's magical powers working. I was both troubled and touched by the spectacle. The swallows grew quiet; all sounds ceased. A red spot grew larger in the clouds near the horizon and the setting sun appeared. Suddenly the birds exploded in song. Their song grew louder and louder until it became just one indistinct note as the red ball descended toward the earth. It was as if the mountain swallowed it. And then suddenly all the birds took flight in indescribable commotion. Swallows were crashing into me from all directions, and I had to put my hands up to protect my head. I closed my eyes, waiting anxiously. Deathly silence followed the hullabaloo.

I opened my eyes on a scene I never would have expected: Stars were spread out over heaven's vault and the cedar's branches were silhouetted against them in a cloudless sky. The night's beauty overwhelmed me. I felt true joy, a deep happiness. The tree's branches seemed to be floating across the sky. Suddenly the diadem the hornbill was holding began to glow brightly. The bird took flight and circled wide, laying the diadem at the very top of the tree. Now the moon was also adding its brightness to the starry vault. The hornbill, back on its branch, contemplated the moon with croaks of satisfaction. Without delay, I started up the trunk to get the diadem. The trunk kept getting thinner and thinner, and yet the jewel still seemed far away. I kept climbing, but then the trunk started to bend over. It was bending from my weight and was about to launch me into thin air. I had to inch back down; the lunar diadem was out of my reach. The hornbill greeted my return with a grunt. And then I spoke aloud to the bird:

"Oh hornbill, how beautiful this moon is, but the next quarter will be more beautiful still."

"Squawk!"

"I know it belongs to you. You're a moon bird, hornbill. I would like to take my turn wearing this moon on my forehead when I visit King Shina. You could give it to me and then follow along when I go to the king's court. And afterward I'll lay it on the ground, and all you'll have to do is fly over and pick it up."

"Squawk!"

The hornbill spread its wings, flew over and unhooked the

moon. It gave the crown to me. Once in my hand it stopped glowing. I expressed my deepest thanks to the bird and climbed back down the tree. Back under the thick foliage, bright daylight awaited me.

I journeyed back to Masangu, having cleaned the golden diadem carefully and attached to it a strap made of plant fibers. As I was walking, followed by the hornbill, I was sure I could sense something else behind me. I turned around several times but never saw anything. I was convinced, absolutely convinced that someone was following me. The image of the leopard entered my mind. And then I thought of King Kilesia's soul, doomed to wander in the forest because his body had not been buried according to the prescribed rituals. In spite of my apprehensions, perhaps protected by the hornbill, I reached the edge of the forest safe and sound. Masangu was deserted, because all the men had been mobilized to invade Kibosho. A few old men were walking about on the paths, with the grave expression of parents whose sons have just gone off to war. A few young boys, more carefree, were playing. Nobody stopped me on my way to the palace.

The guard at the entrance to the stone wall didn't seem surprised to see me. But when I took the crown out of the banana leaf I had wrapped it in and placed it on my head, his expression changed dramatically. He backed up, mouth open and eyes wide, and he didn't make a move when I crossed the threshold. The soldier on duty at the entrance to the palace courtyard barred my passage. I threw him aside violently. I entered the courtyard before he could gather himself together. Dumbfounded, the assembled crowd watched me stride forward, the golden diadem sparkling in the sunshine. Shina stood up, his face frozen in shock. He realized that he was making a mistake by showing how upset he was, and so he sat back down. The spokesman, who hadn't budged, tried to intervene, but I knew he shouldn't speak before I did. I began to address the courtiers without a glance at Shina.

"My friends, I've come to greet my cousin, Nasser Jefar el-Mudi."

I had hit the bull's eye. Shina was thrown off balance. Doubt began to enter the minds of the courtiers, who clearly hadn't known we were related.

Shina pulled himself together. "You've come to greet me with a dead king's crown."

"It belongs to the king of the big cedar, the moon bird."

"And you've stolen it."

"No. I'm its messenger. The hornbill chose me because it knows I'm both a swallow and a human being."

"Well then, what's your message?"

"That the dream of the men of the El-Mudi clan is to understand the tree's essence so as to carve it better, and not to exercise power by linking up with a bloodthirsty animal."

"Then why are you wearing a golden crown, an emblem of power?"

"I'm not wearing a golden crown. My head is crowned with a moon that I took down from the top of the 'cedar with a door.' The cedar let me take it so that I might become like a cedar from the forest on Mount Meru."

"The forest on Mount Meru belongs to the leopard. And to the man who is able to tame it."

"We are the ones who belong to the forest. The dreams of the Mombasa woodcarvers are born from thoughts of trees on Mount Meru. That's what I discovered here, although the elders of the El-Mudi clan had already taught me the same thing."

"That's why I'll never return to Mombasa."

"And it's true that you'd not be welcomed with open arms."

He appeared to be thinking. "And why would I not be welcome?"

"Because I'll tell them the truth about what you've done."

"You ought to think twice before proclaiming such words. You know, a man's honor is greater than life."

"I wouldn't agree. It's not a man's honor, but a clan's honor that is greater than a man's life."

"Tell me, what lies at the beginnings of the El-Mudi clan?"

"There's Badrani Nyuni el-Mudi's dream."

"Yes, and what was in his dream?"

I didn't answer. Or rather, he didn't wait for me to answer, saying himself: "There was a leopard."

At that moment Shina's leopard brushed past me. The big cat was calmly coming back home as if it were the master. Shina had turned the situation around to his advantage. As for me, I had stood directly before the man who had given offense to my clan. I could now leave, but not without one last act of bravado. I threw the diadem to the ground.

"Here, there's the gold you're looking for. I'm leaving Masangu. Goodbye, Shina. Or rather, goodbye, Nasser."

Scarcely had I finished pronouncing those words when the hornbill swooped down from the palace roof. And right under Shina's very nose, and under the nose of his men and the leopard, it seized the diadem in its beak and flew away.

Kabero was both surprised and delighted to see that I was still alive. He had heard that I had fallen into the abyss of evil spirits and thought I was dead. He bombarded me with questions, not sparing me a scolding for my part in the massacre of the circumcised men, which he strongly condemned.

"I was forced to go along, *mzee*. I didn't want to."

"You didn't want to? What kept you from running away?"

"It was impossible."

"Bayu, did you kill any of the men? Answer me."

"No, *mzee*. I didn't kill anyone." I swallowed, hardly daring to keep looking at Kabero. "I quarreled with Shina, *mzee*. It's better for me to leave now. I'm going to Mamtara through the forest."

"Mamtara? Does Shina know? He'll not let you leave."

"I know. If necessary, I'll wait for him in the forest."

As Kabero watched in consternation, I went into the banana plantation. I climbed up the tree in whose trunk I had hidden the weapon the Arab had given me. And then I gathered together my sack, a machete, and some tools necessary for extracting the wild honey I planned to live on. I needed to work quickly. I left Kabero with a heavy heart, promising that I'd be back sometime. With dismay, he watched me walk off down the path.

I entered the forest unsure where I should go. It seemed hopeless to expect to get away and reach Mamtara. The wooded areas that lay before me in the direction of Mamtara were completely unknown to me, and Shina's men would surely be able to catch up with me quickly. For I had no doubt Shina would come. Besides, I was looking forward to the combat.

Suddenly a bird flew by, brushing against me. The hornbill, without the diadem, had come back. It flew off in front of me as if inviting me to follow. It led me to a place in the forest I knew quite well, because it was a place where I had set several hives. A tributary of the Mrusunga had cut a deep gorge that wound through the mountainside, a narrow canyon with steep sides. The ravine bottom was covered with clumps of tree-like ferns, the dead brown stems standing out against the pale green of their toothless fronds. The path winding along the ravine crossed from one side to the other on a log lying across the chasm. That's where the bird left me. On the other side, the path wound around a big rock which would make a good vantage point for me and where I could sit with my weapon loaded, keeping an eye out for Shina. Above the rock stood some trees. One of them sheltered one of my hives. I moved the hive, tying it to a rope hanging directly above the log. All I would have to do would be to cut the rope and the hive would fall and strike the log. I loosened the cover so the bees, angered by the fall, would pour out and attack any men on the bridge. I knew Shina would not be alone, and I knew my own little gun wouldn't be enough to frighten off his soldiers.

I lay there waiting. The wind from the plains was blowing from behind my pursuers, so I knew the leopard would not be able catch my scent. Then I saw some human shapes coming up the path. Four soldiers were walking in front of Shina and his leopard. The group stopped when it got to the log and carefully examined the other side. I was crouching invisibly in the forest shadows, hidden by the foliage. Shina ordered one of his men to cross the ravine. I didn't make a move. The soldier reached the rock I was hiding on.

I could guess what he was doing by watching the men back on the other side as their eyes followed him. He seemed to be inspecting the area. He spotted the hive and pointed it out to the others, but he didn't see that the rope wasn't simply wrapped around the branch but that one end extended down to the ground. A bird landed in a tree and began to sing, and that reassured the scout. He motioned to the others to come across. But Shina stayed back on the other side. He was too far away for me to be sure I could hit him if I shot. The warriors started out over the log. I cut the rope with my machete. The hive hit the bridge right in front of the men, when they were already halfway across. The lid popped open. The bees stormed out of the hive and attacked the men. They screamed with pain as the bees stung them furiously. The first man dove off into the void, and the second jumped. The third man tried to get away by fleeing back the way he had come. He slipped and fell. The men's falls didn't put an end to their suffering. To hear their screams, they were still very much alive. The bees turned on the scout. He ran roaring down the path and then he too tumbled into the ravine.

I had eliminated the four warriors. Shina had found shelter by pulling back from the bridge on the other side, but he could have sent his leopard after me. Why hadn't he done so? Perhaps he wanted to face me on equal terms. Not me. I was hoping to wound or kill him with a gunshot and avoid a knife fight.

I ran deep into the forest with no idea what path to follow. I headed east, toward Mamtara. I walked all afternoon, thinking that surely Shina was doing double time to catch up with me. I didn't waste any time trying to cover my tracks, because the leopard didn't need to see my tracks to sniff out my trail. I came to a large grassy depression between two hills. There were some elephants grazing, perhaps a dozen, tearing off bunches of the tall grass. Some huge rocks had trees growing out of them, the roots nearly covering the stone. Clusters of tiny monkeys were running back and forth from one rock to the other, between two of the elephants. I headed toward the piles of broken rocks scattered over the slope. Seeing the elephant manure gave me an idea; I could coat my body with it to confuse the leopard's sense of smell. I crossed the depression, leaving visible tracks in the mud, and then, once my feet were plastered with elephant manure, I came back and positioned myself in the rocks. If they followed the false trail, Shina and the leopard would be within range.

Evening was falling. There was a risk that night would surprise me at my observation point before Shina appeared. The leopard, difficult enough to vanquish during daylight hours, would leave me no chance in the darkness. Luckily, I didn't have to worry long. The screaming monkeys suddenly began to scatter, and there was no doubt as to why. Shina and the leopard appeared at the edge of the forest. They were running. I got my weapon ready, hoping that Shina and the cat would choose the path I wanted them to.

They were still far away when a thought suddenly came to me. I wouldn't be able to kill Shina. We shared the same blood. Would it be dealing justly with the clan to get rid of one of its members? To be sure, Shina had committed a great offense against the clan and thus had excluded himself from it. But I didn't feel I had the strength to kill him. I needed to gather my courage. Then I realized that if I could eliminate the leopard I would be stripping Shina of his power. With the leopard's help, he could keep himself on the Masangu throne. Killing the leopard would be destroying Shina, preserving Nasser Jefar el-Mudi and getting rid of Masangu's king. So I decided to kill the leopard. It was walking in front of Shina. Both man and beast started out on my false trail. I waited until the animal, or rather its head, came into my line of sight. And I pressed the trigger.

The hammer swung down and struck the flint. A spark shot up. The priming powder burst into flame, setting off an explosion and a cloud of smoke. The noise was horrible and panicked the elephants. Their trumpeting echoed over the hillside, and the dark massed pachyderms rushed toward the forest.

I had hit the bull's eye, but not the target I was aiming at. The leopard was still standing. It began walking around a still form lying there in the grass. I had hit Shina! I had mortally wounded him! Blood was spurting from his abdomen. He would never be able to survive such a wound.

I feared what the leopard's reaction would be. Would it attack me? Although I was trembling, I tensely reloaded my gun, keeping an eye on the leopard all the while. It was nuzzling up against Shina and licking his face affectionately. Pain was beginning to make the man stiffen up. He was bleeding profusely; death couldn't be far away. And then Shina did something heroic, something appalling, something so horrible that I can barely talk about it.

Turning toward the leopard, he began to speak to it. The leopard listened, and it even placed one paw on his shoulder. I couldn't make out what Shina was saying. His lips moved weakly as if he was trying to conserve his strength. Life was surely leaving him slowly along with the blood oozing out of his wound. Shina picked up a knife and gathered his strength. He looked one last time at the leopard, his eyes expressing cold determination. With a sudden thrust—I hadn't seen it coming at all—he plunged the knife into his chest, right into his heart. Instead of burying it deeply to put an end to his suffering, he cut open his own chest. A huge bright red gash appeared across his torso. And that's when the terrible thing happened. With his last shreds of strength, Shina was dropping back to the ground, his face twisted with pain. The leopard placed its two paws on either side of the gash. Pulling violently in order to spread the wound wide, the leopard plunged its jaws into the opening, where Shina's heart was still beating. It ripped Shina's heart out. Shina's body jerked, and he let out a terrible scream. The scream hung in the air. It vibrated in my ears and spread throughout my body. I too probably screamed when the leopard ripped out Shina's heart.

Splattered with blood, the leopard devoured his master's heart. And then, turning its head toward me, it let out a roar.

I ran off as quickly as I could toward the forest, carrying my terror along with me.

It was futile to flee into the darkness of a moonless night, for the leopard could have found me with its eyes closed. But it didn't follow me, remaining to watch over its master's body. I didn't know where to try to sleep, up in a tree or on the ground, for in either case the leopard could attack while I slept. I found a den that would make good shelter. All I needed to do was block the opening with a branch, and the leopard would have to pull the branch back out before it could reach me. I would kill it if it came into the tunnel. I built a fire inside the den and could see by the light of the fire that there were no animals near. I devoured the food Kabero had provided, and then I fell into a deep sleep.

I woke up in total darkness, not remembering where I was. I reached out to touch the walls with my hands, and my nose picked up the smell of the ground around me. In panic, I pushed aside the branch that was blocking the opening and stepped out into the open air, not remembering the leopard that could have been waiting there. The clouds in the sky were beginning to turn gray with the approaching dawn. Insects were chirping, and the forest was breathing softly.

Suddenly, I remembered the leopard. Surely it was looking for me to avenge its master's death. Hiding in some tree, it would leap on me by surprise and kill me.

However, the forest still seemed peaceful. Wind stirred through the tree tops. The breeze moved down along the trunks, bringing with it a shower of yellow leaves. I moved to a cedar tree so I could take refuge behind its huge root system. There I would be safe from a surprise attack. With my rifle loaded, I began to wait. My thoughts drifted back to Mombasa, back to my family and Hasmahani. The girl's surprising words came back to me: "The leopard is your clan's creative breath." What an idea! I had thought of it as one of those typical surprising comments women make, and then completely forgot it. Women are strange people and we can't trust them. Women received the gift of creation, but they also have destructive powers. Their menstrual flow is the blood of children who die before they're born.

I could hear the sap rising under the cedar's bark, gurgling slightly as if the spirits of the Meru ancestors who lived beneath the earth were speaking through the tree.

What was the link between the leopard and the El-Mudi clan? The answer began to work its way into my mind like sap moving upward toward the tree top. We are a clan of sculptors, not simple workmen, but creators of form. We enable shapes unknown to nature to emerge from wood, and we give trees a new vocation. No longer do they guide the earth's energy toward the heavens, but rather they orient it toward works that touch the hearts of men. Our creations invoke destructive forces, and the leopard comes to meet us, reminding us of the risks we run. A leopard had frightened our ancestor Badrani Nyuni el-Mudi, and he had conquered his fear and created an extraordinary mosque. It was now my turn to be creative in order to avoid its claws. But how could a sculpture keep the leopard from attacking me?

There was some rustling in the tree tops. Rain was falling. I heard some rumbling in the distance. I thought at first it was thunder, but the sound was continuous. It kept getting louder as the dark clouds invaded the sky. They dumped floods of water on the mountain. The noise was deafening. A wall of water stood there before me. Water poured down between the branches, flowed over the leaves and ran down along the trunks. I waited patiently in the cedar's shelter. The deluge slackened somewhat, but became a hard, steady rain that lasted all morning long. Termite larvae began to hatch and pour out of the ground. They were flying up by the thousands, filling the spaces between the branches with grayish clouds. Then finally the rain stopped and the sun came out. The ground beneath the trees began to crackle. The smell of wet humus filled the air. Columns of ants began to scurry across the forest floor, which was covered with diaphanous termite wings.

The rain had erased my tracks. The leopard would never be able to follow my trail. I left my shelter to look for a swarm of bees. I came upon a large leafless cedar tree that had been struck by lightning. It was standing firmly in the ground, and its sinewy branches were spread out like a fan. Its sap had dried up, and its heart was dry, though the wood hadn't yet begun to rot. You would hardly have thought the tree was dead, so strongly did it stand.

One of the tree's lower branches was shaped like an animal. I had a sudden revelation. I had to carve a leopard's body in the wood of that cedar tree. My sculpture would sap the animal's life force, and it would become inoffensive. But carving a body would mean transgressing my religion's taboo. In spite of my apprehension, I began to work. But first I offered up a prayer to the tree.

"Oh cedar tree, I am Bayu Ibrahim el-Mudi from Mombasa. My forefather, Badrani Nyuni el-Mudi, is the one who carved the doors of our city using wood from your brothers. Those doors watch over our nights and perfume our dreams. In the country of men, your brothers are now able to sing nostalgic songs of the forest and celebrate their work facilitating communication between two worlds. Cedar, you live within me and in the forest on Mount Meru. Allow me to place the seal of our covenant on your body."

I climbed up onto the branch. I carefully picked out the knots and rubbed the wood with my hands so I could sense its inner power. My carving would embrace the branch's movement in order to match the tree's thoughts. It wasn't easy to complete the first rough cuts without an adze, but at least the first layers of sapwood were easy to work. The body itself would be raised out of the branch, and then, working from a knot, I would carve a three-dimensional head.

I began to work. I brought out the tail, wrapped around the branch, and then I sketched out the shape of the back legs. I truly enjoyed bringing out the animal's shape. When I began to carve the head from the knot, energy suddenly ran through the branch. The sculpture had captured some external force. It struggled with me, trying to get away. I redoubled my efforts, pounding ceaseless on the wood. The head began to take shape. Between its ears I carved a swallow. The swallow would watch over the leopard's head.

I finished the body, but the fur's spots were still missing. Should I carve eyes or simply spots? No answer came to me, so I kept polishing the sculpture with rough leaves. The wood began to be more accepting of me, though I could still sense its life. Beneath my fingers the leopard was alive. Its movements were fluid, its intelligence instinctive. I caressed the feline's body as my ancestor Badrani Nyuni el-Mudi had done in his dream. The leopard told me about walking over the mountain, about ambushes and stalking animals, about its favorite trees for sleeping or hanging its prey, about nocturnal encounters with spirits and animals. But it didn't say anything about the eyes that should cover its coat, because I simply didn't know how to carve them.

I climbed down out of the tree to examine my handiwork. The missing eyes on the animal's coat struck me immediately. The carving seemed incomplete. I tried to start carving again, but the shape the spots on the fur needed to take remained an insurmountable difficulty. I remembered Karagwa. If I were to believe the old man I had met in Mamtara, I needed to walk through bamboo groves in order to understand the leopard.

Night was falling. I lay down beneath the tree. The last picture I remember is the memory I had of Hasmahani. She was waiting for me in Mombasa, the promise of a new life.

When I awoke, I went off to look for food. I walked along a swollen river and crossed it at a ford. The rain was a handicap, and I had to wait until it stopped before I could find a hive and get something to eat. I wasn't able to get back to the cedar by the same path because the rain had swollen the water in the river. I followed the river until I came to a little valley blocked with flat stones. The river formed several waterfalls and then spread out over a flat area strewn with big rocks. The bamboo growing on the other side indicated that the bamboo plantations weren't far away. I walked toward them. Huge evergreen trees rose up like candles, illuminating the sky with their sheaves of light green leaves. The first clumps of bamboos appeared. In the lower areas there were only a few bamboos, but further on they covered everything. A solid wall of green stems, with small plumes of thin, threadlike leaves, rose up before me. It was a forest of long pale green canes among which were mixed some gray dead bamboo stalks. Everything was enveloped in a chilly mist.

The place was noisy. The wind was carving out its passage, tearing screams from the canes. The dead bamboo stalks, no longer supporting life, gave out melancholic sighs. I wasn't fooled. I knew that the plaintive cries were uttered by spirits. Their incessant moaning gave them away as they wandered. They were roaming about, looking for mischief, waiting till nightfall before going down to inhabited areas to trouble human beings. It was clear that the bamboo forest was their domain, and no man could doubt it.

Suddenly, some loud cracks rang out and some black rocks rolled slowly through the bamboos and reached the edge. Elephants were leaving the bamboo forest. I waited until they were gone, caught up in observing the forest. The elephants had made a wide path, a trail they must often follow, because there was a grassless layer of mud covering it. The path must surely lead to grassy prairies and heather that spread out beyond the bamboos and where herbivores could find plenty of pasture. I could no doubt reach the same pastures, but it would be necessary to protect myself at all costs from the spirits.

Nature came to my rescue. A swarm of bees poured out of the bamboos and flashed across the sky before diving into some underbrush. Then they reappeared and flew around a tree. Finally they massed on a low branch. The black ball was crawling with bees clinging together there on the branch to protect their queen. I walked over. I swung my stick into the swarm and the bees scattered, leaving the queen, with her huge abdomen, on the branch by herself. I didn't give the bees time to reform their swarm. I reached out through the buzzing asteroids and closed my fingers over the queen. The bees landed on my hand and my forearm, covering them completely and forming several layers like a protective bandage. I knew they would not sting me as long as the queen was still alive between my fingers. With the swarm on my arm, I brandished it like a torch to light my way and started down the path between the bamboos. Spirits would never dare attack a man protected by a swarm of bees. They would keep their distance from the magician insects, those masters of plant alchemy who could change pollen into honey. Because I had captured the queen, now I was king. I walked for several hours, with the bamboo standing like frizzy hair on both sides of the path. I could hear spirits singing their funeral chants as I walked by. They thought I was already dead. Hidden in the bamboo, they watched me pass. I could ignore their threats. But my arm was beginning to tire, which was worrisome. I had to keep holding it out in front of me. I would have loved to move my fingers a little, but there was the danger that the queen would escape, taking the swarm with her and delivering me up to the spirits. If I were to squeeze too tightly and crush the insect, the bees would dig their stingers into my flesh and the poison would kill me.

The cold was becoming more intense. I was dressed like a Meru, nearly naked, with my loins covered by a goatskin, my bag and gun over my shoulder. Fortunately, the path led uphill, and walking warmed me up. I was beginning to get out of breath and was panting heavily. The fog had lifted, leaving a gray, taciturn, birdless sky, afflicted with the soulless monotony of the bamboo forest. From time to time the bamboos became an immense playground filled with mysterious laughing. I could hear chuckling and great bursts of laughter. Hilarity ruled. Only spirits could enjoy living in such a dismal bamboo forest. I tried not to pay attention to all their shouts that were partially muffled by the sounds of the rustling bamboo stalks rubbing against each other in the wind. I kept climbing up the steep mountain trail. The gray veil obstructing the sky began to break up, allowing the luminously blue high mountain light to shine through.

The elephant path led to a rocky cove where there were many springs. These had created a huge swampy area where buffalo were grazing. I had hoped the path would open out onto vast high meadows, but instead it ended in a cul-de-sac filled with bamboos. I was disappointed and circled around the cove hoping to find a way up the escarpment. I walked through the bamboo wall, moving through the thickets until I reached a clearing.

"And now," I said aloud, "what shall I do?"

As I spoke, I stupidly turned my palms imploringly up to the heavens. I quickly regretted it, for I had forgotten that I was carrying a precious burden. The queen left my arm. The king had fallen. The king watched in dismay as the swarm circled nervously around the edges of the clearing as if the bees, numbed by the cold, were trying to get warm. Without the bees' protection I was lost. Already the spirits' laughter and lamentations were drawing nearer. Suddenly the swarm dropped to the ground and disappeared into a little tunnel leading through a bamboo thicket, probably a game path. I took the same direction and followed them into the gallery leading through the canes. It was indeed a passage; at times an open path, at times a tunnel bored through the bamboos. The bees disappeared. I followed the trail, sometimes bending over, sometimes on all fours, but at all times I kept my back bent, for fear that the spirits, whose shouts I could hear in the distance, might find me. The bamboos began to thin out. At the top of a hill, I could see vast grassy meadows taking the mountain's ample forms. Grassy domes extended one after the other out as far as the horizon, blocking the view of the volcanic peak. Meadows rolled off toward the horizon, full of tall grasses with heavy seed heads, dotted with stands of yarrow and marbled with clumps of heather. There were very few trees in those meadowland pastures, except for some kosso trees with their twisted branches covered with what looked like green algae.

The cold had penetrated deeply. I didn't know where to go. I looked for something to eat, for my strength was ebbing and I was getting dizzy. A flock of water fowl passed overhead. My sisters the storks were back! Their harmonious bodies, like arrows released by the bows of desire, shot through the pure high mountain atmosphere. They gained altitude and then glided toward a hilltop's grassy dome. At its summit a lovely, solitary tree held out its many arms to welcome the storks. They accepted the invitation. Like black and white spindles crowned with red needles, stilts extended, they landed in the tree, weaving a cloak of color around it. The fortunate tree relaxed in the midst of a feathery forest. I went to meet those tutelary birds that had guided me out on the plains and welcomed me at Lake Chana. It was indeed a kosso tree, quite tall. I was relieved to spot a swarm of bees in a hole in the trunk. The cavity was surely dripping with honey at this time of year. It would relieve my hunger, and the fire I'd need to light to gather the honey would provide some warmth. I gathered together a large pile of dry grass and branches and wrapped them all in a sheath of succulent plants.

The storks were upset by the smoke. When I pulled the smoking bundle up into the tree, they all flew off, one after the other. Soon panic struck the bees as well. Some flew out and started to attack me, although I was still some distance from the opening. They were larger and more bellicose than the forest bees. I roared with pain when the first stings dug into my flesh. I placed the smoking bundle just below the hole. And then they all poured out. I screamed. The bees stung me everywhere. My whole body hurt, spotted with welts that turned black around the edges, just like the spots on a leopard's skin.

I reached inside the hole, pulling out combs that dripped with honey and stuffing them in my calabash after biting off big chunks. How good that honey tasted! Smooth and sweet without being cloying, it slipped caressingly down my throat, spreading an unctuous film on my skin. Its spicy taste brought together all the grace of flowers, as if their loveliness had turned to flavor. I climbed back down the tree, warm and no longer hungry, almost happy with the supply of honey I had gathered.

Suddenly, at the bottom of the hill, I spotted an animal shape hiding behind the heather. When it came out from the bushes, I recognized Shina's leopard. It bared its teeth and growled, its ears forward. The leopard started running rapidly up the slope toward me. Taken by surprise, I didn't react quickly enough to take aim with my gun. In my panic, I grabbed my machete. The leopard was already at the top of the hill and was making straight for me. It was about to leap and grab me by the throat.

An instinctive reaction was my salvation. I threw myself flat, and facing the animal, I screamed the scream of a big cat, a lion's roar that rose from my entrails. The leopard braked with all four feet, its claws raking the ground. It lay down, jaws open, showing its fangs, ears laid back against its skull. And then it rose up slightly and, bending backward, tensed its muscles to spring. That was when I had a second reaction that saved my life. On my knees, I held out the calabash of honey to the leopard.

The translucent liquid gleamed like hot flowing golden lava. In surprise, the animal's ears perked up and it cautiously moved near. The leopard sniffed at the container, lapped at it once with its tongue, and then, with a mistrustful glance in my direction, plunged its mouth into the calabash. Honey beaded in great golden drops at the end of its whiskers. It looked at me, grunted with satisfaction and went back to lapping the honey. Then it calmly lay down and began to groom itself. I didn't move. We remained like that for some time until finally the leopard got up, caressed my shoulder with its head and scratched its back against my own back. The white end of its long curly tail brushed against my cheek. The leopard went back to its place, and then it slowly began to change right under my eyes.

Its robe begins to grow lighter. The lustrous bronze tints of its coat are luminous, as if a sun were shining through its hide. White light seems to ooze out of each hair, creating a dazzling halo around its body. The leopard radiates an internal fire that the honey must have lit inside it. The light is blinding, and yet I know that it's the dawn of my own being. It's the same brilliance that has illuminated our clan since the time when I didn't yet exist and yet where I was already.

The luminosity decreases. I can now look at the animal without squinting. Little by little the light exits its body, and the leopard begins to look as it did before. The spots that were so hard to see a moment ago now begin to reappear. They take back their shape and form once again on the yellow-brown coat. They keep moving about on the fur, giving it a bright yellow luster. They begin to darken and expand. The spots are changing. They grow disproportionately larger, darkening the yellow spaces, covering the animal and dominating every parcel of its coat. The lighter areas that still remain soon disappear. Now the leopard is entirely black, totally and absolutely black, as if the animal's coat has absorbed all light. I know that black carries meaning. Blackness is the shadow of our patio during my childhood games and the penumbra in the alcoves of my adult games, as well as the restful darkness in which I will be able to relax as an old man. Black is the color of the depth of our being.

Then the leopard changes back. The black spots begin to break up, and the leopard's coat becomes a yellowed parchment covered with writing. The coat returns to its former state, a bed of yellow with black flowers. But the change is not yet complete. One final transformation comes from the spots. Each rosette is no longer just a series of black spots dancing in the sun. They all take the form of eyes, develop eyelids and pupils in which all the light reflected by the coat is focused. The eyes are alive, the eyelashes move, the pupils dilate and contract, the irises grow alternatively darker and lighter. The eyes give life to the leopard's body. A thousand eyes stare at me so that I'm not sure whether I am seeing them or they are seeing me. I can recognize the eyes of my father and my grandfather, and the eyes of generations of the men from my clan. In my heart, my eyes are looking into the eyes of Badrani Nyuni el-Mudi, the ancestor of our clan, the man who became a leopard in order to move the fig tree from one island to another in order to create a sacred place. His eyes are full of joy, of happiness, and their feminine expression, almost childlike, proclaims great strength. The accomplished man who has had three dreams combines the gaze of three human beings: the child, the woman and the man.

Eyes decorate the legs of the leopard also, but these are not from the past but from the future. They are the eyes of children still to be born, of adolescents, of young adults leaving for Mount Meru. I can see the eyes of my own sons who are not yet of this world, the eyes of my grandsons and even the eyes of their own children and grandchildren whom I will never meet.

The leopard turns and shows me its other side. I see womens' eyes, lovely eyes with long eyelashes, animated with the intelligence of those who can give life. The profound, proud looks of my mother and my grandmother, reminding me I owe them life, the knowing looks of my sisters and close cousins. The leopard's coat is made joyous by the eyes of women who have given birth to the men of the El-Mudi clan and of all the women for generations to come. Proud and noble, those eyes make the leopard's coat come alive with their radiant presence.

Two veins run through a leopard's body, the vein belonging to tough men and the vein belonging to subtle women. They come together and create my woodcarver's sensibility, the intimate calligraphy of my being, the meaning of dreams on Mount Meru.

The leopard gets to its feet. I follow it. We go back down toward the bamboo thickets. We walk through the bamboo and move into the forest. A bird is singing a lovely melody, reminding me of the fossil bird's song. As I look around for it, I come to a clearing. The leopard has disappeared. I move out into the clearing.

On a log sits a young woman dressed in a djellabah, the long robe worn on the coast, and a bird is perched on her shoulder. The bird has a long metallic blue tail, and its head and wings are made of gold. The young woman is Hasmahani.

I move closer. The bird flies off, and I watch as it disappears into the trees. When I look back at the young woman, the décor has changed. We are in Mombasa, in Hasmahani's house. And then I realize that the third dream was the trip to Mount Meru.

I see Hasmahani as she really is and I smile at her.

About the Author

François Devenne

François Devenne was born in Nantes in 1964. He completed his student thesis on the geography and agriculture of Kilimanjaro, and then worked at *l'Institut Français de Recherché en Afrique* in Nairobi, Kenya. This is his first novel, and was written during his long stay in Kenya.

The fonts used in this book are from the Garamond family